AMBER HOUSE
An Emmie Rose Haunted Mystery Book 7

DEAN RASMUSSEN

Amber House: An Emmie Rose Haunted Mystery Book 7

Dean Rasmussen

Copyright © 2025 Dean Rasmussen
All rights reserved.
ISBN-13: 978-1-951120-39-9

This book is a work of fiction. The characters, incidents, and dialogue are drawn from the author's imagination and are not to be construed as real. Any resemblance to actual persons living or dead, businesses, events or locales is purely coincidental. Reproduction in whole or part of this publication without express written consent from the publisher is strictly prohibited, except as permitted by U.S. copyright law.

For more information about this book, visit:

www.deanrasmussen.com
dean@deanrasmussen.com

Amber House: An Emmie Rose Haunted Mystery Book 7

Published by: Dark Venture Press

Cover Art: Mibl Art

❦ Created with Vellum

1

The lights in the Amber House Theater dimmed as a single spotlight focused on the stage, leaving the grand auditorium in shadow. The chatter from the audience faded, and dramatic music rose from an array of carefully positioned speakers planted within the walls.

Leaning forward in her private balcony above the stage, Gloria put one hand over her swollen belly and ran her fingers over the silk fabric of her gown. This should have been a proud moment—an electrifying performance with unarguably the best magician in all of Las Vegas. It was supposed to be her triumphant return after two first-class magicians, Mystic Max and Zack Vayne, had died tragically right there on that same stage only weeks earlier. Instead of joy, a knot of anxiety twisted in her chest.

She took in a shallow breath and fixed her gaze on the side of the stage. Her prized magician, Danny Drake, was standing beside his assistant just out of sight behind the curtain. They were all waiting for Marty to adjust the first prop for the opening illusion. He moved with precision over the casket-sized metal cage, but there was a tension in his stance.

When she'd hired Marty months earlier, his reputation had preceded him. A seasoned professional who had spent years keeping Las Vegas productions running seamlessly, he was the perfect man to tackle the chaos and mold it into magic. But what truly amazed her was how, even after losing his fiancée so tragically, he'd returned to work just a week later. She couldn't even imagine the strength that must have taken, but only someone like Marty could have handled a tragedy like that while also carrying the weight of two demanding theater roles: prop master and stage manager.

The rumors had certainly taken their toll on everyone, and Marty was no different. But he seemed more unnerved than usual. The pressure had eaten away at his confidence. Everything had to go perfectly after all that had happened. It was their last chance to redeem themselves in the demanding eyes of Las Vegas patrons. If the historic theater was to survive, it was now or never.

Marty glanced up from the stage and met Gloria's gaze, giving her a thumbs up.

She nodded to him.

As the music in the theater swelled to a dramatic crescendo, Marty returned to the prop and adjusted the edge of the red velvet curtain. Danny lifted his chin and adjusted his shimmering midnight-blue velvet tailcoat as his assistant slipped her arm under his and straightened her posture. The moment had come.

Gloria shifted nervously in her seat, her rounded belly making each movement slow and careful. Pressing her fingers over her abdomen, a fresh wave of nausea washed over her, but she pushed it away while clutching the armrest beside her. The theater seemed to crackle with life. The lights burst into a grand spectacle worthy of the finest theaters in the world. Danny stepped out onto the stage, accompanied by his radiant assistant, whose glittering white dress sparkled with a different kind of magic.

Marty wheeled out the first prop, positioning the tall metal cage behind the magician and his assistant, before moving back to his place behind the curtain.

Danny's presence seemed to captivate the audience immediately. They had all come there to see one of Las Vegas' greatest showmen, the same illusionist who had recently dazzled American television with his "Phantom Mirage" trick by making an entire luxury yacht levitate over a body of water on live TV before disappearing completely.

Danny moved with practiced ease, circling the cage with confidence as his assistant spun it completely around, allowing the audience to get a view from every angle, before she positioned it in front of him and opened the metal door. Stepping inside the cage with over-the-top bravado, his assistant locked him inside.

Music filled the air again with a dramatic burst as his assistant ascended a dazzling staircase beside the cage and grabbed a metal hook connected to a cable from above. Attaching it to the top of the cage, she gave a confident nod toward the ceiling. The mechanical whir of a hoist cut through the tension as the cable's machinery groaned under the weight while rising into the air. The spotlight followed the cage, casting a long, distorted shadow across the stage floor below.

To add to the grand illusion, Danny's assistant descended the staircase and accepted a torch from Marty as the contraption rose several feet. Using the torch to light a pile of logs and kindling below the cage, the assistant backed away. The audience reacted with gasps and a bit of laughter as Danny played up the drama, feigning distress as the flames rose higher around him, implying that he could not possibly make it out alive.

Gloria clenched her teeth as the drama intensified, watching Marty's reaction as he witnessed the show from the shadows, his nervous expression a reflection of the anxiety that filled her chest. It was undeniable—they were both waiting for something to go wrong.

Danny Drake's voice broke through the music as he

instructed his assistant to step away from the danger. Everything was moving along just as they had rehearsed it. Gloria allowed herself to exhale, just for a moment, as the assistant backed away and spun the cage around again by grabbing a bar near its base.

Maybe they would get through the night without anything happening. Yes, maybe it would stay this way.

Marty glanced at Gloria again from his station behind the curtain, showing the glint of a faint smile that seemed to communicate everything was under control. She nodded back again, taking in a deep breath.

The performance continued to the next step, but something felt... wrong. Maybe it was the weight of her pregnancy, with so much at stake, but there was something in the way the lights had suddenly dimmed... or the way the flames had grown higher...

A shadow appeared near the back of the stage. The silhouette of a figure. Someone who wasn't supposed to be there. She stared at the person nervously as Danny ramped up his dramatic attempts to escape the cage before the flames consumed him.

The assistant seemed oblivious to anything unusual, moving over the stage with graceful confidence as the lights, music, and her distracting elegance helped to make the night come alive as if the very fabric of the theater was holding its breath. Danny had captivated the audience with his illusion. Perfect.

She blinked, and then it happened.

One moment, Danny was following everything exactly as he had rehearsed, playing up the drama to a fever pitch while struggling within the cage as the flames consumed him, and the next —chaos.

The audience gasped, but this time not in awe, as the wire suspending the cage snapped. The cage that Marty had so meticulously engineered and inspected countless times came crashing to the floor and exploded in a ball of fire as the assistant let out a heart-wrenching scream.

No, no, no... Gloria's heart pounded as she struggled to catch her breath. *This wasn't part of the act. Not again.*

Danny slammed against the bars of the cage as his body hit the floor, and blood sprayed into the air a moment later. His face twisted in confusion and terror. The illusion had quickly turned into everyone's worst nightmare. He let out a weak call for help as the flames engulfed his body.

"Danny!" Marty yelled from the side of the stage as he ran toward the magician, but the rising panic of the audience echoed throughout the theater, their shouts drowning out any cries for help.

Gloria stood, although her hands instinctually shot to her belly. A wave of nausea rose in her chest, but she was helpless to do anything more than pray.

Marty joined the assistant, along with another stagehand, as they raced to extract the magician before the flames consumed him. Danny's body slumped to the side against the cage bars. The house lights came on, and the spotlight went dark. As Marty worked furiously to extinguish the flames, the panic seemed to swell and the audience scattered toward the exits.

Danny's assistant dropped to her knees and broke down in tears, screaming his name over and over. The flames seemed resistant to anything Marty did to put them out, instead defiantly rising higher as he shouted for more help. Soon, the flames jumped into the cage and Danny's clothes caught on fire, but the magician lay motionless, his face staring blankly toward the ceiling as the fire consumed him. The theater's sprinkler system finally activated, raining cold water over everything and everyone who hadn't yet evacuated.

Gloria watched helplessly from her seat as her mind raced, trying to make sense of what she had just witnessed. Could all the rumors be true? It seemed unimaginable. Dousing the flames and the fallen magician with the extinguisher's white foam, Marty finally reached the cage's door and unlocked it. The harsh smell of chemical spray filled the air, mixed with the sickening stench of charred flesh. Marty dragged out Danny's lifeless body, while the others tried in vain to resuscitate him.

Her vision spun, and she clutched the balcony railing to keep from falling.

What the hell just happened?

Dropping back into her seat, her body went numb as she closed her eyes and whispered, "Everything... It's gone."

2

Emmie almost missed the message. It had gotten buried within the clutter of her inbox, mixed in with all the other junk emails that seemed to flow endlessly from out of nowhere, and only by chance had she scrolled down far enough to spot the subject line that caught her attention.

Help me, please.

She hovered over it, her finger hesitating to click, believing it was almost certainly junk that had somehow gotten through her spam filter. It *felt* different—there was something about those words, something that tugged at her heartstrings when something was off. She opened it, and her past came rushing back.

Nova Harrison.

Her heart seemed to skip a beat. The name triggered a rush of memories—not all of them pleasant—and it took the combined laughter of her friends across the room to break her out of her thoughts.

"Get over here." Sarah gestured to the cake sitting at the center of Caine House dining room table. Her friend had lit a single candle and placed it in the center with a wide grin. "We have to sing Happy Birthday."

Emmie switched off her phone—the familiar name still

echoing through her mind—and rose from the living room couch. The sweet smell of marble cake filled the air. Jason had put on some jazz music in the background, which helped to lift the mood of the dreary spring weather.

Joining her smiling friends at the head of the table, she drew in a breath, closed her eyes, and paused. What was her birthday wish?

Nova Harrison.

The name flashed across the back of her eyelids. It demanded her full attention, drowning out all other thoughts, until she opened her eyes again and blew out the candle.

A small round of applause erupted from her friends. Sarah smiled at her from across the table. Her empathetic expression showed a bit of concern as Jason stepped around them, pouring red wine into the glasses beside each plate.

"You okay?" Sarah asked quietly, almost in a whisper.

Emmie nodded and took a sip of wine.

She stayed quiet while her friends sang Happy Birthday. Tonight was about letting go, about being present with friends she now considered her family. Still, something gnawed at the back of her mind.

Avoiding Sarah's gaze, her friend who could pick up on even her subtle mood shifts, Emmie tried to push away the name that seemed to almost scream from the back of her mind. Nova Harrison.

"To friendship." Finn raised his glass toward the center of the table.

They all did the same and clinked their glasses together before taking a sip of wine. Jason had picked her favorite, Pinot Noir, and it seemed to wash away some of the anxiety on the way down.

She took another sip before placing the glass on the table and glancing toward the ceiling. "I'll be right back."

No one questioned her, and Sarah even gave a reassuring nod.

Emmie slipped away from them and headed upstairs. While

their voices faded on her way to her room, her pulse thumped louder in her ears.

Nova Harrison. Please help me.

Stepping inside her room, she closed the door behind herself and pulled out her phone. Why did that name rattle her so much? Her hands trembled as she found the email from Nova again.

She hadn't spoken to her friend from college in over a year, not since Emmie had lost her job in California and had moved back to Minnesota. They hadn't grown terribly close in the time they'd known each other, since Emmie had pursued graphic design and Nova had majored in theater arts, but they had seemed to keep running into each other in the hallways, as if the universe had wanted them to stay in touch. Nova's energy and charisma were infectious, and she had a way of commanding attention—sharp, radiant, and stubbornly persistent in chasing her dreams. All the same qualities that Emmie admired. They had shared many hours studying in the coffee shops and restaurants near the college, and Nova had wanted to be a part of her life, but Emmie had gotten caught up in her own world of deadlines and projects, while Nova was on a fast track to stardom it seemed. Her friend had already built a name for herself in the local community theater by the time she graduated and had even developed her skills as a novice magician.

But now, the tone of the email was nothing like the Nova she remembered.

> Hi Em, Remember me? It's been a while since we talked, but I'm back out in Vegas now. Remember I told you my family owns the Amber Hotel and Casino? Well, they also own the Amber House Theater next door and I'll finally get to perform there soon! You've probably never heard of it—it's historic—but that doesn't matter right now. I need to talk with you about something REALLY important. You were always someone I could talk to when things got rough, and God, have things

gotten rough since I moved back here. I remember when you told me about your experience with ghosts, and I'd like to talk about that again. Is that okay? I think this place has ghosts—serious ghosts—and I think they're trying to hurt me.

Emmie's heart beat faster as she continued reading.

I know we had some ups and downs before you moved away, and I'm so sorry for losing contact with you. It's all my fault! Sorry for the short notice, but can you help me? Please? I don't know who else to turn to. I've attached a video to show you what I'm talking about.

Staring at the attachment for a long moment, she finally clicked on it.

The video started with Nova's familiar face, but the confident girl she'd known from college was gone. She was almost unrecognizable now—her hair was damp with sweat, her eyes full of fear, and the camera shook as she moved forward. She was staring into the shadows of a dimly lit hallway.

"This is the place I told you about in college," Nova said. "The theater's been sitting empty for decades, but I convinced Dad to renovate it so I could finally perform magic like I've always wanted to. The place opens to the public next Friday when I give my debut performance, so I've been working my ass off to get everything ready, rehearsing just about every day lately." Nova's breath quickened as a set of ornate doors came into view. "But something's not right. I feel like there's someone here with me. I'm not alone, and ever since I started rehearsing, it's been getting worse. I think they're angry, like they want me gone... Yes, they definitely want me out of here."

The camera wavered as Nova stepped into the theater, revealing rows of empty seats beneath harsh spotlights. A stage loomed in the distance. Her breath was shallow at the edge of panic. "I know I should be thrilled. I mean, I have this beautiful theater all to myself, right? I've waited my whole life to perform in front of an audience, but..." She paused and fixed her gaze on something off-camera. "They're watching me, and I've got goosebumps."

Nova panned the camera around the empty theater. "Can you see them?" she whispered. "It's freezing in here suddenly."

A loud crack echoed through the theater, and she let out a muffled scream. The video flickered then ended.

Emmie sat frozen, her finger still hovering over her phone as Nova's haunted eyes still replayed in her mind. That look... It wasn't just fear. It was the same desperation Emmie had felt as a child, while hiding under the covers from the ghost that had tormented her and her family home.

Silence filled Emmie's bedroom. What should she do?

Switching off her phone, she returned to her friends in the dining room. Sarah met her gaze with an empathetic expression that seemed to recognize the shift in Emmie's energy.

"You're not okay," Sarah said.

"No." Emmie sat at the table in front of a single slice of cake that someone had cut for her. "I need to show you guys something." Her hands shaking, she swallowed and clicked back to the video. "A friend of mine from college—Nova Harrison—she just sent me this."

Jason moved in beside her as she turned her phone toward them and hit play on the video without saying another word.

Their glowing smiles faded when the video started, and the room went quiet while they watched it.

After it ended, Jason let out a slow breath. "Okay... That's not normal."

"No, it's not," Emmie said softly. "I haven't talked with her since we went to college together, but... I just can't ignore it."

Jason rubbed the back of his neck. "You want to go help her, don't you?"

Emmie nodded cautiously. "I know what it's like to be haunted and have no one to turn to. You saw her face—it's not like her to be so terrified. Something bad is going on. It's not just about the ghosts either, this is something else. I don't know how to explain it, but I have this feeling that she's in danger."

Finn sighed and took a seat beside Emmie. "I'm not sure I've fully recovered from what happened at Raven House. It helps that Sarah's accelerated the recovery process—a lot—but her gift only goes so far and even psychic healing takes time. On top of that, Sarah's been working overtime at the hospital, and... didn't we agree to take a break? You've been through enough lately, Em."

"I know," Emmie whispered. "But if I don't go, and something happens to her..."

"*And* she's in Vegas," Jason said. "You know I have a problem with gambling. That's like asking an alcoholic to take a tour through a brewery. We talked about all that. My nickname wasn't Joker back then, just because I was funny and goofed around a lot. I got into some serious trouble with the casinos back then, using my psychic skills on those chumps—I was playing with fire. It was just too easy to manipulate the dealers. Just thinking about it now..." He cringed.

"We don't have to go inside the casinos," she said. "I wouldn't ask unless I thought it was really important."

He looked at her for a long moment before running a hand through his hair. "I support any decision you make, but... It's a lot to handle right now."

"I'm not sure I can change my schedule with a short notice," Sarah said. "Can it wait a week or two?"

"Her performance is next Friday," Emmie said. "She didn't give me a lot of notice."

"You would go alone?" Sarah asked.

Emmie paused to consider her words carefully. "We can't always be together, and I've learned a lot over the last several months. We've *all* grown a lot, in every way, since we met. I'm sure I can handle this one."

They all looked surprised.

Sarah asked, "Is that wise? I mean, you're absolutely right that each of us has grown stronger after surviving everything lately, but don't you think we work better as a team, at least for now?"

"We do, but you heard what Nova said." Emmie picked up her phone. "She's terrified. I know I can help her get through this, even if you're not able to go."

Jason dropped into a chair and let out a sigh. "Can we talk about this in the morning? It's your birthday—"

"That's my birthday wish, then."

Sarah sat beside Finn and met Emmie's gaze. "You need to be sure, Em. This doesn't sound as easy as it seems."

Emmie nodded and glanced toward her phone. The desperation in her old friend's video held something unspoken just beneath the surface. Nova had never reacted like that—with anything. Something had traumatized her. "I can do it."

"When would you want to leave?" Finn asked.

She answered, almost too quickly, "Tomorrow."

3

When a limo arrived to pick them up at the airport, Emmie looked to Jason for an explanation. "I thought you said you called an Uber?"

He shrugged. "We're in Vegas."

The overt pampering was unnecessary, but she didn't complain as the driver took care of their luggage while they climbed inside. She cuddled beside him on the sprawling black seat that resembled a couch.

Jason gestured to the mini-fridge and complimentary bar on the opposite side, stocked with bottles of rum, vodka, tequila, Jack Daniels, wine and champagne. "Can I get you something?"

"Isn't the hotel only a few miles from here?"

He jumped forward. "We better hurry then."

She latched her hand onto his belt, pulled him back, and shook her head. "Maybe later. Better not meet Nova and her parents while slurring our words and falling down."

"You're probably right." Jason dropped back into the seat beside her and stretched out while pulling her in closer. His embrace warmed her heart. Maybe their original plans for a romantic getaway weren't a total loss. They were still in Las Vegas, and the digital billboards and gleaming casinos added a bit of excitement to the moment, even if the weight of Nova's desperate pleas still reverberated at the back of her mind. They could focus on romance as soon as they finished helping her old friend.

Emmie stared ahead through the privacy glass that separated them from the driver as they headed out into the city streets. The congested traffic reminded her of living in Los Angeles, with the limo weaving a path through the Tuesday morning chaos. Brushing her hand against the edge of her purse, she remembered the gift she'd purchased for Nova inside: a small silver pendant in the shape of a magician's hat engraved with the inscription, "For the magic we make, on stage and in life. Your friend always, Emmie." Not the most impressive gift she'd ever given, but she'd had little time to shop, given the urgency—a quick trip to the mall near the airport on the way—and it would help to break the ice when they arrived.

Only a few minutes later, the limo slowed and turned down a street that led them away from the towering casinos and bustling crowds. They hadn't even had time to get comfortable before a flashy red sign came into view. It contrasted against the top edge of a glitzy hotel that rose only half the height of surrounding hotels. The Amber Hotel and Casino.

"At least we're not too far from The Strip." She scanned the property as the limo turned into a driveway. Vintage lampposts lined the sidewalks beside manicured hedges that led them to a wide circular drive at the front entrance. The grandiosity and historical charm of the place struck her. This was no ordinary casino. At the center of the looping driveway stood a grand fountain with tiered basins and water that cascaded down in elegant streams lit from below even as the afternoon sun washed away its full spectacle. The fountains featured statues of jazz musicians and women dancing in short skirts, headbands, and long strands of pearls. A scene straight out of the Roaring Twenties.

"It's not so bad," Emmie said. "Kind of charming, actually." A rush of excitement and awe swept through her. It was like entering a grand movie set or some historical landmark.

"That's what they want you to think," Jason said. "Just remember, all the glitz and glamour are there for the sole purpose of parting you from your money. The theme is designed to pull you in."

"They're off to a good start," she said, "but it feels like we might run into Al Capone after we step inside."

Jason looked at her. "Let's hope not."

The limo's tires rumbled over cobblestone pavement reminiscent of when horse-drawn carriages ruled the streets. That was the theme, of course, the Art Deco and neoclassical architecture of a time when the gangsters rose to power to satisfy the alcoholic thirst of the masses. The intricate stonework and grand columns surrounded them on all sides as the limo made its way to a stop in front of the grand entrance. The dark polished stone columns contrasted with gleaming gold accents.

But despite the opulence exterior, there was a secrecy about the place, an air of mystery reminiscent of the prohibition era. Heavy, dark drapes shrouded the windows, and a high spiked fence lined the property, half-obscured by thick ivy that crept along the stone columns.

The driver's voice came through the speakers. "Here we are, folks—the Amber Hotel and Casino."

Stepping outside into the oppressive desert heat again, someone from the hotel hurried to their car and started loading their luggage onto a trolley at the top of the marble steps. The entrance was marked by a large arched doorway with wrought iron gates and frosted glass panels etched with intricate designs. High above the entrance, a brightly lit marquee glowed with the casino's name in elegant vintage style lettering.

Emmie glanced around while Jason tipped the limo driver. They weren't more than a couple of miles from the popular Vegas casinos, although it seemed they were isolated from the city, set off from the hustle and bustle by a wall of larger structures and surrounded by smaller casinos showing their age that must have thrived a few decades earlier.

As Jason returned to her side, they ascended the stairs, and a tall man appeared just inside the door. He stood with a commanding posture in a tailored suit and stepped forward when they reached the entrance. His steel-gray eyes flicked over them with a cool, appraising glance as he smiled and extended his hand. "You must be Emmie and Jason."

"One and the same," Jason answered.

They all shook hands just inside the hotel's threshold as the doorman had already whisked their luggage inside and was standing patiently beside them.

"Wayne Harrison," the man said. "I apologize for the lack of help at the moment, but as Nova probably already mentioned, we haven't officially re-opened the theater yet after the refurbishments. We won't be completely staffed up again until opening night."

"Nova said it's this Friday," Em said.

"That's right," Wayne said.

"I'm sure you're very busy."

"You have no idea," he said. "It's a special day for Nova, certainly, but also for my family. This Friday, May the twenty-fifth, commemorates *exactly* forty years since the Amber Hotel and Casino, and the Amber House Theater, originally opened. We're ramping up and ready to go." He grinned and stepped aside as they entered. "The gun is locked and loaded, so to speak," Wayne said wryly. "Just waiting to pull the trigger."

"We're looking forward to it," Jason said.

Emmie glanced around the lobby. Two young workers were busy sorting papers behind the check-in counter. Another man stood behind a concierge desk to her left, its brass fittings tarnished in places as if to give the impression that even the staff didn't dare scrub away too much of its past. Their footsteps echoed off the walls and ceiling, where wood beams and dark paneling blended perfectly with intricate Art Deco patterns and golden accents. The metal gleamed under dim lighting that seemed to twist shadows in unnatural ways. It was opulent, but not flashy in the usual Vegas style. This was subtle, like something straight out of an old gangster movie, and there was an undeniable feeling of being watched as they moved inside.

Wayne led them into the lobby until he paused and lowered his voice while turning away from the workers. "You'll meet Nova in a minute, but I should make some things clear first. My daughter contacted you without consulting us first, and although I support her completely, I'm afraid your presence here is a complete waste of time for all of us, but there's nothing I can do at this point. She's determined to go through with this, so we'll just deal with it."

Emmie inched back and her heart raced faster. Everything Nova had said in the video came back to her, that her father openly mocked her pleas for help. "Helping Nova is far from a waste of my time. I went through a similar situation growing up in a haunted house."

"Our theater is definitely not haunted," Wayne said. "Anything you heard is a bunch of BS."

Emmie met the man's stern gaze. Things had gotten tense all of a sudden. "Sorry. I'm just going by what Nova told me. I'm sure we can help her get through whatever she's facing."

Wayne looked at her curiously. "How do you know my daughter again?"

"We were friends in college."

"That's right," Wayne gave a smile that didn't extend to his eyes. "Her time in California. Acting or something."

"I studied graphic design," Emmie added. "We shared some classes together."

Wayne looked them both up and down. "And now you search for ghosts."

"No need to search." Emmie glanced at Jason for support. "They find me."

"You wouldn't believe the things we've seen in the last year," Jason said.

Wayne nodded again. "Nova's facing a lot of anxiety lately. I think the pressure's getting to her."

"I'm sure we can help with that," Emmie said.

"That's fine," Wayne nodded once. "Calm her down and get all this talk of ghosts out of her head. Just make sure you don't interfere with her rehearsals. She's under tremendous pressure to nail this performance."

"Yes, of course." Emmie studied Wayne's face for a moment, looking at the hard lines and tanned skin that stopped at the edge of his glasses. His receding hairline and carefully trimmed hair showed this was a man who did not have time for nonsense.

"Just have it—whatever it is that you do—wrapped up as soon as possible," Wayne said. "I'm hoping this doesn't drag on for more than a few days. And please keep a low profile as I don't want any of the workers to know what's really going on between you and her. If anyone asks, you're here to consult Nova, to help her stay focused on her craft. I'm not sure how much you know about the Amber House Theater, but all the talk of ghosts shut down the theater forty years ago, and the superstition destroyed my mother's dreams. I won't let it happen again."

"Understood." Emmie swallowed and pushed aside the rest of her thoughts, squeezing Jason's arm to relieve some of the tension.

Wayne led them toward a darkened hallway on the left, their footsteps echoing off the walls of the lobby. The faux antique decor eluded perfectly how it must have felt to live in the prohibition era, with dark wood paneling and plush velvet furnishings lavishly displayed in every direction. Ornate chandeliers dripped crystal beads overhead, and framed photos of notorious gangsters and bootleggers on every wall added to the sense of danger. The soft lighting created a mysterious atmosphere as they stepped across inlaid stones in the floor that formed an immense golden letter A.

"Nova is rehearsing." Wayne steered them toward the far side of the lobby where a set of stairs descended beneath the hotel, revealing a hidden passage dimly lit by flickering wall sconces that cast dancing shadows over the entrance. "We'll go in and watch for a bit."

Descending the worn, dark oak steps, their footsteps creaked softly. The railings were made of polished mahogany with brass fittings that glinted in the low light. Exposed bricks lined the walls as if to conceal the secret level beneath the hotel.

Only a few yards from the base of the stairs stood a row of open doors with small brass peepholes in the center like a barrier standing between the ordinary world above and the hidden speakeasy below. A massive brass plaque above the doors labeled 'Amber House Theater' reminded them they were entering an exclusive area.

The air cooled a bit, carrying the faint smell of aging wood and a hint of mustiness. A young woman's commanding voice mixed with dramatic music boomed through a sound system somewhere in the distance.

"That's her now." Wayne slowed, stopped, then turned to them. "Such a tour de force behind the hotel's revival. I had considered selling the place after my mother's decline—plenty of offers—but Nova wouldn't allow it. She refused to give up the dream to bring the theater back to life. She's the driving force behind its restoration—*so* committed to see my mother's dream realized. Everything is riding on its success, with Nova leading the charge. This is why we can't afford any... distractions. My girl needs to focus on her performance, not ghosts. Understand?"

"I'm optimistic we can deal with whatever your daughter is encountering," Jason said. "We can be out of here within a few days, like you mentioned."

Wayne seemed satisfied with his response, and they continued walking toward the black doors leading into the theater. "Now that's the attitude I like. Do your job and get out."

Emmie dug her fingers into Jason's arm a little deeper this

time. It was all she could do to keep from blurting out everything Nova had shared with them in the emailed videos—the desperation, the helplessness, the lack of parental support. The tension between them and Wayne was palpable and it wouldn't make their job easy.

"Opening night is sold out." Wayne lifted his chin. "She's the main event, with quite a following on social media."

Jason nodded. "We did some research on the place before arriving. We watched some of her videos. Very talented."

"Penn and Teller stopped by the other day to watch her performance," Wayne continued. "She's gotten rave reviews from a few other big name magicians around the city. You *are* familiar with Penn and Teller."

"I've heard of them."

Wayne frowned at his response. "Top notch. They've all heard of Nova by now."

"Why is it called Amber House Theater?" Emmie asked.

Wayne paused at one of the doors to the theater, gripped its handle, then turned to her. "The Prohibition theme, you know. A tongue-in-cheek codeword for those seeking a speakeasy. Beer... the color of amber. Get it? You know what a speakeasy was, don't you?"

"Yes," Emmie forced a smile.

"Mom thought by adding the color amber, or gold, in the name would bring her good luck." He scoffed. "Didn't work out that way for her. At least, not in the theater."

The thunderous sounds from inside the theater swelled and Wayne straightened like a proud father and pulled the door open, making a wide gesture for them to go inside. "Nova's near the end of her performance now, but you haven't missed the best part. You won't believe what you're going to see. Nothing like it in Vegas. Nothing."

4

Emmie spotted Nova on the stage immediately. Her old friend was standing at the far side, dressed in a black spandex jumpsuit with rows of sequins that ran down her body and glittered beneath the stage lighting as she moved. Fingerless gloves covered her hands and her feet were bare. A sparkling swim cap crowned her head, although her face was obscured in shadow as she made wide gestures and spoke loudly to an attentive dark-haired young man at the opposite side of the stage. He nodded enthusiastically while focused on her every word, standing tall in a deep red dress shirt with a silky sheen, bow tie, and a black vest and pants that gave him an air of modern elegance, although his outfit was a clear callback to speakeasy flair.

Neither of them seemed to notice as Emmie and Jason followed Wayne toward the front of the stage.

The Amber House Theater was nothing short of spectacular. There were rows of plush velvet upholstered burgundy seats and gold-painted armrests and legs arranged in arcs that mirrored the flow of the semicircular stage. The place had an intimate feel, with box seats on both sides featuring vintage lamps on small tables surrounded by dark wood paneling as one would expect to find in an old historic theater.

The stage gleamed with intricate inlays and small brass footlights ran along the front edge that gave off a warm golden glow like the candle set ups from long ago. The velvet curtains were adorned with gold tassels, and they were drawn open to reveal a large painted backdrop at the back of the stage depicting an opulent 1920s evening cityscape.

A central chandelier hung overhead with cascading crystals that sparkled, leaving a swarm of dotted lights in every direction. The edges of the dome featured hand-painted murals of historical magicians like Harry Houdini, Howard Thurston, and Jean Eugène Robert-Houdin, performing some of their more grand illusions. Rich patterned carpets lined the aisles, with the designs focusing on stars, moons, and mystical symbols.

Wayne escorted them to a row of seats near the front, positioning them just behind a gray-haired man who was watching the stage intently. He glanced back briefly when they arrived, although didn't offer an introduction. Judging by the man's stern expression, he didn't want them bothering him. Wayne ignored the man as they sat down, and they waited patiently in the dim light for the performance to continue.

"There will be music, lights, and drama during this lull while they prepare." Wayne gestured to Nova and the young man on stage.

"Prepare for what?" Jason asked.

Wayne grinned. "Hold on to your seat."

Jason looked at Emmie, shrugged, then glanced around the theater. Emmie followed his gaze. Every detail in the theater exuded an elegance that modern theaters had lost over time. It was hard to believe the place had remained empty and unappreciated for decades before Wayne had renovated it. The dark mahogany wood paneling on the walls had gold trim and Art Deco inspired carvings. Rich, textured fabric covered the lower half of the walls, probably to enhance the acoustics of the theater. And then there were framed vintage posters everywhere of famous magicians from the 1930s through the 1980s. Performers like Doug Henning, David Copperfield, and Chung Ling Soo standing beside his assistant who proudly held up a musket, maybe the same one that later misfired during his famous Bullet Catch trick which ended his life, but the other magicians were unfamiliar. No doubt Finn knew all of their names. Along with those were a series of sepia-toned photographs of the theater in its heyday.

Wayne caught Emmie staring at one of the photos and whispered while leaning toward her. "My mother took those photos only a couple of weeks before the place shut down."

"It's beautiful," Emmie said.

Wayne nodded approvingly. "Couldn't have done it without Nova. She brought the place back to life. Mom will be so proud."

The ambient lighting seemed to come out of nowhere, although hidden seams in the woodwork revealed carefully placed lighting that created the illusion of soft and warm gas lamps. The spotlights above the stage were all modern, but everything else presented an atmosphere of having stepped back in time. There was a subtle smell of aging wood, leather and even a hint of cigarettes, which no doubt filled the theater's air long ago and might never completely fade away without a round of deep cleaning.

Only a moment later, Nova glided out of the shadows near the back of the stage, her movements smooth and confident, while her assistant wheeled in an imposing rectangular apparatus resembling a medieval torture device, reminiscent of a water torture cell like the one Harry Houdini had infamously escaped from. It stood about seven feet high, with a metal frame and glass windows on all sides. The water inside the device sloshed against the glass as the assistant moved it into place prominently at the center of the stage.

Walking around the device, lightly brushing her hands over

the surfaces as she inspected it, Nova met Emmie's gaze for the first time and broke into a wide smile. They shared a heartfelt moment, but Nova continued without a pause. At least Nova knew she had arrived.

The assistant left the stage. Only a moment later, a massive clank, jingle of chains, and heavy machinery filled the air as someone offstage lowered the device's thick cover where it came to a stop at Nova's feet. Hurrying back on stage, the assistant helped Nova attach the ankle stocks as she ran her fingers over the locks and chains, dramatizing the authenticity with each exaggerated click.

Nova was no amateur lounge performer.

Emmie's heart pounded faster, even though she knew this had to be part of the act. They were doing a perfect job of building the suspense. Her assistant double-checked the ankle stocks as Nova maintained eye contact with Emmie and Jason and her dad, with an expression of determination and confidence.

Stepping toward the audience, she spoke for the first time. "Welcome to the Amber House Theater. My name's Nova Harrison, and this is an old but deadly trick, if not done properly. In a moment, I'll submerge myself in this tank, shackled and locked in without access to a key. I'm pretty sure I can hold my breath for sixty seconds, so you'll see the timer counting down as I try to escape. If you see it go to zero, then you know I didn't make it."

Nova stared at her father, and he swallowed but remained silent.

Having shackled herself to the chains, the assistant added another barrier to her escape, slipping her into a straitjacket, straining to tighten the restraints and then left the stage again with Nova sitting seemingly powerless beside the towering device. The stage machinery clambered again as her assistant lifted her into the air upside down. Her body swung helplessly as the assistant maneuvered her above the device and then lowered her into the tank as she took one last gasp of air. The countdown on the massive digital clock at the front of the stage started as soon as her face touched the water. Struggling as she was lowered and then completely submerged within the tank, she twisted as a bit of her hair broke free from beneath the cap and fanned out over her face. Her eyes were wide as she seemed to flounder within the water, the chains clanking against the edge of the glass.

Forty-nine... Forty-eight... Forty-seven... Nova struggled within the straitjacket without progress and her actions slowed almost to a stop as if she had failed to free herself and had given up.

Emmie looked at the assistant. Maybe they had some secret look or gesture—a safe word—that would signal him to stop the trick and rescue her before things went bad.

The theater seemed to go silent. The only sound was of water splashing against the sides of the tank and loud thumps as Emmie let out a loud gasp.

Twenty-eight... Twenty-seven... Twenty-six...

Nova's body went limp and Wayne let out a muffled moan.

Squeezing Jason's hand, she looked at him for guidance. Should she rush onto the stage and stop them? Something had obviously gone wrong, but Jason's wide eyes held no answers.

Fifteen... Fourteen... Thirteen...

The girl was not moving, and the assistant had come out on stage to investigate, staring in at Nova with confusion and concern. It was clear she wouldn't make it out of there within the next ten seconds.

As her body tensed, Emmie shifted forward in her seat, preparing to run up on stage. There was still time to get her out of there.

But only a moment later, the horrific sound of metal screeching came from somewhere above the stage, followed by a loud crack that echoed through the theater. A flash of light and sparks swept through the air. A massive black spotlight crashed to the stage, scattering a mix of glass and metal over the area where Nova had stood minutes earlier.

Three... Two... One...

The theater went dark.

"Jimmy, open the box!" Wayne cried out.

Emergency lights had come on, lighting the exits and aisles, but the stage was dark and motionless.

"Bring up the lights!" Wayne shouted as he rushed onto the stage. "Get her out of there."

Within the dim light, the assistant rushed out with a sledgehammer and maneuvered around the fallen spotlight, slamming the sledgehammer through the glass on one side of the device. Water sprayed out over the stage, and he swung at it again, bringing a torrent this time.

The lights in the theater snapped back on as Wayne had made his way to the assistant, but the cell was empty and most of the water had escaped through the shattered side, having drained into unseen waterways on the floor.

Jason let out a loud gasp. "Holy shit!"

Wayne turned to them with a grin as the assistant looked into the darkness above the stage and nudged him to the side.

Flush with confusion and adrenaline, pyrotechnics exploded across the stage and Nova's voice came from somewhere... behind them. Emmie turned to face the young woman. Nova was dripping wet, standing with a damp towel wrapped around her midsection, but she had somehow slipped out of the straitjacket and stood unshackled. Her face beamed with triumph and pride.

"Did you like it?" Nova stepped toward Emmie, extending her arms until they met in a long embrace.

"I loved it." Emmie squeezed her friend, absorbing some of the dampness into her own shirt.

Nova smelled of pyrotechnics and stale water. "It's so good to see you!"

"And you." Emmie stepped back. "It's been a long time."

Wayne let out a series of boisterous laughs as he came down from the stage. "Isn't she wonderful? What a delight. What a delight."

5

Emmie stared in disbelief as Wayne joined Nova's side, throwing his arm around his daughter in triumph while she attempted to dry herself off with the towel. She removed her swimming cap and her black hair dropped to her shoulders. Water dripped down her legs and pooled near her bare feet. "Simply amazing."

The old man sitting in front of them stared at Nova with a pleasant grin and then stepped over to her with his chin up. "Very impressive," he said with a little bow. "Your grandmother will be so proud, too."

"Thank you, Mr. Spurlock," she said. "That means a lot to me."

He looked at the stage curiously where the assistant and another old man in denim overalls had rushed out to inspect the water torture chamber, then gave a final nod before walking away toward the exit.

All the lights had come on now, and the full spectacle of what had happened became clear. Even from that distance in the audience, Emmie could see that the damage was far worse than it had appeared during the performance. If Nova had stepped anywhere near where the light had fallen, the shards would have sprayed across her face and body, causing serious injury, or worse, and Wayne would now be rushing his daughter to the hospital instead of praising her spectacular performance.

Wayne turned toward the shattered light and shouted at the man in overalls. "What the hell was that, Marty? Seriously, what the hell? Get your shit together."

Marty nodded and lifted his hand as if to calm his boss. "I'll straighten it out."

"Straighten it *all* out. Tighten every bolt and screw." Wayne spoke a little louder. "And then check them all a second, third and fourth time. You don't want to know—"

"It won't happen again," Marty answered without meeting Wayne's piercing gaze.

Nova's assistant scrambled off the stage and returned with a push broom, cleaning equipment, and a large gray bucket. After sweeping up some of the debris, Marty waved him away. "I'll take care of it, Jimmy. Just watch your step."

Jimmy stepped carefully over the scattered bits of glass toward the edge of the stage, glancing up at the rows of lights and then back down to the black casing that had somehow remained intact, although its wiring stuck out from the back like disheveled hair.

Wayne squeezed Nova closer. "You did even better this time, sweetheart, despite the setback. Don't worry about it." He ruffled her hair and looked at them. "I told you she was great."

Jason motioned to the fallen spotlight. "I'm assuming that wasn't part of the performance."

Wayne narrowed his eyes. "We'll get it fixed."

"It was them, Dad," Nova said. "I know it."

"Nah." Wayne frowned while tightening his hand on her shoulder and spoke with a strained grin. "Don't get all superstitious on us again. Nobody saw any ghosts flying around the lighting rig, did they?" He stared at Emmie and Jason for confirmation.

Emmie glanced at Nova then back to Wayne. "No, but we couldn't take our eyes off her performance."

Wayne seemed satisfied with her answer while staring into Nova's eyes. "You see? Just like I said. No ghosts. Just an accident. Another damn accident." He glanced over his shoulder and shouted, "Marty will take care of everything. Right, Marty? Nothing like that will ever happen again, right?"

Marty looked over with a dull stare. "We certainly won't let it happen again."

Jason leaned toward the edge of the stage and strained to get a better view of the fallen spotlight, following its trajectory up to the ceiling as if calculating where it had broken loose. At the same time, Marty carried the shattered spotlight off the stage.

Jimmy came down and stood at Nova's side. The young man held an air of confidence, and up close he looked more like a high school homecoming king ready to take his date to the prom than provide professional assistance to a Las Vegas magician, but he was eye candy after all, strategically positioned on stage to draw the audience's attention away from Nova's sleight-of-hand. He was incredibly good-looking, with slick black hair, a healthy body, and an infectious smile that spread up to his bright blue eyes.

Looping her arm under his, she tilted her head toward him. "This is my assistant, Jimmy. Nothing gets done without him."

"Nice to meet you all." The young man's face held an eager smile as he looked to Wayne and Nova for direction.

"I'm thrilled you're here." Nova grinned while staring into Emmie's eyes. "Absolutely thrilled."

The young woman's eyes seemed to sparkle as they exchanged a silent moment between them. A connection felt on an emotional level that warmed Emmie's heart, a knowing that Emmie had done the right thing in coming to her rescue. Her mouth opened as if to say something then closed again.

"Everything will be okay," Emmie said.

Wayne nudged Nova toward the side of the stage. "Get cleaned up. They'll be here when you get back."

Nova nodded but hesitated as Wayne turned away and took a step toward the exit.

Marty continued sweeping up the glass and clearing off the water with a stoic expression, using his boot to gather the larger pieces of glass and swept the last remnants of water into the drains on the stage floor. He seemed resigned to accept the blame.

"So when you called for Jimmy to break her out..." Jason said.

Wayne stopped and turned back with a look of frustration. "All part of the act. Of course, a stagehand will take care of it during the actual performance, but we've rehearsed the illusion for months now. Nova's a professional. Never mind what happened with the spotlight. Some slack worker took a shortcut during the install. That's why it broke loose. Don't you worry. Do you think I can get up there and check them all myself?"

"No," Jason said. "Never suggested that."

"Too much to do, and it doesn't help that the renovations are taking longer than anyone expected and I'm financially stretched to the limit, but Marty will go through each one of those lights—hell, maybe I *will* get up there and check each of them myself—so don't you worry." He turned back to the stage with a sour look. "Or maybe it's time to get a new prop manager."

"I like Marty," Nova said sharply. "He's been here since the beginning, and he's nice."

"Maybe that's the problem," Wayne said. "You're blinded by your emotions."

Jason glanced at Nova. "How did you escape that thing? Dropping into the floor? How did you get behind us so fast?"

Nova grinned. "You've heard of the magician's code, right?"

"That they can't reveal their secrets?"

"Correct," Nova said.

"She won't even tell me!" Wayne said. "She worked for

months to get it just right, and even I don't know how she does it. Mind-blowing, isn't it?"

Jason seemed to ponder the question for a moment. "I'll figure it out, eventually."

Nova laughed. "Maybe you will, maybe you won't."

Emmie slowed a moment to glance back at the light fixtures, and Wayne seemed to pick up on her interest. He leaned in toward her. "I suppose you're convinced a ghost did this."

"I'm not sure of anything at this point," Emmie said. "We'll have to look around."

"That's a fine answer, for now." Wayne smirked. "You just do your thing and try to stay out of the way. I'm sure you brought plenty of gadgets with you? Electronics to record all the ghosts, just like those people on TV?"

Emmie forced herself to swallow the growing irritation with Wayne's sarcasm, keeping a professional tone. "Two friends of mine, Finn and Sarah, will arrive on Monday. He's the guy with all the fancy gadgets."

"I can't wait to see what you come up with. Maybe I'll change my mind after I see the recordings, but I'm gambling you'll come up a little short—far short—so we can put all those old bullshit rumors to rest. It's an old building and we still have a bit of work to do." He glanced around at the theater. "Not sure if Nova mentioned this either, but I'm afraid we can't pay you for your services."

"We're not doing it for the money," Emmie said.

Wayne nodded. "Perfect. This is all about Nova's peace of mind. She arranged this nonsense, so it's *her* deal." He turned to his daughter and spoke in a condescending voice, "Did you see anything strange up there before this happened, sweetheart? Anything unusual?"

Nova swallowed and looked at Emmie. "Not this time."

"But you still believe a ghost was responsible for that mishap? Knocked that light down, maybe on purpose?"

Nova's gaze dropped, and Wayne continued leading them forward.

Wayne turned back to Nova. "Somehow we've got to get that superstition flushed out of you. Try to see things from a rational point of view... like Jimmy here. You don't believe in all that nonsense, do you?"

Jimmy shook his head, but glanced at Nova nervously. "No, sir."

"Good man. Can't wait to get this cleared up, out of the way, and get back to business." Wayne looked toward Jason. "Please show me the recording of the ghosts when you're done. I want to see the culprit's face myself."

"I'm not sure they have faces," Jason said wryly.

A loud metallic crash filled the air, breaking them from the conversation. Everyone's gaze turned back to Marty on the stage. He'd slipped and was now lying sideways on the floor with one arm draped over the shattered spotlight as if he had failed to lift the thing onto a metal cart that sat nearby. The old man recovered quickly and nursed his hands while struggling to get to his feet again, but after sneaking a glance at the others, his gaze dropped to the floor. "Sorry about that. Hit a patch of water, and the thing got away from me."

Wayne scowled, narrowed his eyes, and turned his face away for a moment before heading back toward the stage while grumbling, "Looks like I've got another issue to deal with."

Jimmy rushed onto the stage and Emmie lurched forward to join him until Wayne gestured for her to come back.

"He'll be all right." Wayne shook his head while trudging down the aisle. "Don't you worry about him."

After Marty stood again without help, she took Jason's arm as they moved forward as a group toward the stage until someone tugged at her arm.

Nova pushed in beside her and met Emmie's gaze, staring into Emmie's eyes with that same frightened intensity from the emailed videos. "Wait."

Emmie let her arm drop away from Jason and stopped. He glanced back with a puzzled expression until he gave a knowing nod and continued alone beside the others.

Emmie stood silently beside Nova until the others were out of earshot before opening her mouth to speak.

Before she could say anything, Nova whispered, "We need to talk. Now."

6

Emmie glanced around the theater for a place where they could talk in private.

As if thinking the same thing, Nova gestured to the far corner at the back of the theater. "Over there."

Emmie nodded, and they made their way up the aisle. The young magician's bare feet left damp stains in the carpeting as the water clinging to her wetsuit beneath her towel dripped down her legs. Nova shivered in the cool air and repositioned the towel around her waist.

"We can wait until after you get cleaned up," Emmie said. "I'm sure you're exhausted after all that."

"I *am* exhausted." Nova shook her head. "But this can't wait."

Cutting across the back row, they took seats as far from the stage as possible, with Nova keeping a constant eye on her father as if he might overhear their conversation. Leaning forward in the plush velvet seat, Emmie turned to face Nova and dug the pendant out of her purse. "Before we talk... I bought you something."

Nova stared curiously, following the pendant from Emmie's purse until it dangled between them, and a wide smile spread across her face as she accepted it. "What for?"

"Good luck," Emmie said.

Nova put it around her neck and adjusted it with a beaming smile. "Love it, but you're the one who's going to need a little luck." Glancing back toward the stage, the happiness in her eyes faded a bit.

Emmie inched in a little closer and lowered her voice. "You can tell me anything, you know."

Nova looked at her with a guarded smile before it melted away and she nodded. "I wish my family felt the same way. I *will* tell you everything, because I can't keep this in any longer, even if I wanted to." Her eyes watered. "Where do I start?"

Emmie held up her hand. "Before you do, I've got a question for you."

"Sure."

"Why *now*? I mean, we shared a lot of great times together in college, and I know you heard all the rumors about me, but I never got the feeling you believed any of the stories back then."

Nova stared into Emmie's eyes with an intensity that seemed to touch her soul. "This might sound a little strange."

Emmie smiled. "Trust me, my life is the epitome of strange."

"Well, it's because of something you told me once over a glass a wine. You shared about that time when you were a child... you found that little boy's body in the lake. The look in your eyes—so much honesty and... trauma. I didn't believe it had anything to do with psychic abilities—not at the time—but later... after this stuff started happening to me in the Amber House Theater... So I decided to look into it. After finding more articles on the Internet, I decided that what you were telling me was true. I knew in my heart that it was all true."

Emmie swallowed. The sudden rush of memories caught her off guard. Her mind raced back to when she had tried to talk honestly about her gift to a journalist after leading the police to Frankie's body, led by her psychic connection to him. The ordeal was something she wished she could forget, but now Nova had rekindled that trauma and the emotional pain swelled again in her chest.

Nova's eyes widened. "Did I say something wrong? I'm sorry, if I did."

Emmie shook her head. "Everything's fine. I just haven't thought about that for a while."

"Sorry."

Emmie forced a smile. "What sort of information did you find about me?"

"A lot, actually. Most of it in smaller paranormal investigator blogs and weird news of social media, but... it got me thinking. You mentioned communicating with the spirits in your house to make them go away. What was it you said to them?"

The memories came flooding back. Emmie remembered when she had defended herself against the Hanging Girl. The little prayer she'd said to herself out loud had helped to calm her nerves but also had seemed to do the same to the spirits.

Now I lay me down to sleep...

"I wasn't really talking to them," Emmie said. "More like praying for them to go away."

Nova's expression seemed to brighten for a moment. "Whatever you did, it worked for me, too. In a way."

Emmie looked at her for a long moment. "Do you also see spirits?"

"I... I'm not sure. They're not... solid. I just see shadows moving from the corners of my eyes and that sort of thing. I don't actually *see* anyone—you know, ghosts—but I'm sure they see me."

"What makes you think they can see you?"

Nova glanced toward the stage. "Because I can feel them watching me, and sometimes they respond when I talk to them."

Emmie's heart raced. "In what way? Do you hear voices?"

"Not like a regular voice—not like you and I are talking now—but like whispering, or sometimes laughing, or even... screaming. There's more than one, definitely, but sometimes they just hover in the background and pass along little signs—leaving things out for me to find, pushing a box around, dropping a book at my feet..." She gestured to the stage. "...and then sometimes, stuff like this happens. It sounds crazy, and nobody believes me."

"I believe you."

Nova smiled warmly. "I need that."

Wayne and Marty's voices grew louder from the stage as their conversation had slowly intensified, but instead of heading back out into the audience, the men moved their conversation further into the darkness where Jason was pointing toward something above them. He held their interest, steering their focus to something up near the lighting rig.

"Do you know who they are?" Emmie asked. "The spirits, I mean."

Nova shrugged. "I suppose they're the magicians who died here—I'm not sure—but I know one thing. Some of them don't enjoy sharing the stage with me."

"You feel they might try to harm you someday."

Nova shook her head. "Not someday." Glancing around the room as if checking for unseen eyes, she slowly lifted her towel and unveiled her arm.

Emmie's stomach churned as the bruises came into view, dark and sprawling across Nova's pale skin. There were cuts too, jagged and shallow, with some of them crusted over and others fresh.

"Nova..." Emmie's mind went back to when she was a child, her life threatened by the Hanging Girl and the terrifying uncertainty of what that malicious spirit might do to her. Reaching out instinctively, Emmie stopped short of touching her friend's arm. "Did you show that to your dad?"

"It wouldn't make any difference." Nova lowered her towel. "He'd accuse Marty or one of the staff."

"Why would the spirits want to hurt you?" Emmie asked.

"I'm hoping you can answer that."

Emmie nodded. "I'll do my best. Have they attacked any of the other performers that you know about?"

"It all seems targeted at me, although not many people have had the courage to get up on that stage after all the performers who died here." She stared at the stage with a nervous grin.

The words hung in the air for a moment between them, until Emmie spoke up, "This might seem like an obvious question, but why keep performing here? Why not go somewhere else? Take your act to a different theater?"

"No way. This is my family's theater, and Grandma Ria never gave up on it. She knows I always wanted to be a magician. As far back as I can remember, I wanted to get out there and perform for an audience—a *real* audience. Grandma Ria always encouraged me to be a performer. She also dreamed of being a singer—she never gave up on this theater or her dreams. This place has sat empty for almost forty years, but that didn't stop me from sneaking in here every once in a while on my own. Do you know there's a ton of props and equipment in storage backstage? They left behind a *goldmine*, and I would play with it whenever I had the chance. It was fun to get up on the stage, pretend there's an audience, and put on silly performances with rope tricks, card tricks, and all the usual cheesy amateur stuff. It was wonderful."

"Your grandmother and dad let you play in here? Even after the stage deaths?"

Nova grinned. "They didn't know, and it wasn't until Grandma Ria's decline that my dad started talking about selling the place. So I raised hell and forced him to keep it."

"Were you attacked back then?" Emmie asked. "When you used to sneak in here?"

"Not as much, although I always felt that I wasn't alone. But it didn't matter. You have to remember that for a kid dreaming of performing as a magician someday, this place was like paradise. Sure, the place wasn't maintained until recently. It sat abandoned for decades after Grandma Ria shut it down in the

'80s, only a couple of weeks after the third magician died right here in front of everyone. Maybe Dad already talked to you about that?"

"A little, not much."

"Well, basically, the place went under because rumors started circulating that the place was full of ghosts and nobody would come here anymore—not workers, not an audience, not performers—so everything just fell apart and died."

"Your grandmother didn't try to sell it?"

"She's so sentimental, I guess. You need to understand that she put everything she had into this place—all of her money, her dreams, her sweat and tears, and then to have it all collapse after a few..." Nova made quotes with her fingers. "...accidents."

"You don't believe they were accidents?"

"I've heard a lot of theories over the years. That the theater is cursed or Grandma Ria is cursed or one of the props is cursed... You get the idea."

Emmie cringed at the thought of dealing with another curse so soon after Raven House. "Is that what you believe?"

Nova scoffed. "All I know is there are spirits here and they want me gone. They remind me every day."

"And you keep coming back."

She gave a wry laugh. "Yeah, I suppose I'm a glutton for punishment for coming back here. But that's where you come in. I *know* you can deal with this better than I can. There's nobody else I would rather turn to for help. My dad thinks I'm nuts, Marty has his own theories, and my friends think it's all a big joke."

"What about Jimmy?"

She rolled her eyes. "He backs me up, sure, when it's convenient, but he doesn't want to upset my dad and sabotage his career."

A silence passed between them until Emmie realized that something wasn't quite right. The theater was completely quiet. The others had gone off somewhere backstage and left them alone. She took a long look around the stage and theater without any signs of spirits.

"The magicians who died here," Emmie said into the still air, "are you sure they died on the stage?"

"I'm sure. Why?"

"I don't see them."

A pained expression swept over Nova's face. "You don't believe me either?"

"I didn't say that. I *do* believe you. It's just that usually I see them near the place where they died. I can feel their presence, but it's a little strange that I wouldn't see them if they died right here."

Nova shrugged. "I'm sure they died in this exact spot."

"Okay," Emmie said. "Sometimes they don't want to be seen."

Nova looked at her curiously but stayed silent.

A chill swept through Emmie as the silence around them somehow seemed... wrong. If the spirits were lurking in the shadows, they not only had their eyes on them, as Nova had said they did, but now a dark energy was moving in closer as if to eavesdrop on their conversation. The jarring unease bristled against her skin.

Emmie closed her eyes for a moment and tried to focus on any spirits nearby. They were there, no doubt, but the energy shifted around them in elusive streams that seemed to dance at the edge of her awareness. "They're hiding from us, but they *are* here."

When she opened her eyes again, Nova was staring at her as if trying to glimpse into Emmie's mind. "What do they look like? When they're not hiding from us? What do you see?"

"Most of the time, they look like anybody else on the street, except for the... trauma." Emmie pushed away the mental images that had formed by the question. "But this is going to take a little time."

Nova glanced around the theater. "I'm not surprised you don't see them. They like to play games."

"Why do you say that?"

Nova leaned back in her seat. "Here's an example. I was going through some boxes behind the stage. There are a lot of things back there left over from previous performers, or maybe some of it belonged to the ones who died. I don't know, but when I was snooping around, I ran across an old wooden box. It opened right in front of me. I didn't touch it."

"What sort of box?"

"Something a magician would use, with a big gold star painted on the side. Not too large—a couple of feet wide—but just big enough for someone with a small frame to fit inside. The thing popped open on its own and scared me half to death." Nova gave a nervous laugh.

Emmie kept silent, but nodded as her friend continued.

"I stared at it for a long time, and then it creaked open a little wider like it was daring me to get closer, to climb inside of it. I couldn't run in that moment even if I'd wanted to, but that wasn't the end of it. Believe it or not, I reached out and grabbed the lid, you know, trying to see how it could have opened up on its own. That's just how I am, I guess. Leave no stone unturned, right? I had to see if it was spring-loaded or an animal had gotten inside or someone was playing a prank on me or maybe a latch had malfunctioned because all the props in that place are rigged for a specific illusion. Marty custom-designs everything, so I *had* to know how it worked. I was running my fingers across the latch to figure it out when something grabbed the back of my shirt and yanked me backwards—hard. My shirt was really tight, so for a moment I couldn't breathe. The box fell over... I fell over..."

"Did you get hurt?" Emmie asked.

"Not that time, but stuff like that happens just about every day here. I never did figure it out."

"Is that where most of the encounters happen? On or behind the stage?"

Nova nodded. "Mostly around the theater, but sometimes in the hotel."

"Have any guests ever complained of ghosts?"

"Not that I've heard, but I'm sure Dad wouldn't tell me if they did. After Grandma Ria shut down the theater, she didn't talk about it much. It sat vacant for almost forty years, even while the rest of the hotel and casino thrived. It wasn't until Dad took control of it recently, when Grandma Ria got sick, that he took steps to open it again. Can you believe that?"

Approaching footsteps and voices interrupted them as Wayne, Marty, and the others stepped out onto the stage again. Their expressions and mood had lightened, judging by the tone of their conversation, although it was difficult to hear what they were saying. Something about keeping the hotel guests comfortable.

Emmie leaned toward Nova again. "The thing that happened today... with the light. Has anything like that happened before?"

Nova nodded and frowned. "What I've told you about the box is only a small part of the bigger picture. I'm always on edge when I'm in here, but I won't give up. I can't. It's not just about my dad's drive to get rich after all the renovations, or even about trying to make Grandma Ria's dreams come true, it's about *my* dreams. This theater is my home and playground, and I've never felt so driven to... shine."

"Nova," Wayne forcefully shouted from the stage, "We've got a lot of work to do."

Emmie stood, and Nova followed as they strolled toward the stage. The cool air, like someone had an open window nearby, seemed to follow them all the way down the aisle and then disappeared after they reached the front of the theater.

Nova gestured to her wetsuit. "I should change out of this and get back to work, but Marty can give you a tour."

"Thank you," Emmie said. "I'm sure you're very busy rehearsing for your performance."

"Very. And I need to squeeze in some time to check on Grandma Ria, too."

"Does she live nearby?"

Nova pointed up. "In the penthouse on the twentieth floor. Well, her penthouse occupies the entire floor."

Before arriving at the stage, Emmie paused to ask another question. "Would your grandmother mind if we talked with her for a bit before it gets too late? She might know the history of the place better than anyone, from how it sounds."

Nova smiled, then looked down with a sorrowful expression. "She would *love* to have visitors, I'm sure, but... she hasn't spoken a word in months."

"Why not?" Emmie asked.

"She's dying of late-stage Parkinson's disease."

7

"I'm sorry," Emmie said.

"You didn't know," Nova said. "Grandma Ria doesn't leave her penthouse anymore. A nurse stops by every day to check on her, and I do the same. I can still take you up there..."

Emmie shook her head. "Maybe later. I suppose it's better to focus on the theater for now, anyway."

Nova nodded. "Whatever you need."

Only moments after gathering beside the stage with the others, Jason swept his arm around Emmie and whispered in her ear. "That was interesting, but we barely scratched the surface. There's a ton of history back there."

At the same time, Nova grabbed Jimmy's arm and steered him toward the exit. Stopping halfway up the aisle, she glanced back and looked at Emmie. "I'll have more time to talk tomorrow. Call me."

"Definitely." Emmie smiled. They seemed to have an understanding between them now that no matter what happened from that moment on, they would get through this ordeal together.

Wayne stepped forward and hovered near Emmie with a curious stare. "I see you're getting acquainted with the star of the show. She's quite busy, so please keep the distractions to a minimum."

"I won't *distract* her," Emmie said, trying to reign in her growing agitation. "Promise. But we'd like to take a tour of the backstage, if that's okay with you. Nova mentioned Marty might show us around?"

Wayne hesitated and glanced over at Marty, who was staring toward the stage with his mouth gaping. "Marty, do you have time to show them around? The faster this is over with, the better."

The old man didn't seem to hear, and even took a step away from them while leaning to get a better view of something near the center of the stage floor.

Wayne spoke louder. "Marty, what the hell?"

Marty furrowed his brow and seemed to snap out of whatever had held his attention. He gave a nervous laugh. "Sorry. Sure, I can take them back."

"Grab a coffee or something," Wayne ordered. "We need to bring our A-game for this opening. Can you do that?"

"No problem, boss."

Wayne nodded as if satisfied with his answer, then stepped toward the center of the stage while glancing around curiously.

Marty wasted no time in following Wayne's instructions. The old man nodded once and looked at Emmie and Jason with a tired stare before gesturing to a door at the far corner of the stage. "See that door? Wait for me there."

"Understood," Jason answered with a little salute, like a soldier being ordered around. His joker side was coming out at a bad time. "Looking forward to it."

Emmie led Jason toward the door and glanced back over her shoulder when they were out of earshot. Wayne whispered something to Marty—no doubt, something about them—before walking out of the theater.

"Where did you guys go while I was talking with Nova?" she whispered to Jason.

"Not far," he answered. "Wayne did most of the talking."

"I'm sure of that. No wonder Nova is stressed out."

Jason laughed. "I'm sure he's under a lot of pressure with the grand opening in just a few days."

Emmie glanced at the stage again as they waited for Marty to unlock the door. There was no sign of anything unusual. No shadows moving or any unusual sensations that someone—alive or dead—was lingering in the darkness. A moment later, the main stage lights switched off. The auditorium's lighting illuminated the stage well enough to get a sense of its depth beyond the towering backdrops, storage trunks, and curtains, but it seemed to go on forever within the shadows.

A moment later, Marty arrived and opened the door, slipping his phone into a pocket on the side of his overalls before gesturing for them to follow him with a smirk. "The boss said to give you the royal tour."

"I'm guessing that's an upgrade from the regular tour?" Jason held back a smirk.

Marty stared at him for a long moment. "Not many people get the chance to come back here. I've given maybe a handful of tours back here since the place shut down forty years ago, so consider yourselves lucky and keep the wisecracks to yourself."

Jason pushed his lips together. "Sorry, I'll tone it down."

"That would help." Marty led them through the door and switched on the lights.

Moving across a wide open space just behind the curtain, the backstage area grew more crowded near the back, branching off in two directions with crates, scaffolding, chairs, tables, tools, ropes and rigging, set pieces in various stages of repair, and piles of cables stacked in every corner. A few tall set pieces stood in the open, their colorfully decorated surfaces shimmering in the overhead lighting.

Several doors ran along the back wall, nearly obscured within the clutter. The main one in the middle had massive double-wide metal doors with a wooden sign above it labeled 'Props & Illusions.' One door on the left had a green sign labeled 'Performers Only,' and another on the right was labeled 'Dressing Rooms.' A constant hum of electricity filled the air.

Marty walked toward the large doors in the middle, glancing over his shoulder at them a couple of times as if they might have wandered off.

Unlocking the prop room with a set of keys from his pocket, he switched on the lights and they stepped inside. The room was lit by a row of dim lights high above them that hardly seemed adequate for anyone to safely move among the maze of stage props that crowded the area. Still, Marty maneuvered around them with ease, pointing out some of the items and explaining their purpose for the show.

"That's for Nova's first act." Marty pointed to a tall, thin staircase on wheels that seemingly led to nowhere. "Jimmy goes up the steps while in a trance, and then he just keeps going until he levitates above the audience. Can't tell you how it works. If you were hoping I'd spill the secrets, you're out of luck. Not that Nova shares much info with me."

Emmie spotted the shattered glass cage that had held Nova during her performance earlier and gestured to it. "The props get fixed after each show?"

Marty followed her gaze. "For that one, we only need to replace a single sheet of customized glass." He turned back to them while making a wide gesture to the closed crimson curtain separating them from the stage. "What do you think of the place? Beautiful, isn't it? Wayne and I worked hard to make it look like it was forty years ago when it opened, just before things fell apart, literally."

"It *is* beautiful," Emmie said. "I'm sure everyone will love the show. We'd love to stay for the grand opening, except Wayne's only giving us a few days—"

"I heard. All the rooms are booked the day after you leave and every ticket to the performance is sold out, at least for the first few nights."

"I'm sure Nova can get us tickets," Jason suggested.

"Doubt it." Marty leaned against a tall wooden structure painted black, a sly grin tugging at the corners of his mouth. "Every seat is filled. But you know, back when this place opened, we had this little trick for getting someone in without a ticket. Called it scoring a 'bootleg pass.' Just a quick detour through the back entrance, bypass security and the stagehands. No one ever noticed. Got a buddy in once to see one of Max's last performances. Front-row view without spending a dime. Pretty slick, eh?" He watched their expressions as if expecting a little praise.

"Is that an offer?" Jason asked.

Marty's eyes widened as he stood straight again without a grin. "That was a long time ago, sorry. Things are very different now with the tighter security. Didn't mean to suggest—"

"It's okay," Emmie said. "We're here to do a job, to help my friend, not to be entertained. We can see her show another time, under better circumstances."

"Sure, you can." Marty glanced around. "And I know why you're here, so just let me know what you need. I suppose you're more interested in the history of the place than the props. Nova thinks we have ghosts, and I can't speak for the things she claims to have seen, but you've got your work cut out for you."

"Why do you say that?" Jason asked.

He glanced at a stack of props in the darkness beside them. "Magicians don't like to give up their secrets."

"So I've heard," she said.

"Nova has a wonderful opportunity here to revive the dying art of illusion—she's intelligent and driven—but she's superstitious as all hell, and I don't understand what she plans to gain by bringing you here." He straightened a tall, black cabinet, pushing it out of the way as they continued forward.

"Maybe she sees and understands things that others don't." Emmie focused on the space around her and sensed a presence nearby, although the energy held no light in her mind as if it was attempting to blend in with the shadows.

"Sure, she's a special kid," Marty said. "I won't argue with that. I just don't see the point. But... I suppose it's not my place to share my opinions. Do you have any questions?"

Emmie didn't hold back and stood directly in front of him while looking at him straight in the eyes. "Have you seen any spirits? Or anything you might consider supernatural?"

Marty's expression didn't change. "Let me just say I understand why people would think the place is haunted. People died here..." A flash of pain seemed to sweep over his face. "...and it's sat abandoned for decades."

"But have you seen anything unusual?" Emmie asked.

"Define *unusual*. The walls are packed to the ceiling with that stuff. Like I said, I used to work here in the 80s, when Gloria Harrison bought this little gem of a theater and attracted some of the biggest names in magic at the time for her grand opening. Anyone can build a casino, but she had an eye for success, and she was driven. Perfect timing. Top-notch talent. Back in the second golden age of magic, everything was looking bright, but..." He gave a little laugh. "...things didn't work out that way."

"What went wrong?" Emmie asked.

He glanced at each of them, then led them out of the room. "We should keep moving."

Emmie touched the top edge of her phone in her pocket. "Would you mind if I took a few photos of this area?"

Marty glanced back. "I expect you'll take a lot of photos during your stay, so feel free. Anything off limits is locked up."

Emmie brought out her phone and snapped several photos of her surroundings. Using her phone's camera was a far cry from the elaborate equipment Finn would have used in a case like this, but the images might provide useful reference later, even if the images didn't contain any signs of spirits.

After Marty locked up the prop room, he took them toward an older section of the backstage. The exposed pipes and ducts revealed an aging infrastructure held up by massive cement columns surrounded by stacks of stage crates and boxes labeled as things like 'white costume' and 'extra ropes.' The musty air reminded her of entering the home of someone who hadn't stepped outside in months, where the possessions had sat undisturbed for years, and the smell of slow decay saturated everything.

"Gloria hired me in 1984." Marty glanced back toward the stage. "She trusted me to take her vision for this place and make it come alive, and I worked my ass off for her every single night—while it lasted—and I didn't deserve the blame when everything fell apart. The theater shut down in 1985, but it didn't have to. Tragic accidents don't necessarily shut down a place like this. The rumors shut it down. Fear and superstition swallowed it whole. First, Mystic Max died, along with his two assistants." Marty glanced down and swallowed. "Max was a character, all right. A good illusionist—not great—and a real pain in the ass. What he lacked in talent, he made up for in ego."

"Why did Gloria hire him then?" Emmie asked.

"I suppose his good looks." Marty gave a sarcastic smile. "But then another performer died, Zack Vayne, in a freak accident during a rehearsal only a couple of weeks later. The audience was full of kids on a field trip to watch a *professional* rehearse. My assistant and I strapped Zack in the saw prop—the one where they saw the person in half—and he held up his hand, just like he would do for the audience, and he said, 'Start the saw, Marty. Let it rip.' I did, and that was that. All those poor students are probably still in therapy recovering from the experience. I've never seen so much blood. You wouldn't think a human could bleed like that. My assistant got a lot of flak for what happened, since he was the last to inspect the prop's safety mechanism, and he accepted a lot of the blame, unfortunately. Nothing about him was reckless, and we never took anything for granted. So when they blamed him specifically for what happened to Zack, of course, he took it hard." Marty wiped his palms on the sides of his overalls. "Shot himself... in his home and I hired someone else, although it was probably already too late by then to save the place."

"Why is that?" Jason asked.

"The rumors were already running wild around Vegas. Some of the workers complained of seeing things—ghost sightings, props moving on their own and stuff like that. It was just a matter of time before they'd had enough. Soon after I got things under control again, another magician died—Danny Drake. He'd just started his performance to a packed audience, and then it all went up in flames. I had thoroughly inspected *everything* before he went on stage. He was supposed to escape from a cage while it hung above a fire, but... the cable broke and..." Marty winced and frowned.

Emmie swallowed. "I'm sure it wasn't your fault."

Marty shook his head. "The device never should have failed —*never*—but it malfunctioned anyway. Damn tragedy. The backup cable also failed. There's no way in hell it should have done what it did—not a chance—but... it did."

"What did the investigators conclude?" Jason asked.

"It was another accident, of course, but I have my opinions."

"Care to share what those are?"

"Not really." He leaned against a tall crate. "I like my job."

"We'll keep anything you say confidential."

He smirked. "It won't make any difference."

"Why do you say that?"

"Whatever is here... isn't going anywhere, no matter how much holy water you throw at it."

"So you *have* seen something?" Emmie asked.

He glanced around briefly. "Listen, I've never told this to anyone except Nova, so you didn't hear it from me, but just before things went... *off the rails* for Danny Drake, I heard footsteps from the catwalk over the stage, but I could see the whole thing clearly from where I stood and nobody was up there. Nobody could get up or down that ladder without me seeing them, and all the cables were controlled from a panel beside me on the stage." His voice faded a bit as he seemed to relive the horrifying experience. "As soon as I heard that snap, I knew something had gone very wrong. Something had malfunctioned deep within the device, and what are the chances that both cables snapped at exactly the same time at exactly the most dangerous moment of Danny's act? I couldn't have executed that if I'd planned it for months. Not pointing any fingers here, but it would take someone with serious knowledge of the inner workings of a theater and magic to pull that off."

"Who was backstage at the time?" Jason asked.

"Just the performers for that night and their assistants. The police interviewed everyone, especially me—thoroughly—although nobody was ever charged."

"That's awful," Emmie said.

"So everyone was in the spotlight for a while, and with that kind of attention, the rumors went wild and the stories snowballed. Some workers claimed to have seen things backstage, and then they quickly convinced the public that something supernatural was behind the deaths. With that much terrible publicity, Gloria had no choice but to shut down the theater, and it never reopened. Well, until now."

"You said you heard footsteps and experienced things you couldn't explain," Emmie said, "but have you ever *seen* anything?"

"You want me to say I saw ghosts?" He grinned and glanced around. "I'm too busy around here to entertain my imagination. But Wayne hired you to make Nova happy, so I'm sure you'll find something to calm her down, right?"

Emmie tilted her head. "That's not how we work."

"I've seen the TV shows, and this *is* Vegas, after all. You're not the only ghost hunters in town. You'll put on a convincing performance for the cameras, make a little money off the video footage, and everyone's happy. Don't tell me you *actually* see ghosts."

Emmie nodded. "Not at the moment, but I sense spirits in this place, yes. And we're not here to make money off anyone."

"You don't need to convince me," Marty said. "Everything in Vegas is a show. It's all an illusion. I get it."

"I can see the dead."

Marty looked at her curiously. "Prove it."

Emmie glanced around. "I don't have to prove anything, but they're here and we intend to find them. You'll know I'm telling the truth when they're gone and the theater is quiet."

He took a step toward them and lowered his voice. "Then keep an open mind while you look around the place. Lots of history here. Lots of secrets. And don't bother trying to convince Wayne that you've seen ghosts, or that Nova is telling the truth. He doesn't want to hear any of that. It won't do any good. He only wants you here to keep Nova on track. To soothe her nerves. Do you think you can do that?"

Emmie leaned back. "So what do you think really happened here?"

"I'm open-minded, for what it's worth, but I won't believe anything until I see it, and if you really do see ghosts and all that, then great, get rid of them, but keep your eyes open wide for me because there's only so much I can do to keep the performers safe."

"You think someone living is trying to harm them?"

"Who can say? Maybe what happened in the '80s actually were accidents, but..." He glanced up toward the lighting rig. "... all those lights are secured with a backup cable in case any of them break loose. The one that fell... it wasn't secured. I checked each of them myself a few days ago, but I can't keep an eye on everything. Understand?"

Emmie nodded. "You're suggesting what happened today might happen again?"

Marty turned away and led them toward the back of the stage. "I'm just saying, watch your step."

They passed several more old crates, outdated stage displays, and stacks of boxes labeled things like 'saw', 'Gigi's costume', and 'cage'. The props seemed to sprawl in endless directions, extending into the dimly lit passageway that narrowed as they continued.

Jason walked over to one of the devices, and ran his finger over what looked like a prop blade for an act where someone gets sawed in half with their toes sticking out one side and the head sticking out the other. He peered inside, lifted the blade from its cradle on the device, then recoiled a moment later while nursing his finger. "That thing's real."

Marty stepped over and grabbed the blade from his hands, returning it to the device. "Not toys. Respect them."

"Sorry."

"If you need to inspect something, I'll help you."

Emmie remembered the box that Nova had mentioned earlier and glanced around. "Nova asked me to inspect a small wooden box that she ran across back here. She said it had a gold star painted on it."

Marty glanced down. "I know the one."

"Can we see it?" Emmie asked.

Marty hesitated. "It's in Nova's dressing room."

"Are we allowed to go in there?"

"For a moment."

He led them back around toward the main area and approached the door labeled 'Dressing Room,' but stopped short of unlocking it. He gestured toward it. "It's in there."

A brief silence fell between them until he finally dug out his keys and opened it for them. Stepping inside, he switched on the lights, but stayed near the doorway and pointed to the box on the other side of the crowded room. "It's over there, in the corner."

Despite the rows of costumes hanging from garment racks on every side, Emmie spotted it right away. An antique wooden box, wide open, the size of a mini fridge with a gold star painted on its side. With Jason beside her, she went to look inside, but moments before peeking over the edge, it snapped shut on its own.

Jason and Emmie exchanged a glance before she looked at Marty. The old man had already turned away from them.

"Did you see that?" Emmie asked Marty.

He shook his head. "See what?"

Running her fingers across the lid, she pulled open the lid again without resistance this time and peered inside. It was empty, except for a gray notebook lying at the bottom. She pulled it out and flipped through the pages. Hand-drawn diagrams and sketches filled its pages, along with detailed notes and measurements for what looked like magician props. Cabinets, decks of cards, handcuffs, chains, trapdoors, a birdcage, a barrel, a lantern, and a guillotine with a crescent blade.

Jason looked over Emmie's shoulder and whispered. "I don't have a good feeling about this place."

Emmie nodded and placed the notebook back inside the box. The presence of a spirit was stronger here, but still no energy had formed in her mind to reveal their location. Someone's harsh gaze fell on her, watching them from the darkness, just as Nova had suggested.

Just after she stepped away, the box's lid snapped shut again. A dark energy flowed around it like twisting blackened fingers.

Marty cleared his throat. "Time's up."

8

A bellhop had offered to help carry their bags back to the room, and Emmie had graciously accepted his offer. Not that they really needed any help—their bags weren't particularly heavy—but the young man's ambitious attitude seemed to lighten the mood after the weight of heavy conversations in the theater. Also, it was a perfect opportunity to get an insider's perspective on what Nova was experiencing.

Emmie stepped into the elevator and huddled beside Jason. The bellhop had stacked their luggage on a cart and rolled it in behind them. His uniform looked sharp: a military-style double-breasted jacket with brass buttons, matching trousers, and a cap. He stood tall, with a mischievous smile as though he were about to break into a joke but was keeping it to himself. A small gold nametag on his chest read 'Charlie K.'

As soon as the doors closed behind them, Charlie pressed the '19' button on the elevator panel, and the elevator shuddered a moment before rising.

"You're going to love the place," Charlie said.

"Depends on how many ghosts we find," Jason joked.

Charlie swallowed. "Nova told me why you're here."

"Have *you* seen anything strange here?" Jason asked.

"Me? No." He gave a nervous laugh and straightened his cap. "I hope I never see anything, but... I've heard plenty of stories."

There was an additional button above their floor labeled 'PH.' Emmie remembered what Nova had said about her grandmother living in the penthouse. "We don't get the penthouse?" Emmie said wryly.

Charlie grinned. "I'm sure Grandma Ria wouldn't appreciate sharing her home, but you have a wonderful room on the floor just below hers—the next best thing—and Nova's just down the hall from you."

"I'm surprised Wayne put us near the top."

"I think Nova had something to do with that. It's a lovely hotel. You're going to love the place. Super quiet. Only Grandma Ria's penthouse above you."

Jason glanced up as if pondering something.

Emmie looked at Charlie curiously. "You're also related to her?"

His smile stretched wider. "No relation. Everyone calls her Grandma Ria. Respect."

The elevator opened, and they walked down the hall to the last door on the left, room 1901. While Charlie unlocked the door, Emmie stepped over to a scenic window only a few yards further at the end of the hall. The view took her breath away. The lights and traffic pulsing on the streets below were mesmerizing, and the mountains in the distance were a stark reminder that the hotel sat in the middle of the desert.

Charlie must have noticed her expression because he swung the door open, stepped aside with a bit of dramatic flare, and gestured for them to go in. "If you think *that's* nice..."

Emmie followed Jason inside. The light immediately caught her attention. It poured in through the panoramic windows that stretched across two walls. For a moment, she just stood there and basked in the golden glow of the Vegas skyline. The city seemed to stretch forever in every direction, yet she couldn't shake the sense of confinement as the wall of competing hotels seemed to stare back at her.

"Back in the '80s," Charlie said, "this hotel was one of the tallest around, if you can believe that. Things have changed a lot since then." He gestured to their luggage. "Where would you like me to put your bags?"

"Anywhere is fine." Jason walked over to the panoramic windows.

The room was just as amazing as the rest of the hotel, but with a strange mix of antique charm and modern luxury. Two queen beds occupied one half of the space with a small living area taking up the rest of the room. The walls were painted in a rich green that reminded Emmie of a vintage cigar lounge. Gold accents ran along the edge of the crown molding, with stylish lamps on every table and an intricate pattern woven into the red rugs.

But it wasn't all nostalgic glamour; there were plenty of modern appliances around the room that seemed to break the illusion that they'd stepped back into the Roaring Twenties. A massive flat-screen TV hung on one wall beside a group of framed photos of downtown Las Vegas in its early days, and a gilded mirror hung above a faux marble fireplace. Emmie had no intention of using it, although someone would enjoy it. A full coffee bar sat in the corner with a state-of-the-art espresso machine, its spotless chrome surface gleaming like a jewel.

"This is nice," Jason said from the window. His voice was casual, but she caught the slight upward tilt of his brows as he glanced around. He was impressed, even if he wouldn't admit it.

"It's… more than enough." Emmie couldn't help but smile. What were they going to do with all that space? And she couldn't help but feel sorry for the hotel staff. The poor workers would have to go around and polish everything they'd touched.

"That's the way Grandma Ria wanted it," Charlie said. "The top two floors all to herself. She liked her privacy."

Emmie's eyes widened. "It doesn't get more private than that in a city like Las Vegas. They did a wonderful job with the renovations."

"The renovations on this floor aren't finished yet," Charlie added, "They completed a few of the rooms, including this one, and Nova's room down the hall, but Wayne insisted they hold off until..." Charlie's gaze dropped to the floor.

"I get it." Jason nodded. "Out of respect for Grandma Ria."

"Exactly." Charlie looked up again and gave a warm smile. "You might see some construction equipment sitting out during your stay—they've used the floor as a sort of storage area recently. The rooms sat empty for a long time, at Grandma Ria's request, until Nova moved in down the hall."

Emmie glanced at him. "Nobody used these rooms in forty years?"

"No," Charlie said then grinned. "I mean, they've all been *cleaned* over the years. And Grandma Ria allowed friends and family to stay here... occasionally."

She turned back to the view, her reflection barely visible in the glass. "After the theater shut down back in the '80s, what convinced Grandma Ria to change her mind and open it again?"

"She didn't," Charlie said. "Wayne made the decision. I'm not sure Grandma Ria even knows about it. She hasn't stepped out of her penthouse in months, but they're planning to surprise her at the grand opening."

Emmie met Jason's gaze. Judging by his expression, he was thinking the same thing.

Surprise her? She turned the phrase over in her mind, and it just felt wrong. The idea of unveiling something as monumental as the Amber House Theater—a place full of so much history and tragedy—without Gloria's full knowledge seemed reckless, almost cruel. What if the old woman didn't approve of it? Or what if the memories were too much to handle?

"What do you think?" Charlie made a wide gesture with both arms. "It's not the penthouse suite, but it's the next best thing...

right? And I'm sure you won't have any problems with the noise from the street up here, and all the other rooms on the floor are unoccupied, except for Nova. Her room is just down the hall, room 1921, on the opposite end, but she spends most of her time in the theater rehearsing."

Jason seemed to take the revelation of the surprise grand opening in stride as he stepped over to the kitchen's full-size refrigerator and opened it, revealing an assortment of beers, wines, and other beverages. "Is this included in our stay?"

Charlie grinned and nodded. "Everything is complimentary... for you."

"Perfect, thank you."

"Don't thank me. Nova insisted we take care of everything."

Jason nodded and closed the refrigerator. "I bet Wayne moaned and groaned a bit about that too. Much appreciated."

Stepping to the window where Jason had stood moments earlier, Emmie tried to take in the overwhelming beauty of the city. "What I wouldn't give to live up here."

"You can, of course," Charlie said. "I think the rooms on the eighteenth floor will go for around *only* a thousand a night. Plus tax and fees. Can you afford that?"

Jason laughed sharply while starting to unpack.

Emmie joined him. "Definitely not. But it *is* beautiful."

Charlie stood watching them from the doorway, his smile never fading for a moment. "Nova shares your sentiment."

Emmie stepped toward the open bathroom door and glanced inside. It looked nothing like a bathroom. There were sparkling surfaces, spacious countertops, gold-plated fixtures, and all of their bathroom needs laid out in a perfect and practical configuration. It looked more like a Hollywood celebrity's dressing room than a bathroom.

Charlie continued, gesturing to an old intercom system beside the door. Its yellowing plastic panel stood out against the freshly painted white walls. "Not everything was scrapped in the renovation, like this little wonder of technology. It still works, and a light on the panel comes on if someone pushes the buzzer outside your door. I suppose they thought it would add to the hotel's speakeasy charm when they built the place in the '80s—you know, forcing outsiders to identify themselves with a secret password before you let them in—and Wayne decided to keep it. There's also a buzzer, but you can switch the entire system off. It's a bit archaic, I know, but it was high tech when Grandma Ria opened the place. There's one in the bedroom, too."

Emmie glanced at the intercom. "I can see where that might have come in handy, before cellphones."

Jason grinned. "We'll need to come up with a secret password."

Charlie remained at attention near the door. "I'll let you get settled in now."

"Thank you, Charlie," Emmie said.

Jason dug into his pocket with wide eyes. "Oh, I almost forgot!" Pulling out several bills, he handed a ten to Charlie. "The tip."

The man laughed and handed back the cash. "Nova took care of the tip too. Save it for the other hotel staff." Turning away from them, he glanced back and looked at them curiously. "May I ask you a question?"

"What's that?" Emmie asked.

"What do you plan to do with them when you catch them?" he asked.

"Catch who?"

"The ghosts."

Emmie glanced at Jason for a moment before answering. "We don't really catch them, like in the movies. We communicate with them and help them move on after we understand why they're here."

Charlie nodded in acceptance. "I suppose that makes sense. I just hope you're the real deal—for Nova's sake. Someone has to get them out of here. They're really messing with her mind."

Emmie took a step toward him. "In what way?"

Charlie opened his mouth, as if to speak, then closed it again. "I better let Nova tell you."

Emmie nodded. "I will, and I promise, we'll do our best. We won't leave until she's safe."

Charlie gave a brief wave goodbye as he turned away. "That won't be easy. It sounds like they would kill us all if they could."

9

Emmie settled into the sprawling red velvet couch beside Jason and placed her phone between them after switching the audio into speaker mode. Finn and Sarah were on the call, no doubt also getting cozy by the sound of sheets rustling in the background.

"Do you miss us?" Sarah asked.

"Every day," Emmie said without reservation.

"How are you getting along without my amazing intellect to steer you right?" Finn asked.

Emmie rolled her eyes, smirked, and turned to Jason while answering Finn. "We're doing quite well, thank you very much—but of course, we miss you both. We *do* work better as a team, but remember what I said earlier, that it's not realistic to think we'll always be together for every situation that comes along. Jason and I can handle this, and you'll be out here in a couple of days anyway, so I'm not worried. Maybe I'll have it wrapped up by the time you arrive. But first, did you get the photos I sent?"

"We did," Finn said. "Lots of history stuffed behind that stage. Lots of fascinating props, although I couldn't see much. Too dark. Adjust the settings on your phone's camera, if possible."

"Sorry," Emmie said. "It was late."

"How's the place?" Sarah asked. "Do you feel safe?"

"I do…" Emmie couldn't hide the doubt in her voice. "But that's the strange thing. I'm not encountering any spirits like I expected. They're not making it easy for me, like I'd hoped. They're here… although I get the feeling Nova is still battling them on a daily basis, judging by the cuts she showed me on her arms. I definitely sense a dark energy in the place."

"If you feel you're in any danger—" Finn started to say.

"I'm fine." Emmie's mind flashed back to the spotlight crashing on the stage soon after she'd arrived. She knew all too well the stark reality she faced by confronting violent spirits. *Anything* could happen if she mishandled the spirits' trauma or underestimated the rage that held them in that ethereal existence between life and death. She had learned that hard lesson at a young age, terrorized by the Hanging Girl for so many years in her home, that ghosts weren't just harmless wisps of energy lurking in the shadows. The charged emotions of a desperate spirit could reach through the thin veil at any time and grab hold of anyone who dared to step within their reach.

"Seriously," Finn said, "if you need help, call me anytime, day or night."

"I can take care of myself." Emmie grinned. "You're like the big brother I never had, you know that? So protective, and I appreciate that, but I also know my limits. This isn't anything that I can't handle. Like I explained before I left, this is an opportunity for me to grow as a psychic. Who knows, maybe I'll discover some new hidden skill out of this." She turned to Jason. "And maybe this is also a chance for Jason to get outside *his* comfort zone."

He looked at her with wide eyes. "I stepped out of my comfort zone as soon as I met you, but I'm not sure I want to develop my skills any further. It's better this way."

Emmie squeezed his hand. "I suppose you're right. Your

support is enough. At least, I don't feel threatened yet, but I'm sure that will change after we know what we're facing."

"I found something that might help," Finn cut in. "I got my hands on the police report for the first magician who died in the 1985 gas leak in the dressing room of the Amber House Theater. His stage name was Mystic Max. Max Donovan was his real name. By all accounts, he was an asshole, to put it mildly. Brash, arrogant but handsome, and a master showman who knew how to draw in the audiences, according to what I read. But he was also a heartbreaker, which I'm sure gained him a lot of enemies. The police scrutinized everything after his death, covering all the bases, but finally concluded that he died from a gas leak—carbon monoxide poisoning—after a valve in the furnace malfunctioned. It left him and his two assistants dead while they were partying in some back room after a show."

Emmie considered it for a moment. "That doesn't explain Nova's claim of a violent spirit. Maybe the violence is coming from one of the other magicians who died?"

"We can look at those too, but don't rule out The Late Great Mystic Max just yet. If he *was* murdered, then there are plenty of suspects. I found an interview with a rival magician named Patrick 'Trick' Spurlock who complained about Max's inappropriate behavior behind the stage. Lots of overt flirting with his assistants and even taking some hotel guests back to his room. Trick had nothing good to say about the man and said all sorts of disparaging remarks about Max's abilities, calling Max a glorified lounge performer and a hack. This was after Trick was hired as the opening act at the Amber House Theater, with Max getting the top billing."

"Sounds like Trick was jealous." Emmie turned to Jason. "We'll ask Marty about the guy the next time we talk, although Marty had nothing good to say about any of the other magicians."

"Who's Marty?" Sarah asked.

"The theater's stage manager, and he also takes care of all the props. He's worked there from the beginning, so I'm sure he can help us paint a complete picture of what happened before the place shut down in the '80s."

"Gloria Harrison owned the place when the theater shut down," Finn said. "If she's alive, maybe you can talk with her too?"

Emmie glanced at the floor. "I already tried—she's alive—but don't expect any answers from her. She's in hospice care. On top of everything else, Nova is worried her grandmother will die before she even gets a chance to perform for her on opening night. I'm sure Nova's heard stories about what happened here in the '80s, but I'm not sure she'd have the insights we're looking for, and getting answers from Wayne seems out of the question. He's barely tolerating our presence and seems determined to see us fail. This is going to take time, which we don't have."

"So you *do* need us," Finn said wryly.

Emmie sighed. "I could never replace you, Finn, but what *I* need is more information about the other magicians who died here. And anybody else. Marty gave us some information about them..."

"I'm one step ahead of you," Finn said. "You might already know this, but the names of the other two magicians were Zack Vayne, who died in a particularly nasty mishap halfway through a rehearsal, and Danny Drake, who died in *another* horrific accident—burning alive in a faulty cage—during his opening illusion on stage in front of a packed audience. Two weeks after Danny died, the theater closed permanently. Again, the police ruled out foul play for those deaths, too."

"How can any theater have so many accidents?" Emmie asked.

"That's exactly how the audiences reacted. News of the mysterious deaths spread through Vegas like wildfire, and rumors circulated that the place was haunted. They blamed everything on malicious ghosts."

"But *what* ghosts?" Emmie held back her frustration. "We need to find out more about Trick's background."

"You're thinking what I'm thinking," Sarah said.

"Someone sabotaged the illusions?" Jason asked.

"Exactly," Sarah said.

"Let's not jump to conclusions," Finn said. "I'll keep digging."

Emmie sank at the weight of knowing they had a long road ahead of them. "If Trick had anything to do with killing one or more of the magicians, then that might explain the violent spirits."

"We have to be careful in how we investigate this," Finn said. "I discovered he came out of retirement just to be Nova's opening act."

"Just like the other magicians," Emmie said. The idea of history repeating itself sent a shiver up Emmie's spine. "On top of that, we need to keep her safe from the spirits. Finn, can you please investigate the history of the place a little more? I know you said that Gloria Harrison purchased it from someone back in the 80s, but I'm wondering if we're missing something deeper here, something that might have happened in the theater before Gloria bought it."

"I'll look again, although I don't remember anything about its history that stood out."

"Thanks. We have to consider all options, at least until the spirits decide to reveal themselves. But if Mr. Spurlock did have anything to do with murdering one or more of the magicians, then we have to be careful in how we investigate this since he'll be working closely with Nova."

"Trick also failed to get top billing anywhere back in the '80s, but he's gained a lot of followers since then."

"You should definitely put him at the top of your list," Sarah said. "Just please be careful."

"I got this under control. And Jason is backing me up, so there's nothing to worry about. Right, Jason?" Emmie looked at

Jason, who had settled further into the couch with his face toward the ceiling and his eyes closed.

He barely nodded. "Right."

"It's been a long day," Emmie said, "so I think it's best we pick up again tomorrow morning."

"We'll meet you there on Thursday," Finn said.

"Em?" Sarah cut in. "Wait."

"What's up?" Emmie asked.

"That picture you sent, the one showing the far side of the curtain. Can you take a look at that one for a moment?"

Emmie flipped through her photos and pulled it up. "What about it?"

"Look in the back. *Way* in the back. Do you see that?"

Em zoomed in, although the grainy texture diluted the quality. Still, she could see it. The faint outline of someone, whether living or dead, standing in the shadows watching them. Flipping to the next picture, which showed the same corner of the backstage from a different angle, revealed that the figure had disappeared. "I do. I guess they know I'm here."

10

Emmie awoke to the sound of scratching in the walls. It wasn't so loud or disruptive like someone doing construction in the next room, but a subtle, yet persistent scratching as if someone were trying to claw their way through the sheet rock a little at a time.

Turning over in bed, she faced Jason and watched him snoring next to her. His chest rose and fell in rhythmic waves, lit by the dim light that spilled in through the cracks of the closed window curtains. Within the pause of each breath, she listened for the abrasive sounds coming from somewhere within the walls. It grew louder by the minute, and it seemed to inch closer and then pause for a long moment as if waiting to gauge her reaction before continuing.

Rats?

It *was* an old hotel, and the renovations had no doubt stirred up more than just debris, disturbing everything that had settled into the safety of the shadows over the years. Lots of critters must have scurried for a new home as the workers swept through the rooms.

Still, the noises unnerved her. It was probably nothing to worry about, but she had learned long ago to always take the bumps in the night seriously, especially when visiting a place with plenty of history. Sometimes it *was* her imagination, ending with a simple explanation, but most of the time her intuition proved correct. Too many spirits had stepped out of the darkness over the years to ever truly regain that blissful ignorance of sleep again.

Grabbing her phone off the end table beside the bed, she switched it on.

2:30 AM.

Jason stirred next to her while cringing in the light of her phone and turned away, taking the warmth of his body with him as the cool night air swept in around her. This was the worst part of waking up to a strange sound. The uncertainty was maddening. She could either wait for the noise to fade away or the weight of the darkness to push her back to sleep.

Instead of letting her mind drift back to sleep, she climbed out of bed and stood in the darkness. Still clutching her phone, she folded her arms over her chest and glanced back at Jason. It wouldn't help to wake him. If she wanted to explore, then she needed to do it on her own. Her flannel pajamas did little to keep her warm as she stepped around the bed, her bare feet scraping over the low-pile carpeting until she stopped and looked from side to side with her eyes closed.

The scratching noises still came from somewhere within the walls on all sides as if the entire room were surrounded by whatever intended to make its way inside. Focusing as best she could within her sleepy daze, she sensed the presence of a spirit nearby. Just like the noises around her, the spirit shifted and faded within her awareness.

Opening her eyes again, she attempted to draw the spirit in closer, but pulling at its energy only generated resistance as the faint sounds eluded her, moving up the walls and scattering across the ceiling toward the living room as if a thousand mice had made a mad dash for the exit.

Their path formed a distinct direction, and she followed

them, moving beneath the sound, carried forward by curiosity and determination to face whatever had awakened her. It *was* leading her out of her hotel room, and she had no intention of stopping to get Jason's help, even as her heart raced faster. Yes, she was scared, a little, but she had faced plenty of moments like that before. Nothing she couldn't handle alone.

"You got this, girl," she whispered.

The noises faded after scraping across the ceiling and out into the hallway. There was no mistaking it now for rats or any animal. A spirit had drawn her attention, but how long would she take the bait? At the back of her mind, she still pictured the injuries Nova had endured at the hands of something supernatural within the place. Would the same also happen to her if she went too far?

Stopping at the door before leaving the suite, she reminded herself that she knew nothing of the entity luring her out into the hallway. Anything could be out there. Clutching her phone a little tighter, she took a deep breath. She *could* wake Jason in an emergency, and she had Nova's number too, but this is why she'd come there, for moments like this, and she wouldn't back away.

This spirit stringing her along held a distinct energy in her mind. A dark intensity mixed with an air of playfulness as if this were some devious child daring her to come out and play. But judging by its light, it wasn't a child. This was a troubled spirit full of pain and fury.

"Where are you taking me?" she spoke into the cool air.

Someone's faint voice, low and full of bitterness, echoed behind the door ahead of her, coming from somewhere down the hallway. It was an adult male's voice, and it caught her off guard. The scratching and scraping in her hotel room had succeeded in getting her out of bed and to the door, but those noises were gone, replaced by a silent stillness between the bursts of grumbling coming from the spirit ahead. She couldn't stop now.

Unlocking the door, she turned the latch slowly, opening it

with great care to prevent Jason from hearing her leave. It was better to let him get a good night's sleep.

Leaving the door wide open, she made her way out into the hallway. The moment reminded her of leaving her bedroom as a child, knowing the Hanging Girl was lurking somewhere out there, watching her every move, waiting for her to come a little closer before...

An icy chill swept up Emmie's spine. Even after years of confronting spirits, it hadn't gotten easier. She'd come a long way, building courage and friendships and tact, but all the fear and trauma of her childhood would forever haunt the back of her mind. Still, she had a job to do and swallowed her fear to face the danger that lay ahead. Clenching her teeth, she reminded herself that Nova's sanity was at stake, if not the young magician's life.

"Hello?" she said into the hallway.

The spirit's harsh voice erupted again, echoing off the walls. Slow and steady footsteps thumped across the carpeting somewhere just out of sight as if someone were pacing back and forth from room to room.

"Hello?" Emmie asked again. "Please come out so we can talk."

The voice came louder this time, echoing just out of sight at the end of the hall. Stepping toward the noises without hesitation, she clutched her phone a little tighter as the sense that someone was watching her grew stronger. The hallway's overhead lights flickered and flared as she moved forward. After passing several doors, the lights went dark.

"Who are you?" She switched her phone into flashlight mode. "We need to talk." The spirit was near. She could feel its dark energy pulling at her own as she moved from door to door to locate the source. Stopping in front of room 1913, she paused and tried the door handle. Locked. The spirit was inside, but no way to get to it. So close.

While debating her options, a latch on the other side of the door clicked open, and Emmie stepped back while gasping in a breath. Jimmy had said all the other rooms on the floor were unoccupied, so when the door rattled and the handle turned sharply, she stared at it with wide eyes.

The door opened on its own. The gaping darkness within the room seemed to beckon her inside as a twisting gray mist spilled out across the floor, unfurling like a carpet made from the breath of a grave. Cold air swept around her as the mist spread out like tendrils, filling every corner of the hallway as it came toward her and crept up the doorway and the walls.

The world around her seemed to vanish, swallowed by a pale, shifting cloud as something dark took shape in front of her. A faint outline, at first, that solidified out of the vapor and merged into the shape of a tall, thin man with hollowed-out features, his gaunt face stretched tight over sharp cheekbones. He wore a magician's costume, but the clothing hung in scorched, ragged shreds, with a bowtie half-melted against his blistered throat. His top hat sat at a crooked angle, charred around the edges, and his blackened fingers poked through what remained of his white gloves. Wisps of smoke rose from his body, rising from unseen embers, and when he moved, his joints cracked with a sickening bone-deep crunch.

He seemed unaware of his tragic state, pacing nervously back and forth within the swirling fog without making eye contact. His gaze frantically darted around the room as if searching for something.

"I'm late... so late... I've got to get down to the stage." He grumbled and lashed out at invisible objects as his hands twitched.

Emmie tensed but stood defiantly. "You're Danny Drake."

Momentarily meeting her gaze, he clutched at his lower chest and scratched at the raw flesh. "I don't have time for talk."

"Please," Emmie said. "I just have a few questions."

"I'm behind schedule again." His voice was bitter and pained as he gestured to a patch of scorched flesh across his arm. "And then *this* happened."

"Who did this to you?" Emmie asked.

"Who?" He paused and looked at her with a moment of clarity. "It was him... Trick... he ruined everything."

Before Emmie could ask him anything else, the man's eyes clouded over, and he turned and ran out of the room. Rushing after him, she caught up with him near the elevators until he disappeared through a wall, leaving Trick's name echoing through her mind.

11

Emmie waited until morning to tell Jason what she'd experienced the previous night, but made sure to repeat the spirit's revelation that *"Trick ruined everything."* It was more than just a revelation. It was a smoking gun, and at least now they had a direction to focus their attention. He listened attentively to every detail as she described the encounter while eating the complementary breakfast that someone from the hotel had delivered to their room minutes earlier.

Jason gave her a quizzical look when she described Danny Drake's appearance. "So three magicians died here, right?"

"Right," she said.

"And if Trick is the culprit behind their deaths, then Nova has a bigger problem than spirits."

"Or the attacks are nothing like any of us think. Trick knows his way around that theater like his own home, and he could slip in and out without anyone noticing. He would have easy access to Nova's props..."

"You think he's behind all of it?" Jason asked.

"Probably not all," she said. "The spirits died unnaturally, if it's true, so they probably have a lot of rage at what he did. You saw what one of them did by opening the box just now. No doubt, they've been trying to communicate with her, and she's misinterpreted their intentions."

Jason nodded slowly. "Makes sense. He's trying to sabotage her performance, like he did to the others, to knock her out of the show."

"Remember what Finn said about him? He failed to headline anywhere back in the '80s, but he's gained a lot of followers since then. I'm sure at his age, Trick believes this is his last chance for fame and save his legacy." Emmie could almost read his mind. She nodded. "We need to check him out right away."

"Finn can take care of that. I'll ask him to research the guy a little deeper, but I think it wouldn't hurt to have a discreet talk with Trick first. Get a feel for *his* state of mind."

Emmie scoffed. "And how would that conversation go? We can't just approach him and ask him to confess."

"Leave that to me. I'm good at stuff like this."

"That's what I'm afraid of." Emmie shook her head. "You can't force him to talk about what happened. Using your psychic persuasion in this case would do more harm than good. He would realize we're onto something and... retaliate. If he murdered the three magicians, he certainly wouldn't have any issues with adding us to his list. But I think we can get him to slip up if we word the questions in a certain way. The murders happened a long time ago. He's probably complacent by now, thinking everyone has forgotten about them."

"How do *you* think we should bring up the subject, then?" Jason asked.

Emmie sat back in her seat and folded her arms over her chest. "The same way I get you or Finn to spill your secrets. Flattery. Just appeal to his ego. After Finn digs into his past, we'll certainly have something to work with."

"But how can we help Nova *now*?" Jason asked. "She's clearly in danger."

"I'll stay with her as much as possible until Finn gets back to us."

"I'll do what I can with Trick." Jason took another bite of food and seemed to contemplate his plan.

"This is way more involved than I expected," she said.

Jason wiped his mouth and leaned back in his chair. "Sarah and Finn will be here on Thursday. As long as we're actively disrupting anything Trick's planning, we don't need to panic... yet."

Emmie sighed. "I wish I could save them the trouble of coming out at all. I had *so* hoped to take care of all this before they arrived."

"I know you did, but these are some big issues at play here. Sarah will help you focus on Nova, and I can work with Finn to nail Trick, somehow. In the meantime, we'll work on gathering information—"

She shook her head. "We've got to do more than just wait for Trick to strike again."

Jason leaned forward and took her hand. "Cozy up to Nova until the others arrive—that's all we can do—and I'll pick Trick's brain at every opportunity."

She squeezed his hand, maybe a little too hard. "But no messing with his mind. If he suspects we're onto him—"

"No psychic stuff." Jason nodded once.

"Promise? It might backfire, if you do."

"Promise."

"Alright." Emmie slipped her hand away and straightened in her seat. "We'll head in that direction."

"Perfect."

"Just one thing I still don't understand. Why are the spirits targeting Nova at all if Trick murdered the other magicians? I mean, wouldn't they attack Trick instead of her if their motivation is revenge? And I don't see him hesitating to step back into the theater where he committed the crimes."

Jason tilted his head and seemed to consider it for a moment. "A criminal always returns to the scene of the crime?"

"That's a myth."

"Maybe not in this case. If Trick is trying to knock Nova out of the show like he did the others, then maybe he's taking advantage of her superstitious nature and making her believe spirits are attacking her just to throw her off. Maybe he's behind everything she's experiencing."

"But... you heard what she said," Jason said. "She's convinced the ghosts are responsible, and could he really pull off all of that without her suspecting?"

"There *are* spirits here, I have no doubt, but Trick's a magician—an experienced, professional magician—and perhaps more cunning than we realize. It wouldn't take much to convince her she's being attacked by the spirits of the dead magicians to mess with her confidence. There's *so much* superstition surrounding the place to help set her frame of mind, and I'm sure she's heard all the stories again and again. She *expects* to encounter ghosts, so he takes advantage of her fears."

"You might be getting off track a bit, but I'll keep an open mind for now," Jason said. "Like we agreed, you stay with Nova as much as possible, and I'll follow the Trickster around."

"Definitely ask Finn to do research on him as soon as possible." Emmie stared into her phone's black screen. "Do you remember how emotional Nova was in the video she sent? She experienced something supernatural, I'm sure. That's the same way I reacted as a child when the Hanging Girl haunted me. She *is* haunted. But either way, we've got to move on this. I don't have a good feeling about any of it."

"I'll get right on it." Jason glanced around the room as if the answer lay somewhere just out of sight. "I'll go straight to the source first thing, but maybe there's someone else we can also ask about Trick's background without arousing suspicion? I know you said the owner—the old woman—isn't... available."

"Sadly, no," Emmie said. "But Marty did say something about having another opinion about what happened. He didn't give a satisfying answer, and I need to know *exactly* what he meant by that."

"I'll talk to him." Jason pushed his plate aside and stood up, stretching toward the ceiling before placing his hands on his hips. "I'll get Finn started with digging into Trick's past, talk to Marty, and then move on to schmoozing with Trick in the theater. If that guy has anything to do with any of the deaths, then I'll get it out of him."

Emmie opened her mouth to speak but stopped after Jason raised his hand.

"I hear you loud and clear," he said. "Don't worry about a thing. I'll only schmooze the old-fashioned way."

Emmie gave him a heartfelt nod. "Just be careful."

"Focus on Nova," he said. "Keep her out of harm's way."

Only a moment later, Emmie received a text message from Nova.

Hey, done with breakfast yet? she wrote. *I'm just about to head out.*

Emmie texted back. *Just finished.*

Want to go up and meet Grandma Ria with me?

Jason peered at the phone's screen over Emmie's shoulder and gave a nod when Emmie glanced toward him.

You aren't rehearsing today? Emmie texted.

Trick's got the stage this morning, Nova responded. *I'll start after he's done.*

"Perfect." Jason turned away and headed toward the door. "I'll see if I can find Trick and Marty in the theater now."

I'd love to meet your grandmother! Emmie texted back.

Come to my room down the hall. 1921.

12

Emmie knocked on Nova's door and only a moment later her friend opened it with a bright smile. Her friend looked just as she had back in college, dressed in street clothes without all the elaborate magician's flare. Her lean frame was wrapped in an oversized vintage band T-shirt with another loose flannel shirt tied around her waist, giving her a relaxed but almost untouchable edge. She wore tight black jeans that were torn at the knees with scuffed boots that looked nothing like the glossy ankle boots she'd worn on stage the day before.

Glancing back into her room, Nova's smile faded. She opened the door wider and stepped aside. "Can you come in for a minute?"

"Sure." Emmie followed her in.

Nova's room was exactly the same as the one Emmie and Jason were staying in—the same furniture, the same themed decor—but she had made the space her own. A sleek vanity sat by the window, cluttered with stage makeup, hair stylers, and a few scattered playing cards as if she'd been practicing sleight-of-hand before tossing them aside. A few stage outfits hung in the closet near the door, with a line of shoes and boots neatly arranged on the floor below them. A large framed photo sat on the dresser showing her as a child standing proudly beside her grandmother in front of the hotel. And despite what Charlie had mentioned about her room being refurbished, there was still a faint but persistent smell of cigar smoke lingering in the air. No doubt, a remnant from the hotel's past that might not ever go away.

"I have to show you something." Nova shut the door behind them and lifted her shirt sleeve, revealing a row of dark bruises along her upper arm and shoulder.

"Oh, no!" Emmie's heart sank. Meeting Nova's gaze, the truth was obvious.

"They attacked me again last night."

A chill swept through Emmie. The encounter with Danny Drake's spirit the previous night flashed through her mind as they stood in nearly the same spot where he had disappeared. Had he traveled on to the theater to attack Nova moments after racing away from Emmie? The thought was heartbreaking. "What happened?"

"I was down on the stage rehearsing again, really late—I guess I should stop going down there alone, but I can't help it. I'm a perfectionist, if you haven't figured it out yet. What can I say? Everything was going slick until I went up a stepladder to put away a prop." Nova cringed. "Someone kicked away the ladder and I fell."

"Jimmy wasn't with you?"

"He's *always* with me, unless I'm training late at night."

"Did you see *anything*?"

Nova lowered her sleeve. "No. Nothing. I'm lucky you're here to help me deal with this because I thought I was losing my mind."

"Did you hear footsteps, or see shadows, or lights flickering?"

"Not this time."

"But you have before?"

"Things like that happen sometimes, but I've never seen the ghosts directly."

Emmie considered the situation, but she had no answers. Not yet. "Can someone stay with you while you're working late? At least, until you get through opening night? You shouldn't be alone, under the circumstances. I can even stay up and hang out with you, if you want."

Nova shook her head. "The problem... I need lots of privacy to prepare the tricks. Not even Jimmy gets to see how I do them. That's how all magicians work. Now *maybe* if you were another magician..."

"But this can't continue."

"That's why you're here, right?"

"But I can't be there to protect you every minute."

"I have faith in you."

The heartfelt expression on Nova's face only added to Emmie's resolve. "Let me ask you something. Back in the '80s, did the magicians stay in rooms on this floor?"

Nova gave a curious look. "How do you know that?"

Emmie shrugged. It was better to keep what she'd seen to herself for the moment. "Someone mentioned it."

Nova nodded. "Grandma provided all the magicians with rooms on this floor. One of the perks for performing here back then, I suppose."

"Did one of them stay in room 1913?"

Glancing toward the door, Nova took a moment to answer. "I think that was Danny's room, if I remember right. The construction people use it for a break room now. Why? Did you see something in there?" Nova's eyes grew wide.

Emmie shook her head. "It just helps to understand how things were back then." Her gaze stopped again on Nova's arm. "I *will* stop whoever is doing this to you."

"I know you will. That's why I asked you to come here." Nova smiled and nursed her injured arm then stepped toward the door. "Let's go see Grandma Ria."

. . .

After stepping into the elevator, Nova used a small key on her keychain to activate an additional button labeled 'PH' above all the others. Her face was full of confidence and composure within the elevator's gentle rattle as it rose as if she'd pushed aside all thoughts of ghosts and bruises. "She's going to *love* your company, but don't ask her any questions, okay? If you do, she'll try to answer you, but she struggles."

"I get it. Just observe."

The elevator doors opened directly into the penthouse, and Emmie gasped. The home sprawled in every direction with light pouring in through floor-to-ceiling windows. A concert piano sat at the heart of the space, with a vast living room on one side and a dining table large enough to seat twenty on the opposite side. In one corner, there was even a cozy library nook with a plush chaise. It was more spectacular than she'd expected of a penthouse, not only because of the breathtaking views but the strange sense that she'd taken a step back into the 1980s. Except for a few modern appliances in the kitchen area, the decor and technology were exactly as they must have looked decades earlier. Earthy-toned wallpaper, plush carpeting, a faded, beige corded phone hung on the wall near the kitchen, a massive CRT TV sat at the center of the living room above a VCR player—advanced technology, in its day, that must have impressed the wealthy back then.

A Spanish woman dressed in violet scrubs peeked her head out from the doorway to the left. She smiled when her gaze stopped on Nova. "I'll be done in a minute."

"Take your time, Camila," Nova answered while leading Emmie toward the kitchen.

The nurse reminded Emmie of Sarah, and she couldn't help but wish that Sarah was there to share the meeting with the old woman. Sarah's medical background and genuine warmth would have gone a long way in a situation like this.

Arriving in the kitchen, Nova made a wide gesture and pulled two glasses from the cupboard. "Do you want something to drink? It's probably too early for wine."

"Definitely too early. A glass of water is fine."

While Nova poured two glasses of water, Emmie glanced around. Linoleum flooring in a pattern of small, beige tiles, and muted yellow-painted cabinets. Rows of framed photos lined the walls in the dining area. Stepping toward them, the faces and locations came into focus. The theater and hotel were there as it stood in its glory days, with proud performers standing beside a beautiful young woman in a dazzling white dress who could only be Nova's grandmother.

Gloria had captured the history of the hotel in her penthouse like an open time capsule. Ornate furniture from decades past sat beside mid-century pieces, while mementos and trinkets were stuffed in every corner and bookcase. A tall piece of furniture in the dining room displayed faded playbills, old postcards, and unframed photos that were stacked, leaning against each other in layers, obscuring whatever lay beneath them.

Nova stepped over and handed Emmie the glass of water. "She won't let us change anything. We've tried."

Emmie glanced around. "The place has a certain charm."

Nova raised her eyebrows. "Not the word I'd use—the colors are depressing—but I guess it somehow makes her happy."

"The past is hard to let go of for some people. It might be overwhelming for her to see how much things have changed since she last went out for a walk."

Nova gave a sympathetic nod. "And things have changed a lot. Once in a while she goes out onto the patio, if I go with her, but I can't remember the last time she left the hotel." Nova gestured to a set of glass double doors just beyond the living room, which separated them from a wide patio lined with flowers and tall plants that sat against the railing.

Seeing a bit of sadness on Nova's face, Emmie stepped toward one of the picture windows near the living room and gestured outside. "Do you blame her? I wouldn't leave this place either if I had this view."

Nova followed her gaze. "It gets old, like everything else in here. I'm like her, a bit of a recluse, since I spend most of my spare time hiding away in the theater."

The nurse stepped out of the doorway again and gestured to them. "She's ready."

Nova turned to Emmie. "Let's go."

As Emmie stepped into Gloria's bedroom, the smell of something medicinal hung in the air. The curtains were only partially closed, casting a dim light across the room.

The silver-haired old woman shifted in her bed and turned to face them when they walked in. She lay propped up against pillows, her small frail body almost hidden beneath a white comforter that extended up to her chest. Her pale skin was almost translucent, revealing faint blue veins bulging from the back of her hands, which lay folded over her chest as if she had made peace with her situation. Despite her age, she looked younger than she was, with a tight jawline, smooth eyebrows, and few wrinkles that didn't match the weariness in her eyes. Plastic surgery?

Gloria squinted to make eye contact with each of them, her body trembling.

Camila stood attentively beside the IV drip and another medical device, glancing at each of them before stepping toward the door. "I need to prepare her food."

"I got this," Nova said, moving to her grandmother's bedside.

The old woman's face lit up when Nova spoke but faded to confusion when her gaze stopped on Emmie.

Nova gestured to Emmie. "Grandma Ria, this is my friend, Emmie. She's staying here with me for a few days."

Emmie smiled at her. "Nice to meet you."

The old woman struggled to answer, her lips quivering as she mouthed a few disjointed syllables in a raspy breath, although the sounds failed to form any words.

Nova leaned forward and held her grandmother's hand, dropping her voice to a soft, affectionate murmur. Emmie couldn't catch all the words, but she felt the gravity of Nova's voice, words spoken not just out of love but out of something deeper—maybe a need for approval. Nova's face softened, losing the tension Emmie had come to recognize in her. She seemed almost like a child again beside her grandmother, someone who desperately wanted to honor the woman who had inspired her so much and built the theater's legacy. The quiet between them spoke volumes, and Emmie sensed there were years of shared stories, expectations, and disappointments wrapped into that one moment.

When the nurse reappeared with a small tray of food, Nova gently pulled away from the old woman with a final warm smile, before leading Emmie out of the room. Heading back into the living room, they didn't speak again until they'd settled into a worn velvet couch, probably a relic of the theater's faded glory.

Nova exhaled slowly as if shedding the weight of the room they had just left behind. "She might make it another month or two—at least, that's what the doctors say—but in my heart, I'm not sure she'll make it through the end of the week." Her gaze dropped, holding a haunted intensity. "I have to put on the show for her, Emmie. I need to stay on schedule if there's any chance to see her vision come to life before..." Her voice trailed off, the unspoken words hanging in the air.

Emmie nodded, sensing Nova's urgency. "I see how important this is to you. We'll do our best, I promise. The pressure must be... immense."

"More than you know." Nova's voice was low but resolute. "Grandma Ria didn't talk much about how things were when the theater failed. Whenever I used to ask, she only encouraged me to keep the dream alive. I'm sure she wanted me to bring the theater back to life someday. 'Don't let it die,' she used to say. 'You have the fire inside of you.'" A trace of pride and defiance glimmered in Nova's eyes. "She worked so hard for this, and I won't let it slip away."

Emmie hesitated, then leaned in, choosing her words carefully. "And Trick... Did he ever perform here, back in the '80s?"

Nova gave a little nod. "He was the opening act for Mystic Max, but then the theater shut down, and he never had a chance to shine. This grand opening next week is a big deal for him too. I mean, it might look like he's past his prime, but I've watched his rehearsals. He's... *amazing.*" She paused as a soft smile tugged at her lips. "I've already learned so much from him, but I'm also trying to push things one step further, using a few forgotten tricks and techniques that I picked up, things most magicians can't teach."

"How did your grandmother connect with him, anyway?" Emmie asked, trying to sound casual.

"Not sure," Nova replied thoughtfully. "He had a reputation back then, so I'm sure it was an easy decision. We're lucky that he was available to perform for our grand opening. Can you believe that our first three performances are already sold out? If it weren't for him, his name, maybe the grand opening next week might not have happened." She let out a soft laugh. "In a weird way, I owe him a lot."

Emmie nodded, her mind piecing together the puzzle that she hadn't yet fully grasped. Nova's words confirmed that Trick had brought credibility to the theater's grand revival, but why now? What could have drawn him back after all these years?

Her gaze wandered to the wall, landing on an old photograph framed in tarnished silver. The images showed Gloria and the magician, Mystic Max, in the prime of their lives, standing confidently in the center of a group of other magicians and performers from the theater's heyday. Max looked confident, with one arm slung over Gloria's shoulders as if he owned the world. But in the background, almost lost in the shadow, stood Trick—his face half-obscured, his eyes dark and piercing as he wasn't looking at the camera but instead staring at Max.

What if Trick had always been more involved in the theater than anyone had realized, watching and waiting, even back then? The pieces were starting to come together, but it left her with more questions than answers.

Emmie turned to Nova, sensing that whatever was buried in Trick's past might be wrapped up in this performance, and as much as she wanted to voice her suspicions, something held her back. She couldn't share her thoughts. Not yet. In a low voice, she said, "Whatever happens, Nova, you're not alone in this."

Nova met her gaze, and for a moment, the weight between them lifted. "I'll always cherish your friendship, and I guarantee my performance will be nothing like anyone has ever seen before."

13

Stepping out of the elevator, Jason nearly collided with two sweaty men carrying a blackjack table. The gold and white lettering caught his eye, radiating over the green surface as it passed beneath the lobby's recessed lighting, along with several silver cup holders embedded within the table's curved black leather edging where gamblers would sometimes stand for hours for the chance to lose their money.

Jason's heart quickened a little as it passed in front of him. Not from almost running into it but from the memories that flooded his mind. When had he last stepped inside a casino? He remembered the trauma clearly. Two years earlier, and the rush of anxiety sent an uncomfortable surge through his stomach.

He took in a deep breath as the workers carried the table past him toward the far side of the lobby. This is why he'd avoided Las Vegas since then. Two casino bouncers in bulging shirts had escorted him into a back room where they'd taken his ID and *detained* him until the manager had gotten a chance to throw a barrage of questions at him.

How do you know the dealer? Who are you with? Where are you staying?

And then the hotel's security officer searched him—thoroughly—without finding anything. The ordeal lasted only thirty minutes, but they'd left a clear impression on him. Allowing him to leave, they politely yet firmly directed him to not frequent their establishment ever again, and if he dared to step inside again, they would *escalate* the matter.

Escalate.

The manager had said the word behind a wicked grin and a piercing stare. Message received loud and clear. It was obviously a thinly veiled threat to kick his ass if he didn't fall in line, and he was well aware of the stories circulating on the Internet about rogue gamblers dragged to the back rooms in casinos only to be roughed up and threatened before getting dumped outside in a dark alley.

Not that he didn't *deserve* the scrutiny. Sure, he had *absolutely* cheated the casino many times, although *they* didn't know that— or at least they could never prove it—but never in any massive way. Never any big stakes involved. A few thousand here, a few thousand there. Just a little psychic fun. Mind games to pass the time.

Gambling wasn't the real problem, so much as the thrill of the manipulation. The slot machines and electronic devices held no appeal. He couldn't manipulate those in any way, shape or form, but nothing was more fun than stopping at an empty blackjack table for a little friendly banter with the dealer before seeing how far he could take it. Any dealer would do, but he preferred a quiet table in a corner, far from the crowds to feed the dealer a slow trickle of suggestions to *accidentally* lift the deck of cards a little too high or turn it sideways or forget to shuffle the deck. Anything to nudge them into breaking the rules at just the right time to gain the player's advantage.

It was a simple thing to do, messing with their minds, and he'd made a bit of money toying with his skill, but more out of sheer amusement than anything else. Pure entertainment. Sometimes he could go for hours before the pit bosses would catch on, but eventually, they all caught on. The thrill was just to see how far he could go with it than anything else. He didn't even particularly need the money—between his family's assets and his business, traveling the world to buy and sell occult artifacts, he was doing quite well.

Now the blackjack table had jarred his memory back to that unpleasant time, and he tried to push it away. He wasn't like that anymore, although the ability to manipulate people was still there, just as he had done in the "good old days," even if it had faded over the years. In a way, he toyed with the idea of stepping back into that same casino where they'd kicked him out just to show them he wasn't afraid, but his senses returned a moment later.

Everything he'd done was water under the bridge, at least in Emmie's eyes, but it was hard to let go of how they had berated and threatened him behind closed doors, although even then he'd used his powers to leave physically unscathed.

Of course, it would be insane to go back to that casino under any circumstances. He couldn't do that to himself or Emmie. With a shake of his head, he focused on the glowing lights of the Amber House Theater's entrance sign at the other end of the lobby and headed toward it. He had work to do.

The lobby was almost empty, except for a few distracted employees hunkered down behind the main reception desk. One of them glanced up and nodded as he passed a young woman with a warm smile and flawless makeup, before her attention jumped back to the computer screen in front of her and a pile of papers scattered over the counter. Another employee turned away, speaking in a polite tone to someone on the phone.

Jason found Trick inside the theater moments later. The old magician was at the side of the stage making wide gestures to a lovely woman in a gold sequin outfit. As Jason walked up the aisle toward them, neither seemed to notice him until he stopped in front of the stage and watched them work.

"Can I help you?" the woman said in a soft, sweet voice.

Trick glanced over, frowning when he met Jason's gaze.

"I'm Jason Reeves," he said. "I'm here with Emmie Fisher, regarding the—"

"I know who you are," Trick said. "What do you want?"

"Just wondering if you can tell me about the theater's history."

"What's that got to do with me?" Trick folded his arms over his chest and lifted his chin. "I'm very busy."

"We were given access to the backstage, so I thought I'd stop by and say hi. Maybe you could show me around, tell me about your experiences here."

"No time."

"I absolutely understand, but you've had an amazing career, and it's fascinating. I'd like to know more."

"You're here to find ghosts. I haven't seen any."

"That's fine," Jason said. "You know, Trick, I've seen a lot of magicians—from street performers to Vegas A-listers—but there's something different about you. You've got this... presence. Like you're not just performing the magic—you *are* magic. It's no wonder you came back to this theater. A place like this deserves a talent like you who understands its history, its energy. I've seen some of your performances on the Internet and they're incredible. No wonder the shows are selling out. What was it like when you first stepped onto this stage? I'd kill to hear how you rose to the top."

Trick looked at his assistant, rolled his eyes, then gestured to a door at the side of the stage. "Come on up."

Jason circled around and met them as they were heading toward the back of the stage. "You must know this theater better than anyone."

"That's not saying much. Nova knows the place better than me. She'll be down after lunch." Despite his silver hair and thin frame, Trick wasted no time in heading toward an unmarked door near the back of the stage. "I'll tell her you stopped by."

Jason stepped a little faster to catch up. "I'd like to hear about your experiences here back in the '80s when this place started."

Trick stopped and glanced back. "It never really started. It bombed right out of the gate, and it's going to bomb again if I don't get back to work."

"That's exactly what I wanted to talk about. You've worked with a lot of top magicians over the years. I'm sure you've got plenty of stories to tell. It must have been a hell of a time back in the '80s, surrounded by all those masters of illusion during the second golden age of magic."

Trick scoffed. "Masters of illusion? A few, I suppose, but Gloria wasn't interested in hiring masters of anything. She was all about the wow factor—the flashiest costumes, the biggest heart-throbs. Whatever grabbed the most attention, that's what she loved. She wasn't interested in the art of illusion, if that's what you're thinking."

"But she hired you."

Trick looked at his assistant, eyeing her costume up and down. "Why don't you take a break, dear, and get changed out of that?"

"Sure, Trick." She nodded and left through the door ahead of them.

Trick inched toward Jason. "I was the first magician Gloria hired after she bought the place. The very first one. She promised me top billing, but I still had to prod her daily to focus on quality over all that flash and flare that the other magicians brought to the table. I may not have the looks, but I have skill. *Real* skill."

"I believe you," Jason said. "So I take it you didn't get along with the other magicians?"

"We got along as far as they stayed out of my way, but I was the only professional in the bunch." Trick looked at him curiously. "What do these questions have to do with your ghosts?"

"Just getting a little background."

"A little background," Trick repeated. "Are you a reporter?"

"No."

"I'm not interested in stirring up any of that superstitious bullshit about the theater."

"I'm not either."

"You'll find everything you want to know about the history of the theater on the Internet."

"I'd rather hear it from you." Jason swallowed. "What was it like working with all those great magicians? I heard you were the best."

"Maybe you're trying to get me to say that we hated each other? Well, it's true. I was the best magician in Las Vegas at the time, but Mystic Max was the chick magnet, and he lowered the bar for the rest of us. Things went to hell after Gloria hired him."

"How so?"

"He flaunted his playboy attitude, and he had no talent. I mean, really, no talent at all. He was the kind of guy you'd find in the back room five minutes after the show crawling into bed with his assistant or maybe a fan or a hotel employee, and everyone looked the other way. They treated him like a rock star. He was drunk half the time, rarely rehearsed, and openly defied Gloria if she dared to speak out against anything he did, which she rarely did. How the hell does something like that happen? No accountability back then. There's a little background for you."

"Do you think that's why the theater failed? Gloria's lack of control?"

"I *know* that's why the theater failed. Hell, I was the only talent in the place, and then she gave that pretty boy Max top billing. Can you believe that? I would've put the place on the map, but Gloria didn't see it that way." Trick laughed. "But you know the saying, a fool and her money are soon parted. Well, she destroyed a good thing, and..." He lowered his voice while glancing around. "Maybe the place should have been torn down a long time ago, except that old woman—" He glanced up. "—can't let go."

Jason studied Trick's face, noting deep lines that might have formed from years of bitterness. Plenty of darkness behind those eyes. "But you're back now."

He stood taller but still frowned. "I deserve top billing, just like I deserved it forty years ago. I'm still the best damn magician in Las Vegas."

"Nova is headlining?"

He pushed his lips together. "There's nothing I can do about that. Her father owns the hotel, so that's the way it is. She isn't ready for the big time, in my opinion. Sure, she'll put in a few good performances, but what happens after that? I'm the one bringing in the sold-out shows. Wayne is a rational man, a practical man. Once he sees the flood of cash I bring in, he'll change his tune."

Trick's assistant stepped out from behind the stage, returning in street clothes, although her black spandex outfit showed way too much cleavage. She smiled at Jason, then turned to Trick, who had picked up a long piece of rope off the stage floor and curled it slowly as he stepped toward his assistant.

Jason followed him. "So you spent a lot of time with the other magicians? Did you know them well?"

Trick glanced back at him curiously. "As well as anyone you might work with. You're sounding more like a cop now than a paranormal investigator." He stared into Jason's eyes. "Why are you *really* here?"

"I want to know what happened back then. From your point of view."

"Well, now you know." He clenched his teeth and went silent for a moment before meeting Jason's gaze. "Do you really want to know about how the place went to shit?"

"I'm all ears."

"The police already questioned me, if that's where this is headed. Max and his assistants died in a gas leak, and the others were freak accidents. Sure, I hated Max. He was a hack, just like the others, but I'm a professional, so if you're headed down that line of questioning, you can just get the hell out of my face, ghost boy." He gave the rope a hard tug.

Jason looked into Trick's eyes. It would be easy to influence him at that moment, if only to calm the man a bit and squeeze more information out of him, but Jason spoke softer instead. "Sorry, I didn't mean to upset you."

"Yeah." Trick gave a sarcastic laugh. "You're not after any ghosts, are you? You're just like all the rest of the pinheads in Vegas. I've been dealing with this nonsense all my life, and I don't deserve it. You think this is easy? I've earned *everything* I accomplished, unlike the other hacks who died here. If you think I had anything to do with what happened, then go talk to the police. They questioned me for *hours*, and I had nothing to do with it. Nothing. So, what are you trying to prove by harassing me?" He looked at Jason up and down. "Are you recording this? You know, it's illegal to record this conversation without my permission."

"I'm not recording anything."

"Stick to chasing the bogeyman and then be on your way. That's what Wayne hired you to do, right?"

"Wayne didn't hire us."

"So why are you coming down here and messing with things you know nothing about? If you want to know about the magicians who died, then do a little research and you'll find Max had plenty of enemies. Hell, Jessica's husband is still alive. If you want to talk about conspiracy theories, go talk to him."

"Who's Jessica?"

Trick spoke in a patronizing tone. "I suspect she's one of the ghosts you're hunting." He made a mocking gesture with his hands and fingers, followed by a haunting ghostly sound. "Woooooo... Jessica Langford was one of the two assistants who died with Max. The other was Vivian Fontaine. Haven't you done *any* research? Her husband was insanely jealous near the end. Hell, he would barge into the green room minutes after the show ended and practically rip her out of there before she even had a chance to change out of her costume. Now, someone should have locked that guy up. A dangerous man, if you ask me, but did the police give *him* the third degree? Nope."

"What's his name?"

Trick stepped away and shook his head. "You met him yesterday, I believe. The guy handling all the props. Marty Winger."

14

Emmie knew the stay in Las Vegas would be difficult for Jason, even if he didn't complain. He hadn't stepped foot inside a casino for years, not since his confrontation with casino security after using his psychic abilities in not the most ethical way. Jason had confessed the entire story of his *dark years*, as he'd called them. So when he hesitated near the entrance of the Amber Casino's buffet for lunch, she wasn't surprised. The buffet was just a stone's throw from the main casino area, where an incessant flow of sounds and flashing lights spilled out. His expression showed tense muscles, but Emmie slipped her arm under his and pulled him closer. "You'll be okay."

He nodded once. "I knew what I was getting into when I agreed to come here."

They walked inside, and Jason kept his face down as if he someone from his past might still recognize him, even though this wasn't one of the casinos he used to frequent. They headed straight to the buffet station, with the clanging, dinging, melodious clatter of slot machines rang in the distance. Jason fixed an apologetic smile on Emmie as if to draw strength from her.

"You don't still feel the urge to go over there, do you?"

"It was... exciting to see how far I could push it," he said.

"But you're over it, right?"

"I don't think you understand. It's been a long time, sure, but it's like walking an alcoholic through a liquor store. Not exactly a comfortable experience."

"I'm so sorry." Emmie pulled him closer. "I didn't realize it would have this much of an effect on you. I'll stay right beside you all the way."

"It's the only reason I've made it this far."

On the way over, she couldn't get the photo of the magicians she'd seen in Gloria's penthouse out of her mind. She'd gone back and forth about what it all might mean and the deeper ramifications of what Gloria might have experienced in her theater over the years. If there was only some way to get inside the old woman's head and extract everything she'd experienced, they might get their answers a lot faster.

Emmie waited until they were seated in the buffet with their food before mentioning her visit with Gloria.

"How did *that* go?" Jason asked while starting to eat.

"Gloria can't talk, just like Nova said, but I saw a photo showing Mystic Max standing next to her, along with the other magicians who died at the theater. Trick was standing behind them, as if they had tried to keep him out of the photo. Something was off—the way they were interacting. I just can't put my finger on it."

Jason seemed to consider it for a moment. "Trick must have harbored a lot of resentment after Max and the others got all the attention. Trick wasn't exactly thrilled when I started asking questions. He definitely holds strong feelings about the past."

Emmie nodded. "I'm trying to keep an open mind with everything Nova told me and what I've seen, but I haven't even communicated with any spirits yet, and it bothers me."

"We absolutely need to keep an eye on him," Jason said between bites of food. "I don't trust the guy. You should have seen his face when I asked him about Max. I thought his head would explode. He did make a good point that Max had a lot of enemies—the guy was a flashy playboy magician in his prime—so I'm also trying to keep an open mind, but... I learned something. One of Max's assistants, one of the two who was killed in the gas leak, had a jealous boyfriend."

"Is he still alive?"

"Sure is."

"Do you know who he is?"

"You do too. It's Marty, the prop master."

"Marty? That sweet old guy in overalls?"

"According to Trick," Jason said. "But I wouldn't put too much weight on what he says—not yet. Marty might have had a motive to kill Max, but what about the other magicians who died mysteriously? Did Marty also murder them out of jealousy? It doesn't add up."

Emmie shook her head. "You need to keep an eye on both of them, for now. Can you do that? At least, until I get through to the spirits."

"Listen," Jason said, "I know we're here to protect Nova from violent spirits, but Trick is giving off some pretty heavy vibes. Nova said she didn't see anyone behind her, right?"

"She told me she hasn't seen anyone."

"Well, he *is* a magician, a master of illusion, and I know we're both trying to keep an open mind, but maybe we've got this all wrong."

Emmie considered it. "You think Trick is trying to intimidate her?"

"We should consider it."

"But I've seen the bruises... Even as a magician, I find it hard to believe that he could do that to her without being seen? Maybe if he was forty years younger, but he moves like a washed-up rockstar at his age."

Jason shrugged. "Maybe he's not threatening her directly, but he could set things up to scare or injure her, thinking that might knock her out of the game."

Emmie let out a sigh. "I see your point, but... I believe Nova."

"I do too, but she's caught up in the mystery of the place, the superstition, just like everyone else. Maybe it's not what it seems here. Maybe *nothing* is what it seems in that theater. Everything is an illusion."

"Nova has seen things, *dark* things," Emmie said. "I can see it in her eyes."

Jason leaned forward. "Just consider what I'm saying, and find those spirits as soon as possible. It seems they're the only ones who might know the full truth."

"They're not making it easy for me."

"When Sarah and Finn arrive—"

Emmie let out her breath sharply. "I need to do this—"

"—on my own," Jason said. "I know you said that, but they can help."

"I know." Emmie took a moment to eat and think about how to proceed. "I'll spend the rest of the day focusing on the spirits. I'll stay right there with Nova the whole time, and I won't step away until I get through to them."

"I know you *will* get through eventually. Didn't you and Sarah run into a similar problem back at Raven House, at the Isabella ruins, where the spirits were hiding from you? It might take longer than we thought."

"We don't have the luxury of time in this case, but I'll work all night if I have to."

Jason looked into her eyes. "I believe you, but I'm concerned we're rushing into this. We shouldn't jump to conclusions. We don't know who or what we're facing yet. Consider *all* possibilities."

Emmie sat back in her seat. "Whether or not spirits are attacking Nova, there's a lot of dark energy in that place. It's like someone's in hiding, staying just out of reach, hidden behind a veil."

"Behind a curtain," Jason added. "Then we should focus on

that for the rest of the day. You'll stay with Nova and contact the spirits. I want to hear Marty's side of the story, regardless of what Trick said, because he's got inside knowledge of what happened back then. I just hope he doesn't take offense to my questions like Trick did. It's been a long time since someone tried to rough me up in Vegas, and I'd like to keep it that way."

15

Jason led Emmie into the theater, and a sudden burst of cool air caught him off guard as they crossed the threshold. He could feel something prickling up his arms, more than just the usual draft from an old building. The place had an unshakable heaviness, like they'd stepped into someone's memory and disturbed it.

Emmie shivered and glanced over at him. "It's colder in here today."

"I'll take that as a sign we're on the right track."

Emmie had already started focusing on the dark corners as if she only needed to stare a little longer at the shadows to extract their secrets. There was tension in her face. Was she holding back, or maybe this place was better at hiding its ghosts than they'd thought?

The stage loomed ahead, dark and ominous, although a few lights near the back confirmed that they weren't alone. Not in any sense of the word. Distant, muffled noises came from someone working behind the stage.

They'd run into Wayne in the lobby, and he'd directed them where to find both Marty and Nova. Marty was in his workshop

—always in his workshop—and Nova was busy rehearsing in her dressing room.

"Better to leave her alone," Wayne had said. Emphasis on *leave her alone*. And the distracted owner had hurried off a moment later, glancing back with an insincere, "Good luck on your ghost hunt."

Brushing off Wayne's cynicism, Jason took Emmie's hand and headed down the aisle, but released it only a minute later when they passed through the side door and stepped up onto the stage.

A glaring overhead light spilling out from the prop room's wide open door, while a softer glow came from Nova's dressing room. Jason and Emmie exchanged a quick nod, like an unspoken agreement, then headed off in separate directions.

Winding around a stack of broken lighting equipment, Jason arrived at the prop room moments later and pushed open the unlocked door. The smell of sawdust and varnish filled the air. There was no sign of Marty, although someone had left in a hurry. There was a set of abandoned tools lying on a nearby workbench, along with a half-finished project of what looked like the frame of a wooden box the size of a football. Jason scanned the room, and his gaze stopped on a door at the back of the workshop. It was the only other door, the one Marty had briefly mentioned earlier as leading deeper into the theater to the lounge where Max and his assistants had died in the gas leak.

Nobody goes in there. Marty's words came back to him. *Not since... the accident.*

Jason opened his mouth to call out Marty's name but hesitated. The door was unlocked, left ajar, and someone's shadow broke the thin slice of light escaping through the opening. He stepped toward the door, his footsteps muted by the worn carpeting in the hall.

Marty?

Peeking through the door's opening, a lounge area came into view. It seemed as if nobody had touched it since that fateful night, left abandoned like a time capsule. Brown leather couches sat in the corner beneath dim lighting, surrounded by antique coffee tables littered with playing cards, coasters, and ashtrays, and there was even the hint of stale whiskey in the air. Everything was as it must have been in the '80s when Max and his two assistants had died, one of them Marty's girlfriend.

Quietly, Jason pushed the door open a little more, revealing Marty standing in the middle of the lounge, frozen in place like a man staring down a ghost, his fingers trembling slightly as he traced the edge of a worn-out chair beside him. His back was to Jason, holding a defeated posture, and Jason hesitated to continue—it was better to leave the man alone—until Marty's voice broke the silence.

"I never thought I'd step foot in here again." His voice was low and rough as if holding back tears. "Not after everything that happened."

Jason moved inside, letting the creaking door shut behind him. Marty didn't turn around, but the weight of his words hung in the air.

"What brought you back?" Jason was careful to keep his tone soft. He had seen the man's stoic nature during their backstage tour earlier, but now the tension between them seemed so fragile, like one wrong move could shatter it.

Marty laughed bitterly. "What do you think, Jason? Ghosts. All this talk of ghosts brought me right back here, like they've been waiting for me all this time."

Marty sat in the chair. Its antique frame squeaked beneath his weight as he leaned forward and buried his face in his hands. His gray hair shifted in the cool breeze that flowed around them from an air duct just overhead. The old man looked even older in this room, like the weight of the rumors had finally caught up with him, breaking down the last of his spirit. Jason moved in closer, wanting to do or say something that might help ease the tension, but gave Marty time to compose himself instead.

"I'm sure someone told you what happened by now." Marty's

voice was muffled as he stared at the floor. "Is that why you stopped by? To hear me tell you how jealous I was of Max and how everyone thought I had something to do with the accident?" He lifted his head and looked at Jason, his eyes tired but fierce. "I didn't. I swear to God, I didn't."

Jason studied him. Marty's hands were shaking, his gruff exterior peeled back to reveal a deep pain that he must have hidden for decades. There was plenty of guilt in the old man's eyes, maybe guilt for things better left unsaid, but the truth was clear. His girlfriend's death had haunted him long before Jason and Emmie had arrived.

"I believe you," Jason said. And he did. Whatever Marty was guilty of, it wasn't for anything that had happened in that room. But Jason had encountered plenty of deception over the years, and there was something more stirring behind those eyes. "So what *did* happen?"

Marty let out a long, shaky breath. "I didn't kill her. I didn't kill any of them, but I wanted to... I wanted to stop Jessica from staying out late. To keep her away from *Max*." Marty said Max's name with disdain. "It was a big issue between us, and I begged her to leave Max's show because I saw the glint in her eyes that he was... getting to her. I knew that something was going to happen eventually if I didn't break her away from his good looks... charm... charisma. He had it all, and nobody could resist a guy like that, not even my Jessica." His voice cracked.

There was a silent pause between them, but Jason held back his questions as Marty continued.

"I should've pulled her out of the theater that day right after the show finished," Marty whispered, his eyes unfocused. "But I got there too late."

Jason narrowed his eyes, sensing Marty wasn't admitting to something, even to himself. "Too late... For what?"

Marty pushed his eyes together and clenched his fists before he opened them with a flash of emotion that surged over the man's face. Was it regret? Fear? Or something darker?

"We had a fight before she left for work that afternoon—a big one. She drove separately and then avoided me all day. I got home first, and after she didn't come home on time—because of the fight—I decided not to go after her." Marty's voice hovered just above a whisper. "I was too angry." He met Jason's gaze. "I should have gotten her out of there right after the show, like I usually did, and apologized. We could have worked it out, somehow, and I actually *did* swallow my pride that night, eventually, and drove over there to straighten things out, but I was too late. I let my Jessica die."

Jason stood there, absorbing the weight of their conversation. This wasn't a confession to a murder, but to something far more tragic. The guilt must have eaten at his soul over the years, and he shifted in his chair when he finished, glancing around the room instead of at Jason as if someone else was in there with them. His eyes held a glint of fear, and something else he hadn't revealed yet.

But before Jason could ask any more questions, Marty stood abruptly. His face hardened again, and the brief vulnerability was gone.

"I need to get back to work." Marty wiped a hand through his hair and stared at the door.

"Sure." Jason nodded and escorted the old man to the door, until Marty turned abruptly and locked the door behind them, even giving the handle an extra twist as if making sure it was secure. "We won't go back in there. Never again."

16

Emmie lingered alone on the stage after Jason headed into the prop room to find Marty. Instead of heading straight to the dressing room to find Nova, she took a step toward the center of the stage and closed her eyes. Focusing on the dark energy within the theater, she pushed her mind to connect with the spirits that she *knew* were there. They were clear in her mind but somehow still eluded her, skirting her awareness as if they knew she was looking for them. It wasn't anything like she'd expected, at least from the way Nova had described it in her video. Where was the violence and confrontation? Instead, the spirits lingered in the shadows like frightened children who had moved off into some dark corner to hide from the bogeyman.

Straining to grasp even one, she counted them. Five spirits. That made sense. Five people had died tragically in that place. At least they were on the right track, but the spirits weren't making it easy for her.

A noise came from somewhere behind her. A woman's voice. Nova.

Within the dim light, Emmie stepped toward the dressing room, scanning the props and stage equipment cluttering the area before focusing her attention on the distant murmurs. Nova's voice, soft but distinct, floated through the air again in broken sentences. Emmie moved toward it while stepping quietly. It was important to respect Nova's privacy and focus on why they'd come there in the first place—to find the spirits haunting her friend—but something about Nova's voice sounded... unnatural. It wasn't the rehearsed, confident tone of someone preparing for a grand show, but softer, more intimate, like a conversation with a trusted friend. Wayne had made it clear that Nova was alone, so had Jimmy joined her on his day off?

Emmie moved carefully between the narrow paths leading to Nova's voice. On both sides of her were piles of tangled ropes, chains, a workbench, and old set pieces. Many of the items showed plenty of neglect, as if someone had abandoned them abruptly decades earlier, but the variety of old and new props was overwhelming. Nova must have found the place a wonderful playground to develop her talents.

Trying to focus on what Nova was saying, the soft conversation ended with no other voice answering her. Was Nova on her cell phone? The way she carried on in a relaxed and casual way...

Moving toward the back of the stage, Emmie spotted Nova's dressing room door, but her friend's voice was coming from behind an unmarked door further back in a shadowed section of the stage. Someone had left the door ajar, but as Emmie stepped closer it creaked open a little further on its own. A change in air pressure from the HVAC kicking in? A spirit guiding her? Judging by the shifting light streaming out, someone was inside.

Emmie approached cautiously—better that she didn't interrupt her friend—and pushed the door open.

Nova was standing in front of a black curtain, facing away, and lit by a single overhead spotlight above. Emmie stopped and held her breath. Nova wasn't on her phone, but instead practicing, just as Wayne had said, but not in the way Emmie had expected. Nova held a commanding posture beside a small table and moved with precision while handling a white rabbit in one hand and a white veil in the other. Placing the veil carefully over the rabbit, she pressed it down a bit, although its shape remained clear and unmistakable.

With the rabbit shifting beneath the veil, Nova picked up a small crate with worn metallic edges. Arm-length chains dangled from its sides, clinking softly as they swayed, and ended in sharp, heavy hooks. The crate resembled an antique toolbox, with a sinister appeal for added danger. Nova lifted it into the air with a delicate seriousness that seemed far beyond her age and made wide gestures, all the time facing into the darkness beside the black curtain as if her audience watched from somewhere just out of view.

Emmie debated whether or not to disturb her but chose to linger in the shadows instead. She would wait until the young magician was finished and then make her presence known, but the longer she waited, the more she felt like a stalker creeping in the darkness.

What am I doing? This isn't right.

Emmie turned to leave but stopped. Something shifted in the air around her. Something cold and thick, and a darkness flooded her mind. The same dark energy she had sensed earlier on the stage. Whatever was in that place held a powerful presence.

Closing her eyes to focus on it, an icy chill swept around her like the frigid winds of a Minnesota winter, and she shivered uncontrollably, almost to the point of convulsing. Wrapping her arms across her chest, she tried to make contact with whatever had caused the disturbance.

Nova's voice broke her concentration. "You like that, don't you?" Nova said in a light, playful tone.

Emmie opened her eyes. Nova hadn't said that to *her*, but was making another wide gesture toward what seemed an invisible audience. The young woman seemed unaware of the change in temperature, not bothered by any threat within the darkness.

Her playful attitude and flair seemed a stark contrast to the heaviness that now sat in the pit of Emmie's stomach. Nova continued practicing, presenting the crate toward the darkness while taking a graceful step backward and opening it as if trying to convince the crowd that she had nothing to hide.

Another chill swept through Emmie's chest, and she shivered again. This time, she stumbled and cracked her arm against a wooden chair while backing further into the darkness to escape the freezing air. The icy chill enveloped her for a moment before she lost her balance again, swirling around her like a swarm of bees, until she crashed to the ground. She screamed when she hit the cement floor, and pain flared through her shoulder and back.

Nova gasped and spun around as Emmie struggled to stand. Their eyes locked for a moment but within Nova's gaze Emmie saw something more than surprise. Hurt. Betrayal.

"What the hell are you doing here?" Nova's voice was sharp and cutting. She backed away from the crate she'd been handling and crossed her arms over her chest as if to distance herself from it. "Were you... spying on me?"

Emmie pulled herself up and stood, wincing at the pain coming from her injured shoulder. "No, I—Nova, I didn't mean to—"

"Didn't mean to what?" Nova's voice wavered, her lips pressed into a thin line. "What were you doing back there? I trusted you, Em. I thought... you were different." The unspoken words hung in the air: *different from everyone else who let me down.*

Emmie's chest tightened. She hadn't expected this, hadn't meant to intrude, but her mind raced to explain her presence. "I was only looking for the spirits."

"While watching me practice?" Nova added. "In the dark."

"I swear I wasn't spying on you. There's a spirit here. I can feel it."

Nova's expression softened, although the wariness remained in her eyes. "The ghosts," she said with a little bitterness. "Of course."

What else could she say? Emmie hesitated to say anything else—it was better not to make things worse—until Nova straightened her posture and looked down at the crate she'd been working with moments earlier. "How much did you see?"

"I'm sorry. I only caught a little. You were showing the audience the prop was empty."

"You know I don't even let Jimmy back here when I'm practicing. I told you that."

"I'm so sorry," Emmie repeated.

The hurt in Nova's eyes dimmed as the moment stretched into a silent pause, replaced by a slight grin and a spark of determination. "I was working on something new. I was going to show Jimmy later this evening, anyway. I can show you... as long as you don't get too close. The illusion is spoiled if you get too close."

"Nova, you don't have to—" Emmie started, but Nova was already lifting the crate, adjusting it with a smooth, practiced ease.

"No, I insist," Nova said, although her tone was more defensive than welcoming. "This trick... it's special to me. I've been practicing it for weeks and you'll be the first one to see it."

Emmie watched her with a growing unease. There was something in the way Nova spoke, something forced, as if she was trying to prove herself. Standing within the light glaring down on them from above, Nova gestured to the rabbit beneath the veil and pushed back the black curtain. Her eyes fixed on the prop as she turned it over, meticulously running through the motions of the trick. But just before she began, her gaze jumped toward the darkness over Emmie's shoulder as if she were afraid to face Emmie directly. "You're still watching, aren't you?" Nova said under her breath. "I'll make you proud. Just wait."

Emmie's skin crawled as Nova's fixation on the darkness continued, and she wasn't sure if she should answer her or not. Playing to an imaginary audience made sense, but it was just the two of them, as far as Nova could see.

Before Emmie could say anything, Nova continued the

trick. Her friend swept the crate through the air, spinning it faster and faster on one corner with the chains and hooks flashing in the light from above. It moved faster than Emmie could observe, and the thing seemed to almost blur out of existence except for the sounds of the chains rattling against its frame.

Nova shifted it over one hand, letting it go with the other, and spun the whole thing in her palm, either through magnets or a gyroscope, while pulling at the corner of the white veil with intense concentration. The rabbit's shape beneath the veil barely moved as the cloth slipped over its form until it disappeared from view. Dragging the veil's corner toward the crate, she brought it to the bottom edge where it met her palm... and something snapped.

A flash of white filled the air as the veil whipped at the crate in a blur of motion and jammed halfway, jerking sharply. The chains and hooks rattled as Nova fought with both hands to maintain control of the illusion. The rabbit squealed, appearing from beneath the veil as its fur caught on one of the hooks. In its panic, it wriggled free from Nova's grip, its claws raking across her arm before it leapt to the floor and bolted out of the room.

"Wait!" Nova shouted while lunging after it, but one of the chains on the crate struck her hand and the wooden prop crashed to the floor. She let out an anguished cry, stumbling back and clutching her wrist.

"Nova!" Emmie rushed forward as blood flowed from the wound.

"It's fine." Nova waved her away. "I just need to fix the timing."

"Fix the timing?" Emmie asked. "Nova, that thing nearly tore you apart! And the rabbit—"

"I'll find him." Nova glanced around with tired eyes. "He'll be fine, and so will I."

Emmie watched her friend react with a mix of fear and frustration. "Forget the spirits, Nova. You're pushing yourself too hard. Why are you doing this?"

Nova's hands dropped to her sides, the blood smearing against her pants. Glancing down at the shredded veil, tangled within the chains and hooks, she whispered, "Because I have to. No matter what the cost."

17

Emmie inched forward to comfort her friend who had retreated into the shadows until footsteps thundered behind them. Jason and Marty burst into the room a moment later with expressions full of fear and confusion.

Nova's eyes were wide as she glanced back into the darkness, as if the invisible audience would react to the malfunction. "I... messed up."

Marty's gaze jumped from Nova to the crate at her feet. "Are you okay?"

Nova extended her arm. "I did it right... didn't I?"

He moved in beside her and inspected the wound. "Let's get you out into the light and check that. Anything broken?"

Nova shook her head and looked at Emmie. "They almost got me this time. It's not supposed to work that way."

Marty carefully picked up the crate and placed it back on the table, rattling the chains and hooks in the process. Examining it a little closer, he tilted his head. "That's not how I left it."

"I told you." Nova turned to Emmie. "It's the ghosts, Em. They want me dead."

Jason took his turn inspecting the broken crate, scrutinizing everything that Marty did to it. Nova jumped toward it and reached out a hand as if to wave them away from it. "You shouldn't touch it. Nobody can know how it's done."

Jason stepped back, shifting his gaze between Marty and Nova. "Who else has access to this?"

"Nobody," Nova answered. "I keep it locked away, except when I perform."

"But not *all* the time," Jason added.

"I don't let it out of my sight," Nova said, "but nobody else would dare to touch it."

Jason looked at Emmie. "I saw Trick back here earlier today messing with something. It must have been this."

"Trick?" Nova laughed. "Let him look at it all he wants. He won't figure it out in a million years."

"But it sat unattended for a while."

Nova's face showed confusion. "So?"

"So, I don't think you understand what I'm saying," Jason said. "I caught Trick doing something back here earlier. I think he had it open before I arrived."

Nova lost her smile. "You think that old man had something to do with what just happened?" Her gaze jumped from Jason to Emmie. "That's your theory after everything I've told you?"

"I'm just telling you what I saw." Jason glanced up toward the darkened corners of the room. "Are there any surveillance cameras back here? Maybe catching him in the act would clear this up."

Nova shot a look at Emmie with accusing eyes. "You're not making any sense. That's ridiculous."

"We've got to keep an open mind about this," Emmie said.

"But you saw what I did," Nova said. "I performed the trick just for you, right in front of you, and you must have seen *something*. You're the one who sees ghosts, right?"

"Not in every circumstance. Sometimes they don't want me to see them."

"Trick has a long history in this theater," Jason said. "He was here when the other magicians died, too."

Nova gave a little laugh and raised her voice. "He's an old man. I can't believe what you're suggesting, after everything I showed you—"

"We aren't suggesting that what you experienced isn't valid," Jason said.

"Oh, I'm so glad you think I'm *valid*. That makes me feel so much better after that thing just about *killed me*."

Emmie extended her hand toward her friend. "I know there are spirits here—nobody's arguing with you about that and I feel them even now—but we should keep an open mind that something else is happening here."

Nova shook her head slowly. "You're wrong. Trick had nothing to do with what just happened. He isn't the one behind anything bad that happened to me. The *ghosts* did it. They're trying to stop me from performing. Don't you believe me?"

Emmie hesitated. The weight of Nova's gaze made her stomach twist. "I think it's important that we don't rush to conclusions," she said softly, although every word felt like a betrayal. She looked to Jason for support, who nodded in agreement. Still, her heart sank deeper with each second of silence.

Nova's face hardened, letting out little gasps as if she were about to explode in a mixture of shock and hurt. "What did you just say?"

"I just—" Emmie faltered, feeling the growing distance between them. "I just think we need to consider all the options, Nova. All the time I've been in the theater—"

"When you were spying on me," Nova cut in.

"—when I was trying to connect with the spirits that *are* here, I haven't encountered any *violence*."

"So, now you don't believe me?" Nova's hands clenched into fists as she stepped back. "You were only spying on me because you're just like all the others. You haven't believed me since you arrived, right? I thought you were going to help me, that you were on my side, and I trusted you. Do you really think I'm making all of this up?"

"No, it's not that I think you're making it up," Emmie pleaded, reaching toward her. "I *am* trying to help you, but we just have to look at all the possibilities. If Trick did something—"

"Stop saying his name!" Nova shook her head, her voice shaking with anger. "It's not Trick! Aren't you listening to anything I'm saying? The ghosts are trying to kill me. You even saw they attacked me, right in front of you, just now. How could you *not* see that?" She glared at Emmie, then turned away and stormed out of her dressing room.

Emmie's eyes started watering, and Jason stepped over and slipped his arm around her waist. She stood there, frozen by the guilt that gnawed at her mind. Wrapping her arms around her chest, she dropped her head and stepped toward the door. "I should go after her."

Marty placed a hand on her shoulder and she stopped. "Give her some time," he said gently. "She needs to calm down before she'll listen to reason."

"I don't know what I should do," Emmie whispered, her throat tightening. "What if something happens to her while she's alone? If I'm wrong..."

"We'll all keep an eye on her," Jason said. "But confronting Trick... That has to be the next step. We can't let him get away with this. We'll need to involve Wayne... and the police."

"Not yet." Emmie's head was spinning, torn between chasing after Nova or following her gut to confront Trick as soon as possible. "We can't let anyone else know what we're doing until we have proof. Sarah and Finn will be here tomorrow," she said, more to herself than anyone else. "At least I think we can still have this mess sorted out by the time they arrive."

Yet something didn't feel right. It wasn't just that she'd lost Nova's trust, or the impending confrontation with a very popular Vegas magician whose arrest would almost certainly destroy any hopes for a successful grand opening, and certainly not with any spirits that she had encountered. It was the nagging voice at the back of her mind asking how she would walk away from this experience with a clear conscience. She had come here with good intentions—to get Nova out of danger—but now she had shattered her friend's world instead.

I did my best.

Emmie turned away and checked the time on her phone. "I'll be in my room."

∼

A COOL BREEZE TUGGED AT EMMIE'S HAIR AS SHE STEPPED OUT onto the balcony. The lights of Las Vegas spread out below like a never-ending carnival midway. From their view on the 19th floor, the city looked alive, pulsing with a chaotic energy, with all the flashing digital signs coming from every direction. There was an eternal rhythm rising from the streets below, almost hypnotic, and the moment did little to help clear her mind of everything that had happened that day.

Jason moved in beside her and leaned against the railing. "I've been to Vegas hundreds of times. Can you believe that?" His voice hovered between vanity and disdain. "It's all built on dreams and lies. How many people do you think came here convinced they were going to make their dreams come true and then lost everything?"

She shrugged and scanned the streets below. "Way too many."

"It's all a mirage," he said, "an illusion. Everything down there."

"And yet it doesn't stop them from coming, does it?"

"Gloria bet her life on that dream too."

"And now it's falling apart," Emmie said quietly. "I just can't get over that Gloria's dream is now Nova's dream, and it's all tangled up in ghosts and lies. And I can't fix it."

"You can't fix everything, Em."

"I sure thought I could," she whispered. "It just makes things a lot more difficult when they don't believe me. Nova doesn't believe me. Wayne sure as hell doesn't believe me. And I know Trick isn't who Nova thinks he is. He's hiding something. I'm sure of it."

"Then it will come out tomorrow," Jason said. "And Finn and Sarah will give us a fresh perspective."

"I should have gotten everything wrapped up by now."

"Says who?"

Emmie glanced over at him. "I do. Nova's life is on the line."

Jason scoffed. "That's unrealistic and a bit arrogant, actually. It's more than okay to need help from your friends. We all have our strengths, and our abilities complement each other. We'll figure something out *together*, like we always do, right?"

Emmie nodded faintly. The lights below seemed a little colder now, a little harsher, as though the city itself was watching them, laughing at them, waiting for their next move.

Jason pushed off the railing and turned to head back inside.

Emmie turned with him, but still gripped the railing. "All those lights and people down there just remind me how small I am."

"You're a beautiful spirit, Em. Don't sell yourself short." He gestured toward the open door. "Come in. You'll need your rest if we're going to catch Trick in the act tomorrow."

Emmie let out a deep breath and followed Jason inside, although an uninvited thought crept into her mind and sent a chill down her spine.

Trick ruined everything... and now he'll ruin you.

18

Sarah and Finn arrived on time the next morning, and Emmie spotted them as soon as they entered the hotel lobby. They were a little overdressed for the Las Vegas heat—Finn in his button-down shirt and khaki pants, and Sarah wearing a denim jacket over a flowery sundress. She held back from calling out to them, to avoid putting any more attention on them than necessary but hurried toward them with Jason at her side.

Finn stood awkwardly beside a hefty silver equipment case, along with a pair of suitcases. He looked around, brow furrowed, as though trying to find something familiar amid the grand lobby. Nobody had come by to help them with their suitcases, and the two employees standing behind the check-in counter had their faces down, too occupied to bother with guests at the moment.

Sarah noticed them first, breaking into a bright smile as they approached. She gave a brief wave, then hurried toward them with Finn following closely behind her.

They met halfway and exchanged hugs. Sarah looked curiously at Emmie, as if already sensing the tension in the air. Wayne, Nova, and even the hotel staff were absent. It was clear that Wayne had given up the illusion that any of them were welcome there.

"Where is everybody?" Finn's gaze drifted around the lobby.

Emmie hesitated, unsure how much to reveal at that moment. "They're... not exactly thrilled we're still here." She exchanged a quick glance with Jason, whose jaw tightened as he put on a brave face for her.

"Don't worry about anything," Jason said while helping Finn with the suitcases. "We'll get through it. It's just nice to see us together again."

Pulling one of Sarah's suitcases, Emmie led them toward the elevator, trying to ignore the sense that someone was now keeping an eye on them. "We'll catch up in the room."

"Shouldn't we get our key first?" Finn glanced back toward the check-in counter.

Emmie continued forward without stopping. "I already picked up your key, and... we have adjoining rooms."

"Perfect." Finn glanced around as the elevator doors opened. "This place is a trip. Can't wait to check it out."

"Don't unpack just yet," Jason said. "We'll explain in a minute."

After arriving at Finn and Sarah's room, they took seats in a sofa and chairs near the window. Before they opened any suitcases, Jason spoke up. "We might have a problem."

"What sort of problem?" Sarah asked.

"We shared our opinions about the situation with Nova," Emmie said, "and she didn't take it well. I wouldn't be surprised if they ask us to leave early."

"So..." Finn said. "She doesn't want our help anymore?"

"Not at the moment." Emmie glanced at the floor. "She's furious that I expressed some doubt about what's going on here. She's more than angry."

"What did you conclude?" Finn asked.

"We believe she's in more danger than she realizes and she's already made up her mind regarding the solution. The thing is, I haven't encountered any violent spirits here—not like Nova explained it, anyway. There is something going on, but we think there's a more rational explanation for this one."

"Rational," Finn said. "Now you're talking my language."

"I'm *so* sorry. I planned to have everything wrapped up by now, but now it's complicated. Maybe I—I pushed it too hard. But I only did it for her own good."

"No need to apologize for anything," Sarah said, her voice calm but probing. "So, what's the plan now?"

Jason glanced at Emmie before answering. "*If* they don't kick us out, we have to focus on the magician, Trick Spurlock. We need to catch him in the act, record him doing something incriminating that we can show to Nova. It's the only way she'll see things from our point of view."

Finn opened the equipment case on his bed and brushed his fingers over the various cameras as if they could offer him guidance. "It's a good thing I brought my toys on this trip, then." Pulling out one of his video cameras, he switched it on and checked the settings. "Battery is fully charged. Ready to go when you are."

Emmie couldn't help but feel a little guilty as she watched her friends going through so much trouble to help her, but she remembered what Jason had said earlier, that their abilities complemented each other. Their unspoken support warmed her heart, the shared commitment to protecting Nova even though they had never met her before.

"We might not be confronting any dangerous spirits this time," Emmie said, "but something even more dangerous."

Sarah reached over and touched Emmie's hand. "We're in this together."

Emmie nodded, feeling the weight of it all settle on her chest. "I'll take you to the theater now."

Emmie watched Finn and Sarah's expression as they headed into the theater. Her friends had the same wide-eyed sense of wonder that she had experienced after entering the place days earlier. Pausing a moment to let them take in the rich Art Deco themes that filled every corner of the theater, Emmie gestured ahead toward the stage. "We should be alone, for now. Marty, the prop master, should be the only one here, but he's behind the stage in his workshop. Nova and Trick won't be in until later, but we don't have much time."

Jason had gone ahead of them and now stood on stage, making a little gesture with his head to let them know everything was clear.

Operating again as a team felt empowering, although Emmie had hoped her friends' first day in Vegas would have gone a lot smoother. Getting Finn and Sarah up to speed regarding everything they had discovered in the last two days would prove difficult because of what had happened between them and Nova.

They moved quickly down the aisle toward the stage, their footsteps echoing throughout the old theater. Emmie led the way, and she scanned the area for signs of anything unusual.

"We have permission to be in the theater, right?" Finn asked.

"Nobody kicked us out... yet," Emmie said. "And they're very aware we're still here."

"Have you seen *any* spirits?" Sarah asked.

"One, a magician, but he wasn't violent. Others are here... somewhere." Emmie stared at the silent darkness behind the open velvet curtains. "Let me know if you experience anything unusual, but I believe Trick is the biggest danger to Nova."

Making their way around to the backstage area, they met up with Jason who kept glancing back toward the prop room. "If Marty comes out, no need to pretend what we're doing, but keep things close to the chest at this point. I don't trust anyone."

Passing under the heavy velvet curtains that loomed around them like a dark wave, a ghostly quiet settled over them as the echoes of the theater faded away. They moved between the stacks of light rigging, tables, and stage sets used by both magicians in their shows.

Finn stopped near a tall set of black cabinets and placed his suitcase-sized silver camera case on the ground. "I'm setting up the equipment here."

Emmie looked up toward the stage rigging. "Try to catch him messing with Nova's props. The ones over there."

Finn followed her gaze. "Plenty of angles to work with. I'm confident if Trick tries anything, we'll record it."

Sarah was quiet after Finn started to unpack his camera equipment. Her eyes scanned the area like she could feel something lurking around them. She rubbed her arms, as if trying to warm herself up. "Do you feel that?"

Emmie shot her a quick glance, but kept her focus on the task at hand. "I felt them, but they don't come out. If you see any…"

"I'll let you know."

Turning her focus back to Finn, she watched him assemble the cameras and step around the stage, peering back at them from different angles.

"We need to be smart about this," Emmie said. "Nova doesn't understand how much danger she's in. She's lucky to have made it through the last couple of attacks."

Jason nodded, moving to help Finn set up the cameras. "Will the cameras pick up his face in the darkness?"

Finn scoffed. "These are the same ones I used to investigate ghosts before I met Emmie. If someone blinks on a moonless night, these will pick it up."

"It's all on you, Finn," Emmie said. "We won't get a second chance."

"I got this." Finn walked over to a metal ladder leading up into the light rigging and swung it from side to side. The metal rattled and clanked. He looked back at Jason. "Would you mind hanging onto this while I go up there?"

"Is it safe?" Sarah asked.

"Definitely not," Finn said. "But I need to get a higher angle or we won't see over the other stuff."

"Be careful," Sarah said.

"When am I ever *not* careful?"

"All the time."

Finn ascended the ladder, the metal cracking under his weight as if it might collapse at any moment. "It's a bit rusty. I see some clamps up here I can use to attach the camera. I switch them on remotely."

"The rehearsal doesn't start for a few hours," Emmie said.

"The batteries will last several hours. We're good."

Sarah's gaze jumped to the edge of the stage, her expression grim. "There are a lot of intense feelings in this place," she whispered. "I can feel a lot of anger... and betrayal."

"That's coming from Nova." Emmie glanced at the floor. "She's hurting because she thinks I don't believe her."

Sarah continued stepping toward the darkness but kept silent as Finn finished setting up the second camera along the opposite side of the stage.

Finn straightened up after climbing down from the ladder. "What if she's right? What if it isn't Trick?"

"If you saw everything we did..." Jason's voice was firm. "All the evidence points to him. He has access to everything—Nova's props, the stage—and he knows this place better than his own home."

Sarah turned to them, her expression still full of doubt. I don't think it's that simple. "There's something deeper going on. I can feel it."

Jason shook his head. "Whatever you're picking up, hold off for now. We can't waste any more time."

Emmie checked the time on her phone, the glare from her screen lighting up their faces like ghosts. "I'm sure Marty will start setting up for today's rehearsal soon, so we've got to get this done fast, and everyone else will arrive shortly after that." She crossed her arms, chewing on her lip anxiously. "None of them will be happy to see us when they get here."

"I can record for a few hours," Finn said, "using the highest resolution. Just let me know when you want me to start."

"Immediately," Emmie said. "Be discreet. We'll need to leave the area during the rehearsal, and I'm *hoping* they'll let us back in when it's done."

A soft click echoed through the air as Finn used a small device to test one of the cameras as he eyed a blinking red light in the darkness above them. "We're ready."

"Let's hope this works," Jason said, looking around the backstage with a sense of finality.

Emmie took a step toward Sarah, whose gaze had narrowed toward the light rigging structures above them. Her friend shivered. "The feeling doesn't go away."

"It will," Emmie said. "After we get a chance to prove it to Nova. She's dealing with a lot of conflicted emotions right now."

"Who's this?" Finn asked, lifting a framed photo out of the darkness. It showed Gloria—Grandma Ria—frozen in time back in the '80s, her face proud and distant. A chill swept over Emmie in the same moment as she stared at it, as if feeling the woman's presence somehow still lingered in that place, watching them, waiting for something to unravel.

"Gloria, the old woman I told you about," Emmie said. "The owner who lives in the penthouse. The one who can't speak."

Sarah's expression softened. "What's wrong with her?"

"She has late-stage Parkinson's."

A flicker of sorrow darkened Sarah's eyes as if feeling the woman's suffering herself. "I wish we had more time."

Emmie looked away, forcing herself to stay focused on what they still had to do. They were too close to solving this. "I won't forgive myself if anything happens to Nova."

Another burst of cold air surrounded them, and in the distance, the echo of footsteps signaled the start of the rehearsal.

Finn clicked a remote and nodded once. "It's showtime."

19

Emmie stood next to Jason backstage, watching Trick's act playing out in a highly choreographed spectacle that rivaled the best magicians she had seen over the years. He was moving with a mesmerizing flare that dazzled them in increasingly greater amounts, starting with throwing knives and wrapping it up with a heart-stopping act involving his assistant getting cut in half. His rehearsal went flawlessly, almost too perfect, and Emmie reminded herself that this was a man who calculated his every move. If he was the mastermind behind the attacks on Nova and the other magicians who had died in that place, then they would have to focus all their attention on him to rise above his sleight-of-hand.

Nova was watching the performance from the other side of the stage, and they had a clear view of each other if Nova had glanced over at any time, although she didn't. The silence between them since their fight weighed on Emmie's heart. Nova seemed to enjoy Trick's performance, her face full of pride.

Emmie glanced at Jason, who stood beside her with his jaw clenched, his gaze fixed on Trick as he wrapped up his last act with a bow. Nova, Wayne, and some of the others erupted in enthusiastic applause until Wayne, standing in the front row, directed him to the edge of the stage where they held a brief conversation.

Jason was still keeping an eye on Trick, while Finn and Sarah had moved off into the darkness to stand watch behind a pile of Nova's props. They had to keep all the angles covered if their plan was to succeed.

Trick finally made his way off the stage and Emmie watched him go, waiting for him to slip into the shadows, to go near Nova's props, but instead of moving in beside them, he lingered at the edge of the stage several feet away and stopped beside the curtain with his arms folded over his chest.

Jason came up beside Emmie and whispered into her ear, "He's not touching anything."

"Watch his hands," Emmie said.

"He's not even close. If he's planning to do something, he's hiding it well."

Emmie's stomach twisted. She hadn't expected this. Trick was supposed to be sneaking around, messing with Nova's equipment, but instead he was observing Nova's performance like a casual spectator.

She briefly met Trick's gaze, and Emmie whispered at the same time, even though he couldn't hear her from that distance. "Make your move."

Moments later, Jimmy and Nova jumped into action. Nova glanced at Emmie for the first time that day, although looked away immediately. Her face showed a deep determination, and there was a tightness in her movements, a stiffness that wasn't there before, and Emmie's heart ached watching her and Jimmy step out onto the stage—danger still hung in the air. Despite Nova's glowing smile as she addressed the empty audience, the chasm that separated them seemed impossible to bridge.

Emmie stared at Trick again, and a flash of doubt swept through her mind. "What if I'm wrong?" she asked Jason.

He seemed to dismiss her concerns. "Jimmy hasn't moved out the props yet. There's still time for him to act."

She gave a little nod and glanced around the stage, focusing in on the lighting rig—no signs of anyone meddling, living or dead—and then the curtain and the props and sets that Marty must have spent so many hours designing. "No," she whispered to herself, "I can't be wrong."

Trick watched with an amused expression as Nova and Jimmy started their first act. There was nothing in his demeanor to show he was planning anything, and maybe they had already missed their opportunity. Had he gone in and sabotaged the props before they'd arrived? A surge of anxiety knocked at her confidence. Trick no doubt was familiar with the stage like the back of his hand—they were on his turf—so catching him in the act would prove more difficult than expected.

Jimmy assisted Nova with the first illusion, one that involved Jimmy dropping into a shallow, black wooden box and disappearing before reappearing a moment later from behind a curtain. Emmie's attention jumped between the performance and Trick. The old magician not only stayed by the side of the stage, but he made no motion except to clap after Nova had finished each act.

The next act was more dangerous, something involving a blade that dropped down near Nova's head, although it was difficult to see the full illusion from where Emmie stood. But Nova emerged unscathed a moment later as Jimmy rushed backstage to get the next prop with Marty's help. Each illusion became more dangerous than the next, with Nova narrowly escaping injury and Emmie's heart skipping a beat each time. There were moments when Jimmy seemed to panic, then break into a grin when Nova emerged unharmed moments later.

Between shuttling the props and sets back and forth from the stage, there were moments when Trick could have stepped forward to touch the props, if he'd wanted, yet he made no motion at all as they passed by. His gaze only followed the objects, as if he were scrutinizing Nova's illusions for flaws.

Emmie watched Nova then Trick, her emotions a conflicted

mess. The acts were going smoothly. Jimmy brought out each new set after Nova performed the illusion with astounding skill and flair. Nothing had transpired between Trick and anything that Nova used, and there was only a single prop left.

As Nova's final act started, it seemed their moment to catch the old magician red-handed had passed, until something cracked above them. A section of light rigging creaked from side to side, almost in the same way it had done when Emmie had first arrived in the theater. A screeching metallic sound echoed throughout the theater, followed by another sharp crack.

Jason rushed up beside Emmie and grabbed her arm while gesturing to the ceiling. "Look out!"

A high-pitched grating sound echoed from the metal scaffolding above them like nails dragged across steel. Jason pulled Emmie to the side. It grew louder as a long black piece of equipment broke loose, swinging wildly from side to side, tearing at ropes and cables along the way. A moment later, it plummeted toward Nova.

Emmie's heart pounded as Jason struggled to pull her to safety until she screamed, "Nova!"

Her cry barely escaped her lips before Trick darted out from where he'd stood watching and rushed onto the stage. His cool demeanor was gone as he surged ahead like someone driven by something deeper than just trying to warn a coworker. He reached Nova a moment before the stage equipment from above came crashing down, shoving her out of the way with a force that sent them both tumbling to the floor. The object hit the stage with a thunderous crash, shattering a row of light fixtures attached to a branch of black clamps. Several ropes and cables came with it and whipped through the air like strands of hair.

Nova landed safely out of the way, but Trick wasn't fast enough to avoid the ropes. One of them swept through the air like a lasso and caught him by the neck. He clutched at the rope around his throat while struggling to stand. The rope seemed to coil tighter and rise as if something from above had begun manipulating him with marionette strings.

Emmie screamed as she watched the scene in horror. Trick was dragged upward as the equipment's weight pulled the ropes tighter, lifting his body into the air and suspending him like a rag doll. For a brief, horrifying moment he dangled there—alive, struggling, his hands clawing at the rope around his throat—before his body went limp and his head drooped to the side at an unnatural angle.

"Get him down!" Nova screamed in terror as she scrambled to her feet, but it was too late.

The rigging gave another sickening groan before dropping further, squeezing the rope tighter around Trick's neck. For a moment, the theater went quiet with only the sounds of the ropes swaying above the stage.

Nova broke down in tears and her cries echoed throughout the theater.

Wayne stood frozen at the front of the stage, his face pale with shock. Finn and Sarah rushed toward the tragedy, and Finn grabbed his phone with shaking hands, dialing a number that could only be 911. Sarah rushed to Nova's side and called out, "Are you all right?"

Nova let out a moan full of pain as she glanced back at Emmie with horrified eyes.

Emmie couldn't move as she stared up at Trick's lifeless body. This wasn't supposed to be how it happened. She had been so sure of everything, so sure that he was the villain. But now, watching him dangle in the air above them, a wave of guilt and confusion flashed through her mind.

Jason's face was pale and his eyes were wide as he caught her attention. "What the hell just happened?"

"I—" Emmie's voice faltered. She didn't know. Instead of harming Nova, like they'd expected, Trick had jumped in to save her, and now he was dead. Everything felt wrong.

Nova still trembled as she stood with watering eyes and

stared at Emmie. "You see now?" she whispered without anger. "It wasn't him... It's the damn ghosts."

Emmie nodded slowly as her breath caught in her throat. She wanted to tell Nova she was sorry, that she had gotten everything completely wrong, that this was just a tragic accident from faulty equipment. But something in the air—the way the ropes had moved, and the way they had lifted suddenly after wrapping around Trick's neck—left her questioning everything.

An icy burst of air caught her attention. A presence hovered somewhere nearby, and it swept around her, intimately sweeping inside her shirt, as if teasing her to act. This was the same familiar chill she had sensed the day they'd arrived, but it was darker now, more aggressive. A shiver ran up her spine as she glanced at Jason and reached for his hand instinctively.

"Nova was right," she said softly. But before she could say more, someone whispered from somewhere above them, an unfamiliar voice that spit out words in short bursts, although the words were lost in the chaos of the rescuers rushing the stage. It was cold, distant and cruel.

Nova stepped toward Emmie as Jimmy was helping her stand, and Wayne was joining the rush to get onto the stage. Nova followed Emmie's gaze to the darkness above. Her friend's eyes were wide with fear again, mirroring the expression from the video that had inspired Emmie to make the visit. "Do you see them? Are they up there? Please tell me you believe me now."

There was something—someone—on the metal walkway above the lighting rig. A shadowy figure wearing a magician's outfit. Emmie nodded slowly as the shadow slipped away into the darkness just above the spot where Finn had set up one of his cameras. "I believe you."

20

The theater was eerily quiet, with only the murmurs of police officers and the occasional burst of static from a police radio to remind them of the tragedy that had just happened.

The steady drone of the air conditioners in the ceiling helped to calm Emmie as she stood with her arms crossed at the back corner of the theater, surrounded by her friends as they watched the crime scene from a safe distance. One of the officers had sealed off the stage with yellow tape, although they were now removing it.

Finn had managed to grab Marty's attention near the stage and discovered that the investigators had already concluded a structural failure caused the incident, based on the witness statements and video footage of the stage that Wayne had provided. He'd been recording everything without their knowledge, using a string of hidden cameras around the theater. He had recorded everything they'd done backstage since they'd arrived too, including their efforts to catch Trick in the act of sabotaging Nova's props. The police had also discovered the cameras Finn had set up, watched the recordings, and had listened patiently as they tried to justify their earlier suspicions about Trick, but had ultimately dismissed their efforts in a condescending tone before returning Finn's cameras.

Everyone was free to go within a couple of hours, after the police questioned each of them, although Emmie refused to leave—she needed to talk with Nova one last time.

Her friend had avoided them since the ordeal, staying by her father as the police had conducted their investigation in a surprisingly casual way. They had rushed to cut down the old magician's body dangling above them as soon as they arrived before putting him into a body bag and carrying him away without fanfare.

As soon as the police removed the yellow tape, Marty started cleaning the area, working expressionless to clear away the scattered debris. Jimmy helped him, although the young assistant seemed lost among the chaos, stepping over the ropes with great care as if they might come alive again and do the same to him. Fortunately, neither of them had the ability to see ghosts, or they would have reacted differently to the ghastly sight hovering over them. After carrying Trick away, his spirit had remained behind, still suspended above the stage in a heartbreaking loop of violence, struggling in vain to remove the rope wrapped around his neck. The old man's eyes bulged while he mouthed something into the empty air, although Emmie couldn't hear him from that distance.

Judging by the way Sarah looked at Emmie, her friend could also see Trick's spirit. Each of them had embraced after the accident, although their muted conversations had focused on how they had failed to stop the tragedy and the powerlessness to see it through to the end. There seemed no hope in trying to convince Wayne to let them stay after this as he moved about the stage slumped over with his head down—a devastated man who had lost everything.

The dark spirit Emmie had seen during the ordeal was gone. She had finally seen what they were up against, although now it was too late. All she could think about was Nova—and how terribly wrong she had been.

Turning to face the stage, Emmie watched Nova console her father just as the steady drone of the air conditioner stopped, and Wayne's voice rose through the air. His face was pale and shaken, his gaze locked on the scaffolding above the stage that had broken loose. "The show is over." His voice was raw and broken. "I shouldn't have bothered. The theater *is* cursed."

The gang exchanged glances as if trying to decide their next step, but before anyone could speak up, Nova responded to her father in a sharp, defiant tone. "No, Dad. You can't shut it down. Not now."

Wayne looked at her with a pained expression. "Nova, you almost died tonight. If Trick hadn't—"

"I've got this, Dad." Nova leaned into him, her eyes piercing. "I have to do this for Grandma Ria. This show is everything to her. You know that. I'm not giving up."

He shook his head. "You saw what just happened. Amber House Theater is done."

Emmie's heart ached watching Nova stand up to her dad. The young magician had so much strength, so much determination, but Emmie couldn't stop thinking about the betrayal that had divided them. The guilt swelled in her chest until she couldn't bear it anymore.

"Nova," Emmie called out to her friend, her voice trembling as she stepped forward. "Can I please talk with you?"

Nova and Wayne both glanced over at her at the same time. Nova held a curious look, and Wayne scowled within his pain.

Emmie took in a deep breath and continued, "I was wrong. So wrong. I never should have doubted you."

Nova stepped toward her and Emmie moved forward to meet her halfway near the center of the theater. The distance between them faded away as Nova's eyes softened. She looked at her dad, then back to Emmie. "I forgive you," Nova said softly, "but you need to trust me now."

Emmie nodded. "You were telling the truth."

"Stop this!" Wayne shouted as his face reddened. His voice reverberated throughout the theater. "I said it's over. No more of this ghost bullshit."

Nova's gaze shifted to her father, speaking in a soft voice, "Dad... you don't have to believe in the ghosts here, but I want you to believe in *me*. I have to do this show. For Grandma Ria. You know that."

Wayne shook his head. "I can't risk your life for a performance. It's not worth it."

"But it *is* worth it. I worked my whole life for this and if you walk away from this theater, she'll never see her dream come true. This place is everything to her. We can't stop now. She might not even make it until Friday. You know that."

Wayne's shoulders slumped, his face weighted down by the decision. "I don't want to lose you too."

Nova's voice softened, but she didn't waver. "You won't lose me. Marty will go through all the equipment again to make sure everything is safe, if that makes you feel better. I know what I'm doing." She turned back and met Emmie's gaze. "And Emmie won't let anything happen to me."

Wayne narrowed his eyes at Emmie and her friends. "I don't want *them* here."

"I do," Nova said. "Nevermind that you don't understand what they're doing. They can watch my back while I'm on stage."

Wayne's gaze moved across the stage. "This place... is cursed."

Emmie stepped toward them. "It's not cursed—at least, not in the way you're thinking—but I've seen who's behind the accidents, and we can stop them."

Wayne looked skeptically at each of them and hesitated. "This can never happen again."

"It won't, Dad."

"How can you say that after what just happened?" he asked.

Nova glanced at Emmie. "Because my friend finally understands. I can do this. *We* can do this."

After a long moment, Wayne sighed, the fight draining out of him. "I'll have Marty double-check all the equipment again—*triple* check everything. We'll go ahead with the performance as planned... but we might have an avalanche of cancellations after the news of what happened today gets out—"

"It was an accident—to them—and nobody remembers what happened here forty years ago," Nova said.

"You won't have an opening act," Wayne said.

"I don't need one. I've got thousands of followers online, and I have plenty of extra material prepared. And Jimmy will help me."

Wayne gave a solemn nod, then stared into her eyes. "Make your grandma proud."

"I will." Nova brightened while looking toward Emmie. "On Friday, everyone in Vegas will know my name."

21

Emmie's mind was still reeling from the experience in the theater as she gathered with her friends back in her hotel room. They had kept their thoughts to themselves until the door was closed behind them. Having Nova convince Wayne to let them stay gave them more time to get it all sorted out, but with Nova's life on the line, every minute spent trying to piece things together felt like a desperate race to avert disaster.

They gathered between the two queen beds and sat as couples facing each other, Sarah and Finn on one side, and Jason and Emmie on the other. There was a sense of completeness now, like four legs of a table that had wobbled until Sarah and Finn arrived. They had each other to rely on—to complement and draw strength from each other now—but Emmie couldn't shake the weight of everything that had just happened.

"I'm so sorry," Emmie said. "I didn't want things—"

"It's not your fault," Finn said. "We've got a lot of work to do. No sense in wasting time blaming yourself."

Emmie leaned forward on the edge of the bed, running her fingers through her hair as her earlier mistakes still weighed on her heart. "I knew the spirits were there, but I still thought Trick…" She looked at Jason for an answer.

"We all thought he was behind the murders," Jason said while leaning toward her. "It made perfect sense to me—until now—but I saw the look on your face when Trick died. You saw something, didn't you?"

Emmie looked at Sarah, and her friend held that same knowing in her eyes that she had in the theater. "I think we both saw him."

Sarah nodded. "The shadow of a man above the stage."

"It was a magician—I recognized his outfit."

"You're sure about this?" Finn asked.

"I'm sure."

"So it's either Mystic Max, Danny Drake or Zack Vayne."

"I passed Danny in the hallway two nights ago. The figure I saw on the stage was definitely not him. And I don't get the sense that it was Zack either. I've seen a photo of him too, and the figure I saw above the stage looked nothing like him."

"So that leaves Max," Sarah said, "but we don't have a motivation."

Finn glanced around the room as if he might see the magician standing nearby. "What's going on in this place where every magician dies? If Mystic Max is murdering the others, then what happened to *him*? Suicide? Murder? The rabbit hole keeps getting deeper."

"Well, we have until Friday to find out."

Jason looked at Emmie as if lost in a deep thought. "When you saw this Max guy, did you see him actually wrapping the rope around Trick's neck?"

Emmie sighed, sensing that Jason had just found the first hole in their only theory, and things were about to fall apart. "No. I didn't see him *directly* interfering with Nova's act. It was just the way he watched the whole thing from above, from the shadows."

"I couldn't see his face clearly," Sarah added, "but I picked up on his intention. His aura was a sharp, bright red. He intended to kill someone."

"Okay," Finn said, "so if we go with that assumption that Max is out to kill every magician who stands on that stage, then... why?"

"Jealousy?" Jason guessed. "Vengeance?"

"He wants to keep something hidden?" Finn added.

"We'll have our answer as soon as I communicate with him," Emmie said, "and I *will* find him, but we have to assume he intends to do the same to Nova. We're running out of time."

"The show must go on," Finn said wryly.

"I'm just so thankful you arrived today," Emmie said, looking at him and Sarah. "I don't know what I would do without you both."

"We wouldn't let you face all of this alone," Sarah said. "We're a team, remember? Psychics 'R Us."

"I remember. It's just that I was trying to spare you the trouble of coming out and having to—it's just, you've been taking so many days off work lately—"

"Never mind my schedule. I can work around it, but nothing is more important than helping my friends, especially with something as grave as this. I know you're committed to helping Nova, but you don't have to do it alone. Maybe one of these days we can all quit our jobs and practice ghost-hunting full-time, but for now, we have to improvise and work around the roadblocks. You're right that we won't all be together someday, but let's not worry about that just yet. For now, we have to have each other's backs."

"So, what should we do now?" Jason asked.

Emmie straightened her posture and tried to shake off the guilt that twisted her stomach. She hadn't been able to see the situation for what it was. And now, because of her failure to consider all options, they were back at square one, scrambling to pick up the pieces. "We need to start over. Go all the way back to the beginning, before the first *accidents*. At least we know where to start, with Max."

Finn leaned back and touched the fingertips of both hands

together. "Max died in the lounge area backstage with his assistants, right?"

"Correct," Jason said. "I found Marty back there yesterday. He was having a sentimental moment when I stepped in and seems to hold a lot of guilt over what happened, but he fiercely defended himself against any notions that he was somehow responsible for the accident. I believe him."

"He told you that?" Finn asked. "So he must have some suspicions of his own."

Jason nodded. "One of the assistants, Jessica, was Marty's girlfriend at the time, and her death must have hit him hard, judging by our conversation. It's obvious he's still not over it."

"We should start there," Finn said.

"He keeps it locked."

"Did you see anything unusual in there?" Sarah asked.

He gave a little smirk. "The place looks the same as it must have back in the '80s. Other than that, nothing leads me to believe that anything... violent happened in there."

"Well," Emmie said, "assuming Max had something to do with Trick's death, we come back to the question of... why? Who is Mystic Max? Where did he come from? What really happened in that lounge with his assistants? Trick mentioned a few things about him before..." She looked at each of her friends. "...what we know now is a murder. We need to find out everything we can about what happened that night to help us get a complete picture."

"Unfortunately, the only person left with all the answers can't talk." Jason shook his head. "A conversation with Gloria—Grandma Ria—might straighten everything out, if only the old woman could give us her side of the story."

"The grandmother with Parkinson's," Sarah said. "I want to see her. Maybe there's some way I can get through to her, even if it isn't directly."

Emmie looked at her curiously. "What are you thinking?"

"Her disease is a big obstacle, I admit. If someone is so close to death, it probably isn't possible to help them in any meaningful way, but maybe I can work around it."

"It sounds like she could go any day," Finn said. "You're planning to try healing? That would take a while, wouldn't it?"

"It's worth a try."

"Be discreet in your questions," Jason said. "Nova is protective of the old woman, and there's a nurse who checks on her every day, but maybe you can get in good with her on a professional level?"

"I can." Sarah nodded confidently. "I can talk the talk."

"All right, and while you're doing that, I'll have a chat with Marty again. I'm sure he knows more about Max's background than anyone else here, except for the old woman."

"What do you think about her son?" Finn asked. "Wayne. He must know what happened around that time, heard stories from his mother."

"Good luck getting *him* to talk," Emmie said. "Now *there's* a challenge to keep you busy. I'm sure Wayne plans to fight us every step of the way. He already thinks we're crazy, but maybe you can use some of that expert experience in journalism to extract a little information out of him."

Finn straightened up. "Piece of cake."

"Just be..." Sarah said, "...tactful."

He rolled his eyes. "You don't have enough faith in me. I've gained a lot of patience over the last year."

"You're going to need it."

"The only thing that still bothers me," Emmie said, "is what Danny said when I confronted him, that Trick ruined everything. If it's not what we thought it meant, then I need to speak with him again."

"Where did—" Sarah cut off.

A loud knock came from the door and everyone jumped. Emmie's heart raced faster as if someone had caught them doing something illegal.

"Wayne?" Finn whispered with wide eyes.

Jason went to answer the door but when he opened it, he glanced in both directions down the hallway then back at them with an expression of confusion. "What the—?"

"Who is it?" Sarah stood to get a better view.

"Nobody's here." Jason gestured to the hallway floor. "But they left something."

Each of them raced to the door and gathered around Jason. A small object lay on the ground just outside the door: an Amber House Casino playing card, facing down.

Jason bent down and picked it up slowly, turning it over to reveal the face to everyone—the Joker card, worn and faded. "I think it's for me."

"Nobody knows your nickname here, do they?" Emmie asked.

Jason swallowed. "Only the people who kicked me out of the casino years ago. Can't imagine how they'd know I'm here though."

"Do you think it's a threat?" Finn asked in a low voice.

Emmie stared at the card and considered where it might have come from. The hallway was empty, and she hadn't heard any footsteps or noises of any kind after Jason opened the door. Had someone dropped it and run? If so, they would have heard something.

Jason scanned the hallway again in both directions. "Someone's playing a trick on us?"

"Whatever it means," Sarah said, "they know we're here."

22

A strange sound coming from the hallway jolted Jason awake that night. A faint but distinct sound, cutting through the silence of the room above the steady drone of the air conditioner. He sat up, taking in a deep breath to calm his racing heart, and the comforter dropped to his side where Emmie lay quietly snoring. He watched the rise and fall of her chest for a moment within the dim light of the open bathroom door.

Had he imagined the noises? Echoes from a bad dream? But then the sound of footsteps caught his attention, light and hurried, that came from the hallway. Judging by the weight of his eyelids, he'd only slept for a few hours. Had Sarah or Finn left their room to explore? Nova had said only they were sharing the floor with her. So, would someone be remodeling or cleaning at this hour?

For a moment, he hesitated to get out of bed, telling himself that it had to be just the hotel staff working overtime to prepare for the grand reopening. But something about the noise left him feeling uneasy.

Tactfully maneuvering out of bed so as not to disturb Emmie, he slipped on his jeans and a shirt—just enough clothing to safely poke his head out the door if he needed to.

Stepping to the door, he looked through the room's peephole first. The faint forms of two people stood at the far end of the hallway within the dimly lit corridor. If it was Sarah or Finn, then shouldn't he at least go out and make sure they were okay? Opening the creaking door slowly, he poked his head out and stared toward the figures in the distance. They stood unnaturally straight, with their hands hanging loosely at their sides. One of them tilted their head as if listening for something, and the other turned one leg outward with a strange elegance.

Meeting their gaze, both of them giggled. Two women.
Definitely not Sarah and Finn.

When they stepped toward him, he inched back into the room, but continued watching them approach as his pulse quickened.

"Please..." one of them said in a soft, seductive voice.

Hotel staff? Late-shift workers? Nova and a friend out for a stroll? Jason strained to make sense of the encounter.

They moved into the light about halfway down the hall. They were dressed provocatively, their uniforms clinging to their bodies in a way that immediately caught his attention in an uncomfortable way. The shorter of the two had long black hair that cascaded over her shoulders like a waterfall of black ink. She let out an intoxicating, melodic laugh. The other gestured for him to follow them.

"What's going on?" he asked.

His question elicited more laughter.

He tried again with, "What do you want?"

"We know what *you* want," the taller of the two women purred, her smile sweet and a bit dangerous, shadowed by long curls of blonde hair. The other black-haired woman tilted her head toward a nearby door, her eyes gleaming with promise. She held two stacks of casino chips and extended them toward him with the overhead light glistening off a ring on her pinky finger. "Free game play. Compliments of the owner. We heard you've got a knack for poker, and we're here to escort you to the VIP lounge. Your friend isn't joining us?"

He stared at the stack of chips, and it sent his heart racing. "She's asleep."

"Shame," the shorter woman said with a frown.

"But you're going, right?" the other woman asked. "We heard you love to play. Just one quick game. It's all free. Nothing to lose."

He understood what they meant at that moment, somehow connecting with him on a deep level. They were appealing to a dark area of his mind that he had given up years earlier, but just the idea of going with them... This *was* Vegas, after all, but his gut twisted with conflict.

Glancing back into the room, he could still hear Emmie's soft and steady snoring. The disturbance hadn't interrupted her sleep. Still, Jason called to her, as if to get permission to leave. "Em."

A brief pause in her breathing, but she continued again.

"Let the princess sleep," one woman said to him. "They're waiting for you."

"Who?"

"The others."

He turned to face them again. "I... I can't go with you. It's late. How did you...?"

"We can't start without you." The woman pushed a stack of chips into his hand. "The boss comped everything. You don't want to waste it, do you? Free money."

Jason clutched the black hundred-dollar chips that easily totaled a couple thousand dollars, but it wasn't their value that energized him. The familiar clay texture seemed to warm his heart and comfort him like an old friend. His heart raced faster as he stood on the verge of shutting the door and going back to bed, although something prevented him from backing away. Why was he still talking to them? "What's the game?"

"Your favorite," the blonde woman said. "Poker, of course."

The shorter woman giggled.

Jason inched forward, then stepped out into the hallway. The door behind him snapped shut before realizing he was standing on his bare feet without a room key.

"Now let's go," the blonde woman urged him to follow her.

How would he justify his absence to Emmie if she woke up and found him gone? His mind clung to the first excuse he could think of.

I needed a strong drink. Something to clear my head.

Yes, it would do. The complimentary alcohol in the room was hardly enough to deal with the issues they were facing. "One stiff drink."

The women exchanged a glance, their smiles widening as he stepped toward them. "Yes, just one stiff drink," they echoed, their voices smooth and silly. "And a game of poker."

As they led him down the hallway toward the elevator, he found himself nodding and clicking the chips together in a steady rhythm. The familiar sensation intoxicated him far more than any drink. But instead of taking the elevator down to the gaming floor, they continued straight ahead, following the dimly lit hallway until stopping at an unmarked door halfway down the hall.

"Where are we going?" he asked.

"The others are inside," the shorter woman said. "You aren't nervous, are you?"

"No," he answered quickly. "Of course not. I've played poker for most of my life."

"Yes, we heard."

The blonde woman opened the door, and he tried to keep some distance between them, but the short woman slipped her arm around his waist and nudged him closer. A familiar scent came off their outfits—faint traces of sweat and perfume mixed with cigarette smoke—rekindled the long-forgotten excitement of his days in Vegas, and he could already feel his adrenaline pumping.

Their feet clattered almost in unison as they stepped inside a darkened room that resembled a maintenance workers' closet. The door slammed shut behind them before he had time to take in his environment. This room wasn't like any hotel room or lounge, but some sort of makeshift break room—maybe for the construction workers?—stuffed to the ceiling with broken tables, spare chairs, light fixtures, a coffee maker, and a full-size refrigerator. It was small and intimate, with only a single light hanging above an old poker table in the center. The decks of cards and another stack of chips were all set up for him, ready to go, and the women laughed as they jumped to their seats on opposite sides of the table, leaving the middle seat open between them. The blonde had dealt the cards even before he had a chance to sit down.

"Where are the others?" he asked while adding the chips in his hand to those on the table but remained standing.

"Oh, they'll be here soon. Don't you worry." The blonde smirked and rolled her eyes. She took a bottle of Jack Daniels from a small table nearby and poured him a glass. "We can't play on the main casino floor, Joker."

"How do you know that name?"

"What name?"

"My nickname. Joker."

"Everyone here knows about you, Joker." The blonde woman tapped the seat next to her and winked at him. "Now sit down and play before I lose my temper."

Jason glanced around. "What is this place?"

The black-haired woman seemed to hold back a laugh. "Heaven."

He eyed the chair before finally taking a seat in it, swallowing the rising unease in his throat. It wasn't like he was going to lose any money. Casinos *did* sometimes comp guests with credits—very special guests—although it was hard to believe that Wayne had done that for them after the recent events. Still, there was no harm in playing one game since he had nothing to lose. He could get through a hand before Emmie woke up, and maybe even make a little money to help pay for the trip. Taking a few sips from his glass, each one a little larger than the last, the effects of the alcohol soon eased his tension and warmed his throat. *Might as well play along.*

The blonde dealt the cards with a sensual flair, playing the first hand slowly as the shorter woman's gaze jumped between him and the cards. Somewhere within the first few minutes of strategizing, something shifted in the air. Something surreal. The women's smiles stretched a little too wide, their eyes narrowed a little too sharply, and their laughter... hollow.

Jason rubbed his eyes, then studied each of them for a long moment. "I can't be dreaming."

The blonde woman laughed. "I hope you're as good as all the rumors we've heard."

"What have you heard?" he asked, taking another drink from his glass.

"That you're the best."

"Where did you—"

"Oh darn," the shorter woman said, laying down her cards a moment later. "I'm out already." Her perfect smile stretched wider, and she met Jason's gaze.

His mouth went dry as an awkward laugh escaped his mouth, trying to deflect his growing confusion. But then the blonde woman also slapped her cards on the table. "I'm out too! Isn't this fun?"

The woman's voice made Jason's skin crawl. "Not really—no."

"That's how *we* play, Joker. You're winning!"

But the shift in tone felt wrong—dangerous. He took a closer look at their uniforms. These weren't barmaid outfits for casino staff, these were costumes, theatrical and outdated. The realization hit him. Magician's assistants.

Jason tried to stand, but the women were on him in an instant. They slid their icy hands across his shoulders, pushing him down and keeping him seated. His heart hammered in his chest. He mumbled, "I—I should go now."

"We're not done playing, Joker," one of them whispered into his ear, her icy breath tickling the skin on his neck.

They weren't asking anymore—they were pulling him in deeper, and he couldn't resist, even as he struggled to break away. Gripping his wrists with the strength of someone twice their size, one on each side, they guided him toward a door at the far side of the room. The playful tone had vanished, replaced now with something cold and harsh.

He stumbled within the daze of the alcohol, leading him through a narrow door as he barely managed to catch himself from falling forward. The space was old and forgotten, like the furthest corner of some utility storage room. A small dusty area lit by a single overhead light that narrowed toward a metal door only a few feet away. They pushed him toward it as his bare feet slipped against the cement floor. He struggled within their grasp as the blonde woman opened the door and the lights of Las Vegas filled his view. A flaking black metal catwalk lay ahead, with only a single rusted railing separating him from the nightlife below.

"What's this?" Jason asked as they dragged him outside into the warm evening air.

"Just a little more fun, Joker." They pushed him forward onto the catwalk, and he screamed in his mind while struggling within their grasp, but the alcohol had taken its toll on his senses.

He could only think of Emmie at that moment as the sense of control slipped away from him and terror washed over him. The women were laughing now in a brash tone, until their voices swept away in the cool breeze just beyond the door.

Certainly, some pedestrian would see the commotion and call the police, wouldn't they?

They moved toward the edge of the catwalk and tightened their grasp on him. The metal scaffolding creaked and clanged beneath their footsteps, and he tried to prepare himself for whatever twisted act they had in mind. His heart raced faster as they inched him forward. Staring down, the glowing top edge of the hotel's marquis came into view below them.

It was clear that they intended to throw him over the edge, but... why? He had done nothing to deserve this. His mind raced back to everything he had done in Vegas years earlier. Had he upset them or hurt them in some way without realizing it? But then, like some sick, twisted magic trick, they slipped a rope around his neck and panic swept through his body. They planned to throw him over the edge and watch him hang above the hotel's marquis like some macabre finale.

Jason thrashed against their grip and the ropes, his muffled cries drowned out by their laughter as he reached toward the railing only inches ahead. If he could grasp it, he could hang on until the police arrived.

I'm sorry, Em. I failed you.

"You certainly have," the blonde mocked. "We'll give her your kind regards."

"No!" he yelled. "Someone call the police!"

"It's too late," the shorter woman said without emotion. "Too late for all of you."

I can't die like this—not for some messed up poker game. Regrets flooded his mind. How had they broken him down and trapped him so easily? His heart sank within the sobering reality of his situation.

"It's not real," he told himself.

"Ha!" The blond woman laughed. "Keep telling yourself that... all... the way... down."

Gripping the cool metal railing in the final moment before they tossed him up and over the edge, he looked at their faces for answers. Within their wide grins, their eyes almost seemed to burn a bright red with deep hatred, and it was clear they intended to do the same to the others.

As he went over the side, his fingers scraped against the railing, but his grip faltered and the lights of the city swirled around him. The rope around his neck stretched tighter until his leg hooked a section of the scaffolding that jutted out, stopping his fall inches before the rope cut off his breath.

Staring up to where the women had stood on the landing, they were now gone. He gasped for air while struggling to recover and spotted a metal ladder on the side of the scaffold. Straining his foot until he caught it, he pushed his weight up onto it inch by inch. Finally, with one last push, he swung his leg over the railing and rolled back onto the metal platform with a shaky cry of relief.

The metal door leading inside was still open and the single light still lit the rope that they had tied around the railing. He pushed through the exhaustion and pain to remove the rope around his neck before the women could return to finish him off.

Heaving in a deep breath, he staggered to his feet and headed back inside the hotel, and didn't stop pushing forward until he was standing outside his hotel room, slapping his hands against the door and calling out Emmie's name. His body shuddered as he pounded on the door again and again until the exhaustion finally took its toll as he collapsed on the floor, his pulse thumping in his ears.

Emmie opened the door a moment later and jumped forward, wrapping her arms around him. "Oh, my God! What happened?"

"I'm sorry," he repeated over and over again. "I'm sorry I ever left you."

Even after she dragged him inside the room and locked the door behind them, the laughter of the women still echoed in his ears. He had almost died, but he couldn't understand how everything had unfolded so quickly.

Emmie's face was full of confusion and fear. "Where did you go? What happened?"

But the weight of what had just happened pressed down on him. How could he tell her how close he had come to making his fatal mistake? He couldn't tell her, or the others. Not yet.

"I failed."

23

After breakfast, Jason still struggled to come up with a way to tell Emmie about everything that had happened the night before. The encounter had left him traumatized and ashamed. His stomach churned while he waited for her to finish getting ready in the bathroom, as all the chilling events replayed over and over in his mind—the laughter of Max's assistants, the cold fingers on his skin, and the way they had violently dragged him toward the balcony like a sack of potatoes. His near-fatal experience had kept him awake half the night, and he had to tell Emmie before it chipped away at his sanity. Rubbing his neck, he could still feel the rope's coarse fibers digging into his skin, and his muscles ached from dragging himself back from the brink of death.

Emmie stepped out of the bathroom a moment later, adjusting her hair and clothes until her gaze stopped on his neck. Her eyes narrowed, but she spoke in a gentle voice. "Did you cut yourself shaving?"

He ran his hand across his chin and glanced away. "Not exactly."

"A rash?"

Her expression showed so much concern. It wasn't fair to

keep it from her—he *had* to tell her—even at the risk of upsetting her. "I doubt it."

Meeting his gaze for a long moment, she asked, "Jason, please tell me what's wrong."

"I'm just not sure how to explain it."

"Try." She looked at him curiously, then took his hand and led him over to the bed where they sat together on the edge.

With the air conditioner rumbling in the background, Jason told her everything—how the two magician's assistants had lured him from the room with the promise of free gambling, the mock poker game cut short, and how they had dragged him out to the balcony with the clear intention of leaving him hanging by his neck over the edge.

Emmie's face grew pale as he spoke, pushing her lips together as he shared every detail. There was no point in holding back anything, and his confession was both terrifying and liberating to finally get everything out in the open. He had messed up, and it was better to tell the truth knowing that the stakes for all of them were too high. Her grip on his hand tightened throughout the story as if trying to keep him from danger. There was no anger in her eyes, just fear and concern. She stayed silent until he finished, but then she nodded and spoke softly. "I'm glad you're safe. Sometimes this happens when Sarah and I work together—when our energies align and the spirits gain enough strength to manifest in the flesh. They can appear just like you or me for someone who normally can't see ghosts."

"That's what happened then." Jason's throat tightened. A throbbing pain gripped his neck and he winced. "I can't believe I fell for it."

She squeezed his hand a little tighter while inspecting his neck. "Finn had something similar happen to him a while back—a feisty French woman with him—so now you two have something in common."

"How does it look?" Jason asked.

"It's a little bruised. Sarah can take a look at it."

"It just caught me off guard, that's all."

"It's my fault for putting you in this situation. I didn't think Vegas would affect you this much. Do you want to leave?"

He scoffed and straightened a little. "Not without you. I plan to see this through to the end."

"If you feel things are… too much…"

"They won't get to me again." He shook his head and stood up. "I promise I'll let you know if I feel… compromised again, but I see now what Nova's up against. Judging by what happened last night, it will take all of us to get through this."

"Just one thing bothers me," Emmie said.

"What's that?"

"If those were Max's assistants, then where was he? Why wasn't he part of the assault?"

Jason considered it for a moment. "He was busy attacking someone else?"

An image of Nova rehearsing backstage popped into Emmie's mind. "Nova. We'll need to find out if she experienced anything last night." Standing up, she held Jason close for several seconds before turning toward the door that adjoined their rooms and knocked. "We shouldn't keep the others waiting."

～

THEY GATHERED IN FINN AND SARAH'S ROOM A FEW MINUTES later. Jason shut the curtains against the glaring morning light, then he turned back to them and folded his arms over his chest. He recounted his harrowing late-night encounter with the two assistants, detailing his brush with death above the hotel sign, and making it clear that he wasn't proud of what he had done by venturing out on his own in the middle of the night.

"We all get duped once in a while," Finn said while opening his silver suitcase and pulling out one of the larger cameras.

"The larger concern," Sarah added, "is that these spirits have shown they won't hesitate to target each of us."

"So what's the plan?" Finn asked while powering up the camera.

They mapped it out quickly. Jason and Emmie would go down to the stage. Finn and Sarah would go to the penthouse to meet with Nova and Wayne.

"Her performance is tomorrow night, so we don't have much time," Emmie said. "Don't expect Wayne to be a river of information."

"I have plenty of tact when it comes to interviewing noncooperative witnesses," Finn said. "I'm sure I can handle him."

"Don't be so sure," Emmie said. "You might have met your match with this guy."

"That bad?" Finn asked.

"Keeping the man calm seems to go a long way," Emmie replied. "We'll meet up this afternoon and exchange notes, but contact the others if you run into any issues."

Emmie glanced toward the door. "I also need to make a detour to room 1913."

"What's in 1913?" Finn asked.

"Maybe nothing, but it's where I first encountered Danny's spirit. It's time that we finished our conversation."

24

Emmie found the door to room 1913 unlocked again and pushed it open. Stepping inside, she flipped on the light and a rush of cool air swept around her. The makeshift storage room looked the same as it had before, with disassembled furniture, construction equipment, and tools lying across the floor in every direction. Even without focusing, she could feel Danny's presence. He was there, somewhere, but evading her attention.

Taking a step inside and shutting the door behind her, she spoke into the silent room, "Danny."

No response.

"Danny Drake," she said a little louder.

Something shimmered across the room, flaring through one of the antique glass lamps stacked in the corner. The bristling energy grew stronger until a man's figure formed out of the shadows. Danny Drake. His charred flesh and tattered magician's outfit clearly stood out, although his spirit seemed even more distressed than before.

"I'm late," he said in a low, strained voice, his gaze darting toward the door. He leaned forward as if he might hurry away at any moment.

"You're going to the stage again," Emmie said, stepping into his path.

Meeting his gaze, his bristling energy seemed to encompass them both, and the clutter around them faded in her mind's eye. Danny's past came into focus, playing out around her like a forgotten movie. His memories became her own and the decades peeled away. She could hear the young magician's laughter echoing faintly, blending with the shuffling of playing cards on a worn velvet table in the corner. This room was where Danny Drake had spent his time preparing for his illusions. She saw flashes of him, his hands expertly practicing an impossible trick, his face half-lit by the glow of a bedside lamp. There had always been a restlessness about him, a look on his face like he was chasing something forever out of reach. There was so much pain in his eyes too—isolation. That had been his greatest illusion, to hide his true emotions from the world.

"Danny, wait," she said. "We need to talk."

His form flickered, flaring with a bit of irritation, but he didn't move past her. "I need to... get down to the theater."

"I just need... can you help me answer something? Earlier, you said that *Trick ruined everything*. What did you mean by that?"

Danny froze, his shoulders tensing as if bracing for a blow, his eyes narrowing in sharp pain. "Oh, it doesn't matter anymore," he said, clenching his teeth and inching forward as if attempting to move past her.

"It *does* matter," Emmie said, holding her ground. "Why the rush to get to the stage now?"

"I have to stop her."

"Stop who?"

He glared into the distance with that same pained look again. "Nova."

"No," Emmie said. "I won't let you get near her anymore. You're trying to kill her, aren't you?"

He looked up at Emmie sharply. "Kill her?"

"You attacked her two nights ago in her dressing room after we talked. You were in a rush to get down there, I remember. I saw the bruises."

"For her own good." He gave a pained expression. "I will do whatever is necessary to stop her."

"And then you tried to kill her again yesterday while she performed on stage. Trick died trying to save her."

He shook his head. "I'm not sure what you mean. I'm not trying to kill anyone, but someone has to stop her."

"What do you mean by *stop her*?"

"She must never perform on that stage again. He'll destroy her, just like he destroyed me... and Zack..."

"Who will destroy her?"

"Max, of course."

The mention of Max struck Emmie like an icy chill had stung her chest. "Destroyed you? You said *Trick* ruined everything. Trick killed you."

Danny shook his head, his eyes showing a bit of confusion. He spoke softer, yet tinged with bitterness, glancing down at his scorched outfit. "Trick and I were... We planned to do an illusion together as a team. Gloria wanted something grand, something spectacular to revive Amber House Theater after what had happened with Max and Zack. We'd planned the act for weeks, and it was going to be something huge, something no one had ever seen before—with his showmanship and my precision—we were going to give Gloria everything she dreamed of, to shake off the rumors and superstitions surrounding the theater, to lift the theater back to greatness. We intended to demonstrate the finest magic in the world."

"What happened?"

His voice cracked, and he clenched his fists. "Trick bailed on me. Out of nowhere he backed out, leaving me to start from scratch. I had to redesign the entire performance alone in a matter of days. Sure, I made mistakes and rushed decisions.

Dangerous ones. He ruined what should have been a truly spectacular performance."

"Why did he back out?"

Danny's expression changed from anger to despair. "I suppose the superstition... I thought at that time that the superstition had gotten to him, that all the talk of ghosts had finally freaked him out, but that wasn't why. In fact, the reality got to him. Somehow, Max got to him. Max never left Amber House. He and his assistants are still here, and he twisted Trick's mind, stirring up his fears, making him believe the only way to save himself was by leaving." Danny's voice grew darker. "Max needed me to stand on that stage alone. He wanted me vulnerable."

"To kill the performers."

"Much more than that. He wants to destroy Amber House. Everything."

"Why?"

"He can't let go—" He looked sharply toward the door, his face filled with fear as his eyes widened. "Nova is heading down to the stage. I've got to stop her. Max wants something bigger, something darker."

"From Nova?"

Danny nodded, his expression haunted. "She's his new star. He's feeding her ambition, making her think she's unstoppable, making her trust him. I have to stop her from completing his... nightmare. The only way is to disrupt her performance before it's too late, but he's gotten into her mind. The lure of Amber House stage becomes like a sickness once it takes hold, and I can only do so much."

"Danny..." Emmie started, trying to keep him in the room a little longer. "What is Max planning to do to Nova?"

His voice became sharper and more frantic. "God help us if he succeeds. Max is going to finish what he started if I don't get down there. She doesn't understand the depths of his manipulation, what he's planning, what she's gotten herself into."

"How do we stop him?" Emmie asked.

Danny glanced around the room and whispered, fear growing on his twisted face. "He knows we're talking. I have to get down there and stop her from rehearsing. I have to break her from the dream before it's too late."

Before Emmie could press him further, the air around them shifted. A sudden wave of cold air rushed out of the room, and the bulbs in the overhead lights shattered with a sharp pop, plunging the room into darkness until her eyes adjusted to a crack of light peeking through the window curtain.

Danny was gone. The air in the room had dropped several degrees within seconds. Emmie's heart beat faster as his warning ran through her head. She had enough pieces of the puzzle now to form a picture, but the missing pieces terrified her. She had to get down to the theater and do everything she could to stop Nova, even if she didn't fully understand everything he'd said.

25

The hair on the back of Jason's neck bristled after stepping inside the theater. He wasn't scared, but he couldn't shake the feeling that someone was watching him. He held a defensive stance while moving forward, keeping an eye out for anything out of the ordinary. After his confrontation the previous night with the two assistants, anything was possible. Murderers were roaming the darkness somewhere in that space, and only the distant noises of construction workers echoing in from down the hall broke the silence. There was no sign of spirits, although he couldn't shake the nagging sense that someone was ready to pounce as soon as he let his guard down.

He found Marty working quietly at the edge of the stage, repairing a wooden strip from part of a broken set piece. His back was turned as Jason approached, and after stopping at his side, Marty didn't even look up, his focus seemingly glued to the task in front of him.

A knot grew in Jason's throat. How was he supposed to approach the subject of the tragedies in the theater without ripping open old wounds?

"Marty," Jason said carefully, "I was wondering if you had a minute."

Marty's hammer paused mid-swing. His face tensed, but he didn't respond. His gaze remained fixed on the wood as if hoping Jason would walk away and leave him alone. "I thought you'd stop by again."

Jason continued, "I'd like to know more about Max and, more importantly, his assistants. What was their relationship with him? You said one of them was your girlfriend, right? Jessica?"

At the mention of Jessica, Marty's body stiffened. His face twitched, and Jason could feel an emotional wall slamming down between them. Their last conversation had been full of emotion with talk of the tragedy that had claimed his girlfriend's life, but Jason needed to push it a little further if they were going to get the answers they needed.

"Was Max married?" Jason asked.

"No." Marty spoke firmly. "And I'm sure you can get all that information off the Internet."

"But I heard something strange," Jason said, trying to sound casual. "That Jessica wore a ring on her pinky finger. Is that right?"

Marty's face went pale. His hands seemed to stop working, and the hammer slipped from his fingers and clattered onto the stage floor. He turned to Jason, his eyes wide with shock and pain. "You've seen her, haven't you? My Jessica..." The old man's voice was a whisper, as though saying her name out loud caused him physical pain. "She wore that ring on her pinky because I messed up her ring size. We'd just gotten engaged the day before... before the accident."

Jason swallowed hard. The last thing he wanted to do was drag Marty's grief back to the surface, but there was no way around it. "I didn't know it was her at first," Jason admitted, his voice shaking. "But it's like she was out to... Marty... The spirits are still here, and they're aggressive. Dangerous."

"My Jessica wasn't... *dangerous*." His expression hardened as his eyes narrowed. He looked like he was teetering on the edge of storming away while still clinging to the hope that Jason's words were true. His eyes held a glint as if he was holding something back.

"I've seen... things," Marty confessed quietly. "For years, and I've heard things I can't explain, but lately... it's been worse, especially since Nova started rehearsing. Now that Trick died, I'm afraid it might get worse."

Jason's heart beat faster as the image of the two assistants wrapping the rope around his neck flashed through his mind. "I need to see the furnace room where the gas leak happened."

Marty hesitated but eventually nodded. "I can take you there."

He led Jason through the dark corridor in silence until they reached the cramped, suffocating room just a short distance from the lounge door that Marty had vowed never to enter again. Moving inside, the air was stale as Jason scanned the room. The massive HVAC units took up most of the room, stretching back several yards into the darkness. Now they were silent and covered in dust.

"It happened in December," Marty said. "Right before Christmas, which is the only time of year we fire up the furnaces. We don't use these anymore." He gestured to one of the units. "Too old. Too many problems. Wayne installed a new system on the roof. A lot safer."

"Which one malfunctioned?"

Marty seemed to understand what Jason was referring to—the one that had leaked the fatal gas into the lounge. He gestured to the one on the left. "That one."

Jason stepped toward it and inspected an open panel on the side of one unit as if he knew how the thing operated. The ductwork ran across the ceiling and passed through an opening into the lounge next door. "Who had access to this room back then?"

"The police asked all those questions. I had access, along with every other theater employee. We never kept it locked back then."

"Did you see anyone come back here before the leak?"

"More of the same questions the police already asked me. No. Nobody saw anybody come back here before it happened, but—" Marty's eyes darted around nervously, and he whispered in a raspy tone with his shoulders slumped forward, almost as if confessing to a sin, "There's something I never told anyone. Not even the police."

Jason turned at him sharply. "What's that?"

Marty's voice was tight, almost trembling as he started to speak. "After the accident... I noticed the door was open, so I came in to look around. I found something, something I didn't tell the cops about." He glanced toward the open door as if afraid someone outside might hear him. "I didn't mean to hide anything, but I couldn't leave it there."

Jason leaned toward the old man. "What did you find?"

Marty stepped to the unit, pulled out a small flashlight from his pocket, and switched it on. Aiming it through the open panel, the light revealed an intricate web of pipes and valves. He pointed to the bottom ledge of the opening. "I found a wrench, the kind someone might use to adjust the pipes. It wasn't full of dust, like everything else back there, and the exact one useful for tightening or loosening the fittings."

"A wrench?"

"*My* wrench." Marty nodded, his eyes wide with something like fear. "It was sitting just below the gas valve that the police concluded had failed, opened just wide enough to loosen it. Whoever put it in there knew what they were doing, maybe to set me up to take the blame. It wasn't an accident."

Jason's heart beat even faster. "Why didn't you tell the police about it?"

Marty's face was pale now, his voice shaking. "I panicked. If they found that, with my fingerprints all over it, after everything that happened, it would have looked like I did it."

The startling confession caught Jason off guard, but he could understand why Marty had hidden it. All eyes would have shifted to him, and already devastated by the horrific loss of his girlfriend, Marty would have been an easy scapegoat. Someone had turned the wrench into a murder weapon.

Jason chose his words carefully. "Do you think Max somehow sabotaged the gas line? Maybe intending it for someone else?"

Marty shook his head, his gaze distant. "Doubt it. Max was a reckless asshole, but not smart enough to pull something like this off. This was planned."

The weight of Marty's words hung in the air between them. What now? The realization that Marty had been living with the secret all these years, fearing that he might be blamed for murdering three performers, including his girlfriend, sent a chill down Jason's spine.

"What are you going to do?" Marty asked, turning his face away.

Jason understood what the old man was really asking: Are you going to turn me in to the police? "We're going to find the person who did this before Nova gets back up on that stage."

26

Finn took a seat at the kitchen table in Gloria's penthouse and opened his laptop while he waited for Sarah to get back. She'd gone with Nova into the old woman's bedroom, and he could hear Sarah's soft voice, trying to keep things light in a room weighed down by so many harsh realities.

Across from him, Wayne stood at the kitchen counter facing away, pouring himself a glass of bourbon with trembling hands. He glanced around as if wondering if anyone was watching him. It must have been a great weight on his shoulders to handle everything—the casino, the ghosts, Trick's death, and now his mother's rapid decline—and it seemed like he might be on the edge of collapse. At least he had Nova to keep him going through it all, although their world seemed headed to fall apart at any moment.

Absentmindedly drumming his fingers on the edge of his laptop, Finn tried to think of something he might say to break the ice. He asked quietly, with an air of humor, "Do you have an extra glass?"

Wayne glanced over and gave a subtle grin before pouring another glass and sitting down across from Finn, sliding it beside

Finn's laptop. Wayne's eyes were bloodshot but sharp. "You're not planning on posting any of this online, are you?"

"No, sir."

"Keep it that way."

"No problem." Finn sipped his drink. "You know, it's an amazing accomplishment, everything your mother built here. Buying a hotel, casino, and theater back in the 80s as a young woman. What was she... thirty?"

"Thirty-eight."

"It's remarkable, really."

Wayne managed a small smile, though it didn't reach his eyes. "Yeah, she's something else."

"Ambitious," Finn said. "Did your father share your mother's dream?"

He shook his head and glanced at his drink. "I never knew my father. She did all of this—worked her way through college, climbed the corporate real estate ladder, bought the casino, and took care of everything, including me, on her own."

"She didn't get help from her family?" Finn said. "That's a lot to take on for one woman."

"It *is* a lot." He shook his head. "No help from anyone. She cut ties with her family before I was born. Bad blood."

"Cut ties?" Finn raised an eyebrow. He hadn't found any of that in his research. "Why is that?"

Wayne shrugged, pulling his glass a little closer but not drinking it. "She said they didn't get along. Old-school type. They didn't understand why she wanted to invest in real estate so soon out of college, especially in Vegas. Back then, it was too... risky, I guess. She stopped talking to her family after she left college and never looked back."

"So she raised you all alone, on top of everything else?"

"All alone. I never knew my father, and that's just fine with me. Mom said he was a real piece of shit, anyway. Life in prison, she said."

Finn nodded, trying to mask his curiosity. "What made her want to tackle Vegas alone?"

Wayne's expression softened. "Her dream was to sing on stage one day. She has the voice of an angel, although we'll never get the chance to hear it again in any meaningful way. The disease stole that from her."

"She must have loved the theater," Finn said.

"Loved it all. Musicals—Broadway, especially—and the dream of standing in front of an audience always fascinated her. That's why she bought the place. She didn't buy the casino to get rich, she bought the casino because of the *theater*. Amber House Theater wasn't just a playground for magicians, it was for *her*. Everything else was just a gateway to her stardom, she figured."

"That's one way to climb the ladder," Finn said. "Cut out the middleman."

"Even with that, it wasn't easy for her. She started small right out of college, just managing a few properties around the city, but by the time the Vegas boom hit in the '80s, she was already ahead of the curve. She knew how to play the game by then, especially when it came to casinos." He lifted his chin then sipped his drink again.

"And you've done a hell of a job keeping it all going," Finn said, not out of flattery but because it was true. "Especially with all the... complications lately."

Wayne gave a dark laugh, shaking his head. "You mean all the rumors? The ghosts? Trick's death?" He set down his glass and rubbed his face with both hands, clearly overwhelmed. "But if you want to know the truth—" He leaned in toward Finn and lowered his voice. "Finn, despite what just happened and everything Nova told you, you guys are *completely* wasting your time. There are no ghosts in this place. None. People are just superstitious and that's the problem. Rumors spread like wildfire, and now, after what happened to Trick..." His voice trailed off.

Finn leaned in, trying to keep the conversation going. "But

Nova—she's keeping things together for you, right? I mean, from what Em says, she's incredible."

Wayne nodded. "Nova's the only one holding this place together at this point, but I'm not blind. This theater is bad luck —cursed, but no ghosts—and the news of Trick's death will drag this place into the ground. The worst part, my mother might not even live long enough to see Nova's performance. That's the hell of it. I don't care if the theater fails anymore. I just need Mom to hang in there a little longer. You know, she used to go down to the theater's entrance all the time and sing through the open doorway, although she never stepped inside again after what happened to Max and the assistants."

Wayne's heartfelt words hung in the air between them as Finn tried to gauge how to respond. Wayne's face showed strain now, and there was exhaustion in his voice. He seemed to be holding himself together with every ounce of energy he had left.

"It wasn't just about building another casino in Vegas," Wayne continued, "it was about creating an experience, something different... Magical, literally. She wanted it to be like nothing else that came before. Legendary. I guess in a way, it is now, just the legend."

Finn leaned in slightly, trying to keep the casual tone but trying to pull in Wayne as much as he could away from the heaviness without pushing him too hard. "What happened back then? I read the story on the Internet, but is that what really shut it down?"

Wayne met his gaze as if trying to decide whether or not to tell them everything. "I don't have much to add. I mean, I was born a few weeks after the theater finally shut down, so it's not like I was there for any of it. Mom shared a few things over the years, bits and pieces. She always said it wasn't the business itself that failed—it was the people."

"The people?"

"The magicians, mostly." Wayne spoke with a bit of growing

frustration. "Max, Trick, and the others. They were supposed to draw in the crowds for Amber House, but there was always so much drama. Fights, jealousy, all of them had big egos, strong personalities. Nothing ever went smoothly for long, from what I was told. Max was the worst of them. He was a party animal, always pushing things too far, going overboard with the women. He never took anything seriously."

"What were his assistants like?" Finn asked.

Wayne shrugged. "They had their own issues. Drugs and alcohol, mixed with Max leading the charge over the cliff—and I think they all took advantage of my mom's generosity. Max was the biggest offender, if you take Marty's word for it, although every one of them had big issues, from what he said. Mom told me once that everything became a competition as soon as any of the magicians stepped onto that stage. Trick was a little younger, a little more competent, and very ambitious... Probably saw Max, Danny, and Zack as inferiors standing in his way. But it wasn't just about skill back then. Sure, Trick wanted more than just to perform—and he *was* a great magician—he always wanted to own the spotlight. That guy had a chip on his shoulder he carried with him to the day he died."

"Why do you think your mom chose Max to be the face of Amber House? I mean, if he was such a wildcard?"

Wayne hesitated, taking another sip of his drink before answering. "Because he *was* a wild card. Max had *charisma*—is the way she described it—he could charm his way out of anything, get away with things that most people couldn't. She said he used to stroll around with a smoldering cigar in one hand and a glass of bourbon in the other like he belonged in the Rat Pack. And yeah, he was handsome. That didn't hurt. Trick never stopped bad-mouthing Max over the years, so you can see how deep the jealousy cut into him. Trick insisted Max wasn't the best magician in Vegas, not by a long shot, and maybe that's why an elitist like Trick couldn't stand him."

"So why Max, then? If he wasn't that great, what convinced

your mom to pick him over a more qualified magician? Was it only about his looks and charisma, or did she see something else in him?"

Wayne seemed to think about it for a moment. "I think she liked his style more than anything, that flashy, unpredictable flare that attracted an audience back then. Trick just didn't have that. Max was a spectacle. A big risk, but a big reward, if it paid off. But yeah, he had a lot of enemies—so maybe that's why things spiraled out of control so quickly after he was gone. She gambled big with him and lost that bet."

Finn nodded, trying to process everything that Wayne was telling him. "Did your mom mention anyone besides Trick who might have wanted him... gone?"

Wayne's expression changed. Finn had broken their conversation and now the man had switched back to formal mode. Wayne glanced toward Finn's laptop screen. "You aren't recording this, are you?"

"No," Finn said, turning the screen a little toward Wayne. "Not recording anything."

"Max died in a gas leak, as I'm sure you've heard." Wayne spoke a little louder. "I wasn't suggesting anyone murdered him."

"I—"

Before Finn could smooth out the moment of tension between them, the nurse came rushing out of Gloria's bedroom, breathless and wide-eyed.

"Wayne!" she cried, her voice full of urgency. "She spoke! Grandma Ria... She finally spoke!"

Wayne bolted up from his chair, his face full of disbelief and a bit of fear. He shot Finn a quick, haunted look before rushing toward the bedroom.

Finn hurried after him. Coming into the bedroom, they were all gathered around the old woman's bed. Nova stood on one side as Sarah sat on the other side with the old woman leaning in against her shoulder. Gloria's mouth hung open as the nurse jumped to Sarah's side.

"What did she say?" Wayne asked desperately.

Before anyone could answer, Gloria sang in a weak, raspy voice.

> I held the stars, but let them fade,
> The lights so bright... now fall to shade.

27

As soon as Sarah walked into Gloria's bedroom, the familiar smell of antiseptic and body odor caught her attention. She wasn't just visiting someone's grandmother for a friendly chat—she was meeting a patient in hospice care. The old woman was lying beneath a neatly folded blanket on a giant bed that contrasted with her tiny frame, with her unwavering gaze turned up toward the ceiling.

Nova stepped over to her grandmother's bedside and kissed the old woman on the forehead. The nurse was busy switching out an IV bag from its stand beside the bed, resetting the device with a series of beeps, then checking on the line that led into the old woman's wrist. Routine care for a patient who only needed to be kept comfortable.

Nova spoke softly to her grandmother and gestured to Sarah. "Hi, Grandma Ria. This is my friend, Sarah. She's also a nurse."

The old woman gave no indication she'd heard Nova's voice, except for the constant trembling of her small frame. The nurse attending her glanced over at Sarah, giving a little smile and a nod before going back to her duties.

"Hello, Mrs. Harrison," Sarah said to the old woman and the nurse. "Nice to meet you."

Again, no response from her.

Nova looked down on her grandmother with her arms crossed over her chest and her lips pressed into a thin line. It was clear that she was doing everything she could to hold herself together. She brushed away a few stray hairs from her grandmother's forehead with careful tenderness, as though the slightest touch might shatter her. "Are you comfortable, Grandma? Everything okay?"

The old woman's eyes fluttered open. No doubt, the disease had stolen so much from her already. Her dull gaze shifted down from the ceiling, over to Nova's face, then finally stopping on Sarah's face for a long moment.

"Sarah wanted to meet you, Grandma," Nova said. "She's here to check on your progress."

"I've heard a lot about you," Sarah said politely. "You should be proud of everything you've accomplished here."

The old woman's body ceaselessly trembled beneath the sheets, but she remained silent.

Sarah turned to the nurse. "What's the outlook?"

The nurse gave a detailed response, speaking in terms only a nurse would understand, and Sarah tried to hold back her disappointment. The outlook wasn't good. Gloria was nearing the end of her life. "Has she eaten anything lately?"

The nurse slowly shook her head. "The doctor suggested that we do our best to make her comfortable."

Another bad sign. A clear sign that the doctor had all but given up hope.

The nurse moved methodically around the room, checking on some medications and typing notes into a laptop. Her motions were precise and efficient, but devoid of any emotion as though she'd seen too many patients slip away to allow herself to feel anything anymore. The aura radiating from her face and hands showed a mix of bright greens but also plenty of gray. Most nurses had that same mix of colors—strong greens, stemming from a nurturing nature, which had probably driven her to become a nurse in the first place—mixed with the dull grays of stress that had probably grown stronger after so many years of working with the dying. It was the same at the hospital where Sarah worked, a challenging cycle of joy and heartache she encountered every day.

The old woman gave a labored breath as the nurse monitored her breathing. Sarah stepped in beside the nurse to get a better view of the woman's sparkling eyes. Behind that debilitating disease, there was still a spark of whatever had driven her to build the casino in the first place.

Nova leaned in and glanced toward Sarah, her eyes momentarily brightening with a glimmer of trust. "What do you... see?"

Sarah met her gaze. Within Nova's desperation, a clear message came through. Please help her. No doubt Emmie had told Nova all about Sarah's psychic past, and maybe even that she had the gift of healing, although it came at a cost. "Your grandmother has a strong spirit."

After the nurse stepped away to review Gloria's charts, Sarah moved in and met the old woman's gaze as Nova stepped back and watched them with her arms still wrapped around herself as if bracing for a miracle.

"Let me have a look at you." Sarah spoke quietly while placing a hand on Gloria's arm. The woman flinched at Sarah's touch, but Sarah held on and quietly shifted her energy through the old woman's aura, surrounding her in a golden light only Sarah could see. The energy flowed back and forth, connecting them in a profoundly beautiful way, and she felt all the woman's hopes and fears—

The flow ended abruptly. A darkness had formed like a wall between them. The disease had taken away the woman's ability to walk and talk, but something else, deeply embedded and overpowering, weighed on the woman's mind. Sarah struggled again to find a connection with her, somewhere that she could move the energy within hers. The warmth flowed again, but the darkness returned a moment later, moving around the woman like a black cloak, suffocating her light as Sarah struggled to connect with her. Something oppressive, a heavy force like death itself had its grip on the woman, and it seemed to pull Sarah in deeper.

Sarah held on, straining to get beyond the disease. Every patient she had ever encountered held some level of dark energy, usually manifesting as a thick mass embedded within their soul, but she'd never encountered anything like this. The strain to help the woman was almost unbearable, draining her energy with every second, yet she pushed forward—she couldn't stop now. She might not get another chance to get close to the old woman. Even worse, the disease had taken its toll, and it was clear from the resistance that the woman might not even make it through the night, much less live long enough to watch Nova's performance.

Gently maneuvering her energy around the woman in waves of light, she broke through the dark sickness that had encased the old woman's spirit like a tomb. Checking the woman's pulse and heartbeat beneath her hand, Sarah infused a bit of her own energy, like striking a match in the darkness. Gloria's eyes widened for a moment and her breathing eased, her frail chest rising a bit more steadily. With whatever gift of healing she had developed up to that point, Sarah filled the woman with as much light as possible. The dark energy remained, but maybe it was enough.

Light flowed from Sarah in waves that left her lightheaded, with her hands trembling after she withdrew. Opening her eyes, Sarah released the old woman's hand and lifted her head, startled that she had collapsed against the old woman's shoulder.

"Sarah?" Nova's voice came from somewhere far away, tinged with concern.

Sarah forced herself to look up at Nova and offered a weak smile. "She's... she's okay, for now."

Nova let out a deep sigh and moved in beside her grandmother, taking her hand. "Thank you," she whispered to Sarah. "I think that helped."

Gloria stared into Nova's eyes with a curious expression. The old woman's eyes were somehow sharper, wider.

"Does that feel better, Grandma Ria? Sarah's here to help you, too."

Sarah took a shaky step back. The room seemed to spin, until out of nowhere she heard someone's voice rise from the bed. A voice, so faint, she thought at first she was imagining it.

"Max..." Gloria whispered with trembling lips. The old woman turned her head slightly and stared into Sarah's eyes with an intensity that sent chills down her spine. "He won't let it go..."

Sarah froze, her heart racing as she glanced toward Nova, who seemed as oblivious as she was. The nurse had already jumped back and grabbed her phone. She now stood with her back turned and dialed a number.

Gloria's eyes hardened as a sudden, shocked expression crossed her face. Her eyes seemed to dig into Sarah, as though accusing her of something unforgivable. "What did you just do to me?" A mix of clarity, pain, and fear in her eyes.

Sarah recoiled inwardly, shaken by the old woman's silent outrage.

A moment later, the nurse turned back toward them and met Nova's gaze for a moment before rushing out of the bedroom, her voice breathless with excitement. "Wayne! Grandma Ria... She's spoken!"

Nova stood wide-eyed with a surge of hope spreading across her face. She turned to Sarah with a grateful smile. "It's a miracle!"

Sarah could only stare back, the cryptic words still echoing in her mind as Gloria's piercing gaze lingered on her.

28

Emmie's footsteps echoed off the walls of the stage, leaving Jason and Marty to talk alone while she focused her mind's eye on at least one spirit hovering somewhere ahead at the edge of her awareness. There was Danny nearby, watching them all from a distance with his expression full of nervous tension, but someone else was there, a lingering presence that seemed to pull at her with the same dark energy she'd felt so many times before. Someone was urging her to move deeper into the heart of the theater.

Trick's spirit was still there on the stage, struggling within the web of ropes that had ended his life the day before. His ghostly form flared and faded as his emotions shifted from anguish to rage while straining to escape his trauma. His hands clawed at the ropes around his neck and body, his expression distant. He couldn't see her, so lost in the moments of his death.

Glancing back, Jason was actively engaging Marty in conversation, and she was free to explore the area on her own, but she moved closer to Trick and tried to catch his attention. She wanted to reach out to him, to pull away the ropes and break him from the trauma, but it rarely worked out that easily.

"Trick," she whispered to him.

No reaction.

He can't hear me. He's too far gone.

Still, she tried again. "Trick. Who did this to you?"

Moving to within inches of him, the magician gave no indication that he recognized her, yet she focused her mind and pulled at his spirit, hoping to break him out of his cycle of trauma even for a moment. A dark cloud enveloped him, trapping the dim energy of his spirit like a cocoon. She still needed him—needed to get this piece of the twisted puzzle from him—but his attention was too far consumed by himself, trapped in his own personal hell.

Even if she could talk to him, he probably hadn't seen his attacker. The frustration weighed heavy in her stomach. She had come so far to solve the mystery, yet it seemed that everything might slip away from her before Nova's performance.

Emmie scanned the area. There were other spirits nearby—more opportunities to get the answers she needed, but they seemed even more distant than the hopeless connection between her and Trick. Four magicians had died in that place, according to everything she had discovered so far, and she had come face to face with three of them. So where was the other one? Why hadn't she encountered him yet?

Digging through the darkness of her mind, the last magician couldn't have gone far if he had died in such a tragic way.

More than one presence hovered not far from where she stood, although they seemed to evade her. Moving toward the farthest corner of the stage, she let the spirits' energy guide her beyond the props, crates, and equipment cluttering the area. Lit only by a few small lights high above, she felt her way through the shadows toward a doorway ahead, her throat tightening with a sense that someone was watching her—waiting for her.

Straining to see more than a few feet into the darkness, a sense of failure washed through her chest. She had hoped to solve this mystery before her friends had arrived, if only to prove to them and to herself that each of them could function independently, but that theory was falling apart and now she couldn't imagine facing all of this without them.

A presence shifted in her mind up ahead as she weaved through the back stage toward the far corner. It was evading her, even as she moved faster toward it. It was a faint presence, its energy twisted and cowering among the shadows as if it were trying to hide, but at least it was reacting to her.

Turning down a hallway lit only by an exit sign, she spotted a man's spirit.

Found you.

He was hunched over and trembling with a bloodied shirt, torn wide open as if something had nearly sliced him in half. His spirit wavered, half collapsed in a heap, like he was trying to make himself small, invisible. She approached him cautiously, sensing his fear. His spirit was nothing like Trick. Something had traumatized this man in a horrifying way, yes, but he wasn't just frightened, he was terrified.

"Hey," she said in a soft voice while reaching out her hand as if approaching a wounded animal. "It's okay. I'm here to help you. Please tell me what happened to you."

It had to be Zack, judging by the bloody wounds slicing deeply through the magician's chest. Blood flowed out in endless cascading waves over his pants and pooled on the floor before disappearing. His eyes flickered wildly toward her, recoiling in silence with a bit of panic. Shaking his head, the man glanced to the side with a bit of madness as if he expected someone or some *thing* to strike him at any moment.

"Who are you hiding from?" she asked.

He whimpered and sank even further, as though the question itself was a threat.

Emmie inched forward with her palm out further, hoping that he might also reach out to her. "Who is after you?"

His jaw and lips quivered as an icy chill swept through the room. Someone else had arrived nearby, and their dark energy seemed to eclipse any light between Emmie and this magician.

The magician's eyes widened as he pointed and shook his hand violently over Emmie's shoulder, toward the far side of the stage.

Emmie's heart raced faster as she turned slowly, dreading the presence that she recognized as the one who had taunted her from the shadows since the day she'd arrived.

Then she saw him. The same shadowy figure she'd seen above the stage after Trick had died. He stood in the open at the edge of the stage beside a row of magicians' props, watching them both with a malevolent grin—a twisted smile that didn't spread up to his eyes.

Max.

In the same moment that she met his gaze, the air around them seemed to warp. One moment, she was facing Max, and the next, she found herself standing at the center of the stage in front of a packed audience. Darkness shrouded the faces of those in attendance as the rows of glaring spotlights blinded her. A layer of fog floated in from every direction, spreading out and obscuring the stage as Max came around from behind her. He made wide gestures toward the audience, gripping her hand and raising it into the air as if to present her to them like someone who had volunteered to take part in one of his grand illusions.

She tried to pull away from him, but her body trembled within a strange paralysis. Finally releasing her hand, he stepped back as the floor beneath Emmie shifted suddenly, and she stumbled forward as a trapdoor opened inches in front of her feet, its edges sharp and gleaming. The sound of grinding gears came from somewhere beneath the layer of fog is it swept down into the opening as if the theater itself had come alive and planned to swallow her whole.

She shook her head. *No, this is just an illusion. None of this is real.*

The audience gasped. Their style of clothing was reminiscent of an '80s sitcom, and the air was filled with the smell of old wood and an icy fog. This was the theater as it must have existed in the 1980s, and somehow it was flawlessly displayed around her like a vivid dream. An urge came over her. Something in the dark behind her was compelling her to step forward, even as she teetered on the edge of falling forward, her instincts screaming in her mind to step back. A rising tension filled the air as she struggled to distinguish reality from whatever Max was doing to her mind.

Get out of there, Em. Her heart pounded in her chest as she struggled to wake herself up.

Max moved in beside her and whispered in a low, velvety voice. "What are you afraid of?"

His words clouded her mind. *What was happening?* This was the man she had come to face alone, but now a wave of doubt crashed over her. She might have already gone too far. Her team had arrived, but maybe it was too late.

"Why are you doing this?" she asked.

The audience seemed to pick up on her words, giving a little laugh as if she had made a joke.

"They came here to see me perform an illusion." He made a wide, grand gesture. "Let's give them a night to remember."

The grinding gears beneath the stage echoed up through the opening, drowning out her shaky breaths. It seemed that the best she could do was resist him at that moment, until his two assistants came up beside her, positioning themselves, one on each side, each gently, elegantly taking a hand and nudging her forward.

The assistants held an air of professionalism, although their expressions were distant and hollow as they bared wide grins. Their vacant eyes were full of pain and pleading, filled with something much darker than hatred. Still, there was a quiet desperation in their movements, as if they were bound to perform this terrible task, compelled by the same darkness that now controlled Emmie. Their grip wasn't violent, but it was relentless—a quiet, eerie determination guiding their actions. A faint trace of perfume came from the shorter woman on the left, mixed with the musty odor of an unwashed costume and sweat. The other woman's outfit, a glittering sequined dress, was dull and faded beneath the stage lights. She wore a ring on her pinky finger that almost slid off as she dragged Emmie forward.

Max loomed in front of them, the sharp lines of his face barely visible through the shadowy haze surrounding him. His expression was tight with anger, but the hunger for revenge was clear just beneath the surface as he seemed determined to see his grand illusion play out to its grisly conclusion. His stony gaze locked onto her for a long moment and there was a twisted satisfaction in the way he watched her struggle, the pleasure he found in pulling her toward the edge.

"Don't fight it," Max said in a calm, desperate voice as the assistant's fingers tightened around her hands. "The audience is waiting!"

Emmie let out a few ragged gasps as she fought to break away. The floor creaked beneath her as something metallic, like rust or blood, filled her senses.

She shook her head as the trapdoor seemed to widen further, along with the horrifying realization of what was about to happen. Her feet slid forward as she tried to piece together why —Why were they doing this? Why *her*? Why now? Had the same things happened to Nova?

"Why?" Emmie cried out.

Max's eyes seemed to gleam with a dark satisfaction. "Because the show must go on."

The show must go on. What show? Panic rose in her throat as she struggled to breathe within the terror.

Inching forward, she closed her eyes for a moment and caught a glimpse of their dark energy in her mind. Her instincts took over and with a surge of adrenaline, she forced their spirits closer, moving them toward the trapdoor at her feet. At the same time, the assistants lost their grip and her mind sharpened on them as she refused to be literally dragged into their illusion. She could still feel Max's gaze on her, but with a final burst of strength, she hurled herself backwards with her eyes still closed and crashed to the ground with a sickening thud.

Pain jolted through her body a moment later, surging up her spine and throbbing against the back of her head, and she let out a guttural cry that echoed throughout the theater.

Opening her eyes, the sounds of the empty theater returned. Max and his assistants were gone, leaving Emmie writhing on the floor alone in the cold, dark space.

"Emmie!" Jason called out from somewhere behind her, along with his approaching footsteps.

"I'm here." She tried to stand before he arrived, but toppled backward as she still struggled to get a grip on reality. They had tried to kill her, but for what purpose? And, most importantly, how close had she come to being lost in that illusion forever?

29

Emmie hurried through the hotel lobby with Jason at her side, her mind swirling with confusion and dread. What had she just experienced in the theater? The weight of everything seemed to press down on her, making it hard to breathe.

A security officer watched them with a curious stare as they passed. Had he watched the whole incident from a hidden camera? Forcing herself to stand tall and keep moving forward, she swallowed her emotions and kept a straight face.

Jason, for once, was unusually quiet. They hadn't spoken more than a few words since leaving the theater, and the silence between them seemed to build with every step. Emmie couldn't help but keep replaying Max's last words in her mind, feeling the magician's hate behind his voice. There was so much depth to his rage, something she hadn't expected. His grin was still etched in her mind—the way it had twisted into something so wrong, so cold, before he'd disappeared. And worse, the other magician had cowered in the corner, too terrified to speak. It seemed they were no closer to a resolution.

After the elevator doors had shut, Emmie let out a slow breath as the tension around her chest seemed to ease a little. Jason watched her as though waiting for her to speak first. They shared a knowing glance into each other's eyes on their way up to the room, but she held back. She didn't want to say anything until they were safely behind the privacy of their closed hotel room door.

Sarah and Finn were already in their adjoining room when they arrived, and the door between the two rooms sat wide open. Finn was immersed in something on his laptop, but broke away when they arrived, and the four of them gathered near the center of the room.

Sarah rushed to Emmie's side. "What happened?" Her intense concern helped to soothe Emmie's unease as she sat beside her and leaned in.

Emmie waited until Finn and Jason had settled in beside them before speaking. She was relieved that they were all together again, that she had their support, but she still felt no closer to keeping the promise she'd made to Nova in the first place—to rid the theater of ghosts.

"They knocked me down. Literally." Emmie told them everything—about the cowering magician, hiding from something far worse than death, and then about her encounter with Max—the way his spirit had twisted with anger in the most inhumane way. "He doesn't just want Nova gone, there's plenty of hate to go around—she's right that he wants her dead. I could feel the hate, and he wanted to harm me like he did everyone else he encountered in that theater."

Finn's expression showed that he had shifted into his analytical mind, trying to fit this new piece into the rest of the puzzle. "Why the chip on his shoulder?"

"I asked him. He said *the show must go on.*"

Finn tilted his head slightly. "He wants to give a final performance?"

"Max died after completing his show for that evening, so I'm not sure what show he's talking about."

"Then he's refusing to share the stage?" Sarah suggested.

"It seems that way after attacking everyone who dares to step up there," Jason said. "And now he's turning his attention to us."

Emmie nodded. "It's not just Nova he wants now, and I don't think we've seen the worst of it yet."

"We might have a chance to get some answers," Sarah spoke just above a whisper. "Gloria spoke today."

The room fell silent as each of them gazed toward her, and Emmie's heart skipped a beat. "She spoke?"

Sarah nodded, exchanging a glance with Finn before continuing. "Not much, but I think if we can get some time alone with her..."

"What did she say?" Emmie asked.

"Something about Max not letting go. Then she sang a few words. Maybe you can talk Nova into letting us visit her again? If only we could talk with her alone for a few minutes. After Wayne and Finn came in, I couldn't follow up on what she said."

"How was she able to speak and... sing?" Emmie asked. "I thought she had Parkinson's?"

"I helped her... just a little," Sarah said. "Not much, but it took more out of me than I expected. It won't stop her decline—nothing can prevent that—but it might keep the door open long enough to finally get some answers."

Jason turned to Emmie. "Do you think Nova would let us talk with her again, under the circumstances?"

"I'm not sure," Emmie said. "I can certainly try."

"If we do," Finn said, "I have a few questions I'd like to ask her."

"Like what?"

"Like who is Darlene Harken? And what happened to her? Gloria has some connections with the woman, but they don't add up. It's like Darlene just disappeared in 1981—a true magic act—right around the time Wayne said that Gloria cut off her family and moved to Las Vegas. Yet, no police reports of foul play, and I can't find anything else about Gloria prior to that."

"Nobody reported Darlene missing?" Sarah asked.

"It seems that way," Finn said.

"Nobody *noticed* her missing," Emmie said. "What was Gloria's connection to her?"

"I'm not sure," he said. "Roommate? Friend? Both names appear on some rental documents I found online while I was researching Gloria's past, but then... No more Darlene."

"If we do get the chance to talk with Gloria again," Sarah said, "we should choose our words carefully. It won't help to upset her. Nova and Wayne were *so* elated to get her back, even if it only lasts for a little while. Everything will take time."

Finn sighed. "Which we don't have."

"I'll speak with Nova as soon as I can about Gloria's condition." Emmie tried to piece together the new information.

"Sarah's right," Finn said. "It won't help to toss a barrage of questions at the old woman moments after she recovers."

"And something else bothers me about Max," Emmie said.

"What's that?" Jason asked.

"He was so full of hate, but the shadows I saw earlier in the theater when we first arrived, they were different."

"Different like *how?*"

"Like there might be more than one spirit trying to kill Nova."

30

Nova agreed to let Emmie and Sarah inside Gloria's penthouse a few hours later, but Wayne balked at allowing them all inside, insisting his mother's recovery was turning into a spectacle, so Finn and Jason stayed behind in their hotel room to do more research on Gloria's past.

It seemed they might finally get answers when Nova met them near the elevator with a wide smile. "Grandma's doing *amazing*."

"Did she say anything else?" Sarah asked.

"Not... a lot."

Nova took them up to the penthouse. When the elevator doors opened, the light flooded in around them. The massive windows in the penthouse cast a late afternoon glow over the room, creating long shadows that stretched across the carpet like fingers.

Stepping quietly inside, they followed Nova to the bedroom where she sat at the edge of Grandma Ria's bed. The old woman's frail fingers brushed against the plush bedding. Her eyes were half-open now with an expression of resolve as she struggled to pull herself up on her own.

The nurse sat positioned like a silent guard at her side. She leaned forward with her hands outstretched to steady the old woman, but Gloria dismissed her with a sharp shake of her head while mumbling a string of garbled sounds.

Nova spoke up, "She can do it. I'm here to help. If she wants to sit up, let her sit up. If she wants to get out of bed, let her do it. She can do anything she wants."

The nurse mumbled a few words, then turned away and left the room.

The old woman's gaze jumped to Emmie's face. Her eyes narrowed and her brow furrowed before she looked at Sarah, then turned back to Nova, as though her granddaughter's attention alone could bring her some peace.

"Do you want to get up, Grandma Ria?" Nova asked, her voice filled with quiet encouragement. Gloria's fingers grasped Nova's forearm, but it was clear the woman had no strength to complete her wish.

"Take it slow," Emmie waited by the doorway, feeling like an intruder in the tender moment but also sensing the weight of urgency settle heavy in her chest, sensing the weight of urgency to deal with the bigger issues at hand. Emmie cleared her throat. "Nova... could we talk for a moment?"

Nova glanced back at them, showing a flash of frustration before it formed into a patient smile. "Sure. Just... give me a second."

She helped her grandmother settle back into the pillows, tucking the blankets around her small frame carefully. The old woman's gaze stopped on Emmie again as if demanding to know why she was still in the room.

Nova stepped over and paused in front of them. "What is it?"

Sarah spoke up, "May I have a moment to check on your grandmother?"

Nova's eyebrows went up. Then she stared back at her grandmother for a long moment before finally answering Sarah with an air of uncertainty. "Maybe later? She's exhausted."

Emmie gestured toward the living room. "Can we talk alone?"

"What's this about?" Nova didn't move.

"It's about the theater..." Emmie spoke gently, but her pulse raced as the memories of the spirits waiting for them danced at the edge of her thoughts.

Nova nodded once, and the three of them left the nurse and Gloria alone again, closing the door behind them on the way out. "What about the theater?"

"I don't think it's safe," Emmie said.

Nova let out a little laugh while heading toward the elevator. "Let's take a walk. I need a coffee. We'll come back later."

She punched the elevator button and the doors opened immediately. After stepping inside together and the doors had closed, Nova pressed the lobby button, then continued as the elevator descended, "Of course it's not safe. That's why you're here, right? How's that going?"

"What I meant to say is, I think you should postpone the performance until after we get this under control. The danger—"

Nova's laughter cut her off. Her friend had a bright, almost manic sound that didn't match the tension in the room. "Listen, Emmie, I know you're worried. I'm worried too, but you have to understand that I can't back out now. This is my family's future. This is *my* future, so it's impossible to stop the train now. You don't know what this place means to me, and I might never get the chance to perform for Grandma ever again. This is it."

Emmie's stomach twisted. There was something wild in Nova's eyes that hadn't been there before—an intense spark and a stubborn stare as if she were looking past Emmie into something that only she could see. Emmie swallowed, glancing at Sarah. "Just a little while ago," Emmie said, "I encountered all four of the magicians on the stage, Trick, Zack, Danny, and Max. Max almost killed me."

Nova looked at her for a long moment, then broke into a confident smile. "Well, you must be used to it by now, with everything you've told me about your life. I'm sure you've seen your share of ghosts."

"I'm not worried about me," Emmie said. "It's you I'm worried about."

Nova glanced down and stayed quiet.

Sarah broke the silence, her expression showing a bit of desperation. "We need to talk with your grandmother about what happened here when the theater shut down in the '80s. Time's running out and she's our best hope for getting answers."

Nova shook her head but met their gaze. "That's not a good idea. She only spoke her first words in a long time *hours ago*."

"I know, and that's why it's so important that we talk with her now," Emmie said. "Before it's too late."

Nova looked away. "Leave Grandma out of this. Do you know how much shit she endured back then? She still hasn't recovered from it."

"Yes," Emmie said, "and we're trying to prevent it from happening again, but more people will die if we don't sort this out. Something else happened here around the time the theater shut down—something the police missed or the spirits would have left long ago. You can be there when we talk to her. Just for a few minutes."

Nova showed a pained expression. "I hardly think it's a good idea to force Grandma to relive that trauma at this stage of her life. Can't you please just deal with the ghosts without bothering her? You're the expert, right?"

"Yes, but we can only do so much. We've hit a roadblock."

"I can't help that," Nova said.

"Then I strongly recommend that you postpone or cancel the show," Emmie said. "It's too dangerous to perform. Can you do that? At least, until after we've got this figured out."

Nova frowned. "You said you could do it."

"I think we still can, but we just need more time."

The elevator stopped descending and the doors opened to the lobby. Stepping out, Nova's expression changed sharply as if she'd snapped out of something, and her face brightened. "No, Emmie. I can't cancel anything. I feel something incredible about this performance. I've got something no one has ever seen before, a trick like nothing else, and I haven't shown it to anybody. Not Marty, not Jimmy, not you. It's going to change everything for this place, trust me." She made a wide gesture. "The audience will love it, Em. They'll all be chanting my name. Can you imagine that?"

As they stepped toward the lobby together, there was a strange giddiness to Nova's words, an energy that chilled Emmie's skin. It was like she was now talking to someone entirely different, someone who'd never been afraid of ghosts or the theater or performing in front of an audience.

"Listen, Nova, listen to yourself," Emmie said. "I'm afraid something's going to happen."

"Emmie," Nova spoke sharply, and it cut like a knife. "Just do your thing, and... deal with whatever is going on down there in the theater. My performance is tonight, and Grandma is recovering but she's not up for an interrogation." She glanced toward the Amber House Theater entrance across the lobby as if filled with quiet pride. "That means everything to me. This show is more than just a performance; it's going to keep her going. I need to do this, and she needs to see me do this. Don't you understand?"

Nova stared pleadingly, almost wounded, and Emmie couldn't look away. How could she tell her friend that she did understand, that she had her back, but the words caught in her throat? "I won't let you down."

Nova inched closer to Emmie, her tone dropping to a whisper. "I've been dreaming of this for a long time, and soon—tonight—everyone in Vegas will know my name."

Her words hung in the air between them until a man's harsh voice came from not far away, from somewhere behind them. "I've had enough!"

Turning around, she spotted Wayne rushing toward them,

accompanied by a beefy security guard. Both of them had expressions showing that they were in no mood for games.

"I heard everything you said in the elevator," Wayne said. "You've manipulated my daughter long enough with your ghost nonsense, and now pressuring her to get my mother involved in your wild theories is borderline criminal. Pack your bags and check out. Now! If I catch you wandering anywhere near this hotel again, I'll have you all arrested."

31

Emmie couldn't help but feel powerless as she stood with her friends outside the theater an hour later as a line of guests arrived from every direction. So many families were completely unaware of the dangers that awaited them inside. There was even a pregnant woman holding the hand of a small boy, his free hand clutching a Nova-themed souvenir program. The woman laughed at something her husband said while the other hand rested protectively on her swollen belly. A little girl skipped beside them, her sparkly shoes catching a bit of light from the marquee overhead.

Emmie turned away. She couldn't take it anymore. Clenching her jaw, she scanned the faces of her friends; their expressions showed they were as stunned as she was. The hotel staff had cleared out their rooms and brought down their suitcases even before they had a chance to pack anything themselves. Now they stood on the curb waiting for their ride to the airport while the Amber House Theater's glowing marquee blazed Nova's name above them in brilliant golden letters that seemed to shine brighter as the sun dropped below the horizon.

"We were almost there," Emmie said. "How did things go so wrong? It was supposed to be easy."

Jason put his arm around her and pulled her in closer. "It's out of our control now."

"I hope we're wrong about Max and his intentions," Sarah said.

"We're not wrong," Emmie said. "That's the hell of it. There's got to be a way we can get back in there and stop all this."

"You heard what Wayne said," Jason replied. "But I'm okay with taking a few bruises for the team if we come up with a plan. I've dealt with—"

"That's the last thing I want for us." She looked into his eyes. "We need to fly under the radar somehow, but we also can't just walk in there and pretend nobody will recognize us."

Dread surged in Emmie's stomach.

"If it'll help," Jason said, "I'll run back in there and create a distraction so they have to cancel the performance."

Finn seemed amused. "And how do you propose to do that?"

Jason formed a sinister stare. "I'll hit the fire alarms, like in high school."

"We don't need you spending the night in jail," Emmie said, "and I doubt that would stop it, anyway."

Finn ran his fingers through his hair. "So what's the plan, then? What options do we have left?"

Emmie looked into his eyes. "Can you somehow get Marty's phone number? Maybe we can send him a text message to let him know we still want to help stop this."

"I can try." He sat on the curb and dug into one of his silver suitcases, pulling out his laptop and starting it up. "What do I tell him, assuming I can get his number? Nova's about to start and I'm not sure he's available to help us, anyway. Even if he does believe us, he has a job to do, and I'm sure he doesn't want to lose it because of us."

Emmie checked her phone's screen. The show would start in less than thirty minutes, and the thousands of guests would be settling into their seats soon.

"I know it's a sold out show," Sarah said, "but someone *always* sells their tickets online at the last minute. We could change our clothes, put on sunglasses, wear a hat..."

Emmie shook her head. "Someone would still recognize us. I'm positive Wayne has his security focused on us right now, and we couldn't make that happen in less than thirty minutes anyway. We have to somehow get backstage. If we could only convince Nova to delay the performance for just a few more days, I think we could get this resolved. But it's like she's hell-bent on going through with it tonight."

Scrolling through a few websites on his laptop, with Emmie watching him over his shoulder, Finn stopped on one page and let out a sigh. "This is going to take a little time," he said. "And I'm not sure I can get it all done before the show starts."

Only moments later, Jimmy stepped out from the side door of the theater, his posture stiff and apologetic. He ran over to Emmie and held out a small object in his open palm. "I have something for you." It was the pendant she'd given Nova earlier. "Wayne forced her to give it back. She didn't want to."

Her heart sank at receiving it. "Thank you, Jimmy."

"Nova told me to bring it out to you myself," he said and gestured to their suitcases with a pained expression. "I hate that they treated you like this. I really do."

Emmie shook her head, her voice a whisper, while slipping the pendant back into her purse. "It's not your fault. You're just doing your job."

"Yeah, I suppose, but it doesn't feel right. I know you all care about Nova. I can see that. After this is all over..." His words trailed off as he glanced toward the theater doors. The crowd was slowly filtering through the entrance. He looked back at them with an expression of concern. "Do you really think something's going to happen tonight?"

"I hope not." Emmie's chest tightened. He turned to leave, but she caught his arm and he turned back. "Would you mind passing along a message to Marty for me?"

"Marty? Sure. What do you need?"

"Tell him we'd like to score a few bootleg passes. Right away."

He frowned. "The show is sold out. I'm sorry."

"No, please just tell him that. He'll know what it means."

Jimmy's confusion deepened. "Uh, okay? I can pass that along, but—"

"Just tell him," Emmie spoke in a sharper tone. "Please."

Jimmy nodded. "Sure, no problem. I have to run now." Jimmy gave a wave then hurried away, glancing back while security opened the side door for him before slipping inside the theater.

When the door slammed shut, the weight of the situation crashed down on Emmie again. Would she ever talk to Nova again?

The four of them stood in silence as the crowd's laughter and excitement continued to grow as the line finished moving inside.

Finn gestured to a car that stopped beside the curb a few yards away. "We're out of time," he mumbled.

The driver stepped out and met their gaze. "Someone called for an Uber? Emmie Fisher?"

Emmie raised her hand. "Here."

The driver gave a wide smile and stepped over to them. "Not going to the show?"

Before Emmie could answer, the side door to the theater burst open and someone called her name. It was Marty.

"I've got four bootleg passes available," he said with a little grin. "But you'd better hurry. Things are about to get strange."

Finn handed the driver some cash as they scrambled to get their suitcases inside the theater before Marty closed the door behind them.

32

Even within the darkness of the backstage, Emmie moved forward with her face down to avoid being recognized by security. The others were doing the same as they hurried along behind Marty, who led them through a dim, winding passage crammed with all the abandoned props and equipment since the theater opened. They had left their baggage behind at Marty's direction, leaving it just inside the door after covering it with a white silk sheet that a performer might have used in an illusion. Marty steered them away from the stage, where security stood watch over a flurry of stagehands who were busy preparing for Nova's performance.

They finally stopped near a shadowy prop storage area and paused to listen to the rustling of the audience. A Prohibition-era jazz number was playing over the loudspeakers, no doubt intended to put the audience in a festive mood for Nova's performance.

"This is as far as I can take you," he said. "I have to get back out there before someone notices I'm gone. Security rarely comes back to this area, although if you run around making a scene..."

Emmie nodded once. "We'll fly under the radar."

"Do what you need to do," he said in a somber tone. "Don't let anyone stop you if you feel you're onto something, and I'll try to watch your back."

"Thank you." Emmie gave a sincere smile. "Before you go, maybe you can answer something for us. Nova said she was planning something special tonight for the audience. She said it was something nobody had ever seen before. Do you know what she meant by that?"

His eyes lit up. "Yes, although I'm not allowed to reveal—"

"Nobody here is out to steal her secrets," Jason jumped in. "Under the circumstances... It might save her life."

"It involves a guillotine," Marty answered. "I designed it myself, following Nova's exact specifications. It's completely safe, and—"

"What sort of guillotine?" Emmie cut him off. "What does it look like?"

Marty looked confused. "Several feet tall with dark-stained wood, like one from the Medieval times. We wanted it to look like something a wealthy mob boss might have displayed in his home to intimidate his enemies. We thought it helped to enhance the hotel's theme. It's *very* realistic, but with plenty of safeguards, so nothing to worry about. We worked hard to give it an authentic design, with a crescent blade—"

"Crescent?" Emmie's heart seemed to skip a beat. "When is she performing the illusion?"

"It kicks off Nova's performance. She wanted to start the show with a bang."

Jason straightened his posture and looked at each of them. "I don't like the sound of that."

Marty's phone dinged twice and he stepped toward the stage. "Listen, I'm sorry, but I have to go."

Finn checked the time on his phone, then looked at Emmie with wide eyes. "We've got less than thirty minutes."

"Is there anything I should know?" Marty's face showed a growing fear. "How can I help?"

"Don't let her go through with the act," Emmie said.

Marty swallowed. His phone dinged two more times. "I'm not sure that's possible... I have to get out there." Marty hesitated before leaving, rubbing the back of his neck. "Listen, if you see my Jessica, tell her I'm sorry. Tell her I should have gone with her that night."

Emmie nodded. "We will," she promised, although her mind was racing now, not sure if any of them would survive long enough to deliver the message. Marty looked at her for a moment, then turned away and disappeared down a long, narrow corridor leading to the stage, his footsteps drawn out by the music coming from the theater.

After he left, they each looked at each other in the darkness. She could see their faces, and a sense of uncertainty hung in the air between them.

"What's so important about the crescent blade?" Finn asked.

"I found a notebook that Max left behind backstage after his death," Emmie said. "It was full of his plans for illusions, with diagrams and notes showing how each of them would work. Max had planned to use a guillotine with a crescent blade for one of them. I think Nova's taking directions from his spirit now, and I promise you, the show will definitely end *with a bang* if she goes through with it."

"Where's the notebook?" Finn asked.

Emmie pictured it in her mind and glanced in the direction of Nova's dressing room. Would her friend still be getting dressed so close to showtime? "Follow me."

Circling around behind a line of props, they entered the main dressing room door and found Nova's door cracked open with the light off. Slipping inside, Emmie closed the door behind them. The small wooden box sat a few feet away on her friend's desk, the lid wide open like a gaping mouth.

Emmie stepped over and peeked inside. The notebook sat alone at the bottom. "It's here."

Finn reached in and pulled it out before she had a chance. He flipped through the pages, studying the notes like a boy with a treasure map. The pages were stuffed with diagrams and notes.

When she spotted the guillotine and the crescent blade diagrams, she stopped him and gestured to it. "Nova was looking at this when I accidentally interrupted her private rehearsals."

Finn continued moving through its pages. "This is what she used to build her props? She's stealing all of her ideas from Max?"

"Not stealing," Emmie said. "He's guiding her like a mentor, passing along all of his knowledge."

"Then why go through all of this if he intends to harm her?" Sarah asked.

"I think Max has something else in mind," Emmie said, "something bigger than any of us realize, although I'm not sure what that is yet."

Finn was silent as he seemed to study the pages. Instead of waiting for him to look up, she asked, "What do you think?"

He nodded. "I think you're right, and I wonder if Marty knows about this."

"He didn't mention it."

Finn glanced toward the stage. "While you're busy here... Marty needs to see this."

Before Emmie could say another word, Finn hurried out of the room. Turning back to Sarah and Jason, she sensed the presence of more than one spirit nearby, as if their presence had electrified the air itself.

"We can't. Some of them are here, but..." Emmie narrowed her eyes and focused on the charged energy. "Max is still out there somewhere, maybe on the stage near Nova."

Sarah moved in beside her. "Then let's draw them all away from Nova. Pull them back here where we can deal with them directly."

"You read my mind." Emmie glanced around the area. "I'll start now. Jason, would you mind standing outside the door and distract anyone who tries to get in here while I'm trying to contact the spirits? Keep them away from us, if you can."

"I won't let anyone stop us." Jason cracked open the door and peeked out before leaving.

Sarah glanced around the room with a curious stare. "There's something here," she whispered. "Can you feel it? Like static in the air."

"It's not just you," Emmie said, scanning the shadows. The air was thick with a bristling dark energy. "Max and the assistants are close by. I can feel them."

Sarah took in a deep breath and closed her eyes. Her hands trembling, she stretched them out in front of her as if to grab the ghosts and pull them in herself.

The air seemed to shift, growing colder and heavier. Emmie started her focus. Her face contorted with effort as she reached over her head, connecting with something ethereal. "He knows what we're trying to do. I can feel so much hate in his spirit."

The temperature dropped, and a low guttural moan echoed through the air, followed by the sharp clatter of falling props.

"Someone is coming, all right," Emmie said, "and they're not happy at all."

33

Taking the notebook with him, Finn moved through the darkened corridors of the backstage and spotted Marty only a minute later. He was alone, thank God, and it was easy enough to catch his attention in that moment after he glanced back and met Marty's gaze. Marty rushed over with fear in his eyes and kept looking over at a group of stage workers who had assembled near a large set piece. Finn recognized the massive device a moment later—the guillotine. Its sleek blade perched at the top looked even more ominous in the darkness. Nova stood behind the curtain, glancing back into the darkness with a frown and calling out Marty's name.

Marty pulled Finn back. "Someone's going to see you. You need to stay away from this area."

Finn scrambled to open the notebook and show him the diagram for the guillotine. "Is this what you used to build that thing?"

Marty ran his finger over the diagram. "I've never seen this before. Where did you get this?"

"It belonged to Max."

He studied it closer this time, paying special attention to the blade. "This is exactly what I built. Well, almost." Marty pointed out the structure's ropes and mechanisms near the top. "This is all different. Did Nova give this to you?"

Finn shook his head. "She doesn't know we have it."

"This is everything she instructed me to design except..." His face showed confusion as his eyes widened. "I think what I built is flawed."

"What do you mean, flawed?"

Marty swallowed. "I think I made some mistakes. Nova made it clear what she wanted, down to the last details near the top. I checked and double-checked everything." Marty looked at the design again. "No, this is different than what Nova had me build. This one is..."

"What?"

"This one is correct."

"Correct? What do you mean?"

Marty glanced back at the guillotine. The stage workers were moving it out onto the stage now. It was too late. The show had begun.

"Nova couldn't have intentionally designed that thing to fail for her act. That's impossible."

Finn dropped his voice to a harsh whisper. "Not Nova, Max."

The weight of those words seemed to hit Marty like a punch to the gut as his face drained of color, and his gaze jumped back to the towering guillotine being pushed out onto the stage. The grinding of its wheels echoed through the backstage corridors like the cry of a waiting predator.

Finn tried to steady his breathing. "If it's flawed, how bad are we talking?"

Marty's aging hands trembled as he pointed to different sections of the diagram in the notebook. "The mechanism for the blade... it's supposed to stop automatically when the trick reaches a certain point. But if it fails, if the tension is too high or the release jams, it... won't stop. It'll continue straight through. I built in a fail-safe, but after seeing this... my backup won't work."

He looked at Finn for a long moment. "And they would have blamed me for her death."

"We still have time to stop it, right?"

Marty stared at Finn without blinking. "It's out on the stage."

"Well, pull it back in."

He shook his head slowly. "Nova would never allow that. It's too late."

Finn gestured to the diagram. "But, if we can... The thing is rigged to lock into place at the center of the stage, right? And then a rig from the floor takes over. It's all masked out by mirrors. What if someone could get down there and hold that thing in place manually..."

"It's heavy," Marty said, "and you'd have to squeeze in there."

"I'll do it."

Marty glanced down at his overalls. "I wish it was me. It's very dangerous down there between all those gears."

Finn could see the powerlessness in Marty's expression, the realization that Max had somehow intentionally convinced Nova to compromise the safety of the guillotine. But Marty's shock only lasted a short time as he waved away workers while leading Finn across the backstage and down a dim passageway that led them beneath the stage, where only the muffled sounds of the audience above created a strange disjointed rhythm. The musty air smelled of old wood, and the rhythmic hum from the machinery sounded like an opponent daring him to come closer.

Marty gestured to a narrow crawlspace in the far corner, framed by a web of pipes and grinding gears that churned and hissed with mechanical precision. A rope snaked its way through the gears, its tension visible even in the dim light. "There," he said, his voice urgent but laced with guilt. "That rope controls the blade. If you can hang on to it throughout her act, then even if it does fail, you can stop the blade from crashing down on her. Even if you could just delay it for a minute or two, it should be enough for someone to get Nova out of harm's way."

Finn eyed the space. The crawl area was barely wide enough

to squeeze into, and the constant grinding of the gears made the task look like an illusion in itself. "I have a feeling OSHA would have a problem with this."

Marty gave him a grim look. "If I could get in there... these old bones... Do you think you can do it?"

"Sure," Finn said without thinking. He clenched his jaw and started climbing the metal ladder as Marty watched with a helpless expression. Finn wasn't a fan of tight spaces or being surrounded by industrial-grade cheese graters, but he had faced plenty of dangerous situations before. "Sure, I can do it."

The crawl space was tighter than Finn expected, and the grimy walls pressed in on him as he wiggled forward on his stomach. He struggled to breathe in the thick, hot air. The grinding gears drowned out any noises from above, and Marty's voice had faded to nothing. He tried not to think about the fact that one wrong move could leave him with fewer body parts.

Reaching the rope that flowed along the circumference of a larger gear, he grabbed the cool metal and felt the vibrating tension. A bit of sweat formed on his forehead and dripped down his cheek as the gears around him stopped moving.

"The guillotine is ready," Finn cursed under his breath, adjusting his position beneath the rope to prepare for the relentless weight of the guillotine's blade if it were to fail, like Marty said. He tried to brace his legs against the walls of the crawl space, but he had little leverage. There was no way to know when the blade might drop, so he could only wait and grip the rope. The tension in his arms made his muscles burn after only a minute.

Marty's voice echoed faintly from the opening to the crawl space. "Hold it steady! I'll tell the others!"

"Yeah, no rush!" Finn shouted back, his tone laced with dark humor. "You'll know where to find me."

The stage above vibrated with the sounds of the music coming from Nova's performance. The gears had stopped, at least temporarily, and all the muffled reactions from the audience came through the floor. Finn's heart pounded, and he couldn't help but think of his friends who were backstage racing to deal with the ghosts who had set all of this motion, their own lives in danger.

As the rope shifted just a little, he tensed, and every muscle in his body strained to prepare for the worst, although its full weight hadn't yet been unleashed. "Come on, Marty," he whispered through clenched teeth. "Get Nova out of there."

34

Emmie could see them in her mind's eye. The spirits held a heavy presence as she stood with her eyes half-closed, her breathing deliberate, reaching out with her senses to draw them in.

"They're here," she said with strained concentration.

The faint shapes began to take form: a man with a commanding presence flanked by two women, whose dark energy radiated with restlessness. Max and his assistants. There was no mistaking the strength of their twisted energy.

Sarah stood beside her with her hands out as if she might embrace them when they arrived. "I feel them now," Sarah said quietly. "We should expect a fight from them. They've got a lot of anger built up."

"At Nova," Emmie finished, pressing her lips into a thin line.

The energy shifted in her mind as the forms sharpened, hovering near the stage. Max was like a churning storm cloud of razor-sharpened intensity, and he had somehow tethered himself to Nova like an invisible chain. How long could he maintain that hold on her, twisting her thoughts with the sheer force of his rage?

"He won't let go of her," Emmie said. She dug deeper, her

mind reaching out toward the spirits with waves of intensifying energy. "He's not making it easy."

Sarah's hands curled into fists. "Just get them close enough so I can connect with them. You only need to hold them."

"No. No," Emmie said. "He doesn't want to let go. I've never seen so much hate and determination to harm others. I think he'd love to destroy the theater and everyone in it."

Emmie focused on the two women first. They resisted, although their spirits weren't as strong as Max. Their forms wavered in the darkness, their energy turning toward her slowly.

"Come on..." Emmie whispered under her breath. "Just let go. You don't need to stay here anymore."

"The assistants," Sarah's voice broke through the rising tension. "Their auras are eclipsed by Max, but I can sense their emotions shifting now. The hate—betrayal—it's fueled by him. Since they all died together, I'm sure he has a hold on them, too." Sarah took in a sharp breath. "Max is... he's digging in. His rage is out of control and he knows we're here. He's feeding on Nova's obsession to succeed."

The tug of war continued as Emmie focused harder. "It's like trying to drag an elephant through quicksand."

"Nothing we can't handle." Sarah's voice was firm. "Just don't let up."

The two assistant spirits flickered closer, their presence almost tangible now, only a few yards away. Although Max was still refusing to budge from his place beside Nova, he lingered in the darkness, his energy circling Nova like a noose.

Just when Emmie was sure the assistants would materialize at any moment, Jason's voice cut through the tension and broke off their concentration.

"Hey," he said in a careful, nervous tone.

Emmie could hear the undertones of a warning in his voice as her concentration faltered, and her eyes snapped open to see Jason standing only a few feet away. He was looking back toward the edge of the stage, focused on someone approaching.

Emmie's heart sank. They were so close to ending this, or at least closer. Nova was there, standing near the shadowy outline of the curtain, obscured in darkness. Although Emmie didn't need to see her expression to know that she knew something wasn't right.

"Damn it," Emmie whispered, curling her fingers into fists. The connection Emmie and Sarah had worked so hard to establish with Max and the assistants now wavered, her grasp slipping away from them. As the assistants' spirits retreated, their energy snapped back toward Max as if he held them with a powerful magnet. Whatever chance they'd had to diffuse the situation had been shattered when Nova had come between them.

"It's not what you think," Jason said to Nova.

"Where's Emmie?" Nova asked. "Where's the rest of them?"

"We're trying to help," Emmie called out. There was silence between them for a moment as Nova stepped into the faint backstage light, her silhouette sharp against the glow spilling from the stage. Her face was unreadable at first, cloaked in darkness, but as she moved closer, the tension in her expression came into view. Her eyes carried a mix of curiosity and suspicion, although she wasn't angry at them—yet.

"What are you doing?" Nova demanded.

Sarah remained in her trance, as if refusing to give up on the constant connection to the spirits. Emmie hesitated for a moment, then gestured toward an open area, motioning for Nova to step aside with her. There was no need to break Sarah's concentration.

Leading Nova away from Sarah and the stage lights, they stopped beside a stack of crates as the faint hum of the audience beyond the curtain filled the air. Nova was in full makeup and her costume was stunning, even in that darkened space. She was moments away from stepping on stage, and they would only have a short time to talk.

"I'm sorry," Emmie said, "but we had to do something."

Nova's expression softened. "Where's Marty? Did he let you in?"

"We convinced him to help us. We just couldn't leave you in danger like this. None of us want to see anything happen tonight."

"Nothing bad's going to happen." Nova gave a little grin. "I know you're just trying to help, and I love that about you. Don't worry, I won't call the police on you or anything. I was going to call you as soon as the show was over to thank you for everything. Sorry about my dad forcing you to leave. He overreacts sometimes. Listen..." Nova reached out and took Emmie's arm gently. "I'm not afraid anymore. Just having you around these past few days has helped me a lot to face my fears. I've never felt so confident about anything in my life before."

Emmie shook her head. "No. You can't go on with the performance."

Nova's hand dropped from Emmie's arm and she stepped back. Her expression held a bitter grin, as if Emmie had made a bad joke. "I'm not afraid of anything in this place anymore. Marty even triple-checked all the props and the rigging, and I trust him completely." Her face lit up. "You won't believe the illusions I've got prepared for tonight. If only you could be out there in the audience watching the show."

"It's more important that I stay back here. The danger is stronger than ever. Please cancel the show."

Nova frowned and stiffened. "I'm sure the ghosts are gone by now. I haven't had any trouble so far today, so whatever you did, it seems to have worked. Maybe just your presence scared them away."

"It doesn't work like that."

Nova shrugged. "Seems like it did."

Emmie's heart raced as she searched Nova's face, trying to find the right words to get through to her friend. "Spirits don't just leave when I show up," she said finally. "They're still here and they're planning something again. Something awful."

Nova glanced back toward the stage while rolling her eyes. "They're gone," she said with a small laugh.

"They're not gone," Emmie snapped. "You have to believe me. You were right all along about how dangerous it is here. We wouldn't be risking everything to help you unless we knew you weren't safe. They're watching you and me right now, waiting for the right moment to strike again. We also found the notebook."

Nova gave a confused expression. "What notebook?"

"The one from Max. The notebook showing diagrams for all his illusions."

She furrowed her brow and frowned. "You shouldn't have looked in there. That's for a magician's eyes only—*my* eyes."

"Is that where you got your ideas?"

Nova scowled. "My ideas came from me, not from anyone else, not from anyone's notebook."

"Max is here, and he's been manipulating you. He's been guiding you, hasn't he?"

Nova gave a sarcastic laugh. "Nobody's been manipulating me. Is that what you think now? That I'm a fraud?"

"I'm not saying that."

"Sure sounds like you are."

"What I'm saying is that Max's spirit is still a powerful force in this place, and he intends to kill you."

Nova rolled her eyes again. "Nobody's going to kill me. I'm really sorry now that I got you involved in all of this."

A thick energy swept through the air, the same kind of energy that Emmie had recognized the first time she stepped foot in the hotel. A spirit had arrived over Nova's shoulder as a wave of icy air rushed in around them. Emmie shivered as the figure took shape behind her friend. The form stood only a few feet away, translucent with dark eyes fixed on Nova with a chilling intensity.

Max.

Nova tilted her head and folded her arms over her chest as her gaze became unfocused for a moment. Max leaned in closer to her, whispering something in her ear. Emmie strained to hear, but the magician's voice was too soft from that distance. Nova gave a faint reaction, her eyes widening with a little smirk as she shivered.

"When I'm done with my illusions, you'll owe me an apology," Nova said.

Max stared at Emmie with an icy gaze. He whispered again, but this time loud enough for Emmie to hear. "Just stay on schedule like we planned," he said, "and the world is yours. Everyone in Vegas will know your name."

Nova repeated his words without hesitation, her voice filled with reverence. "If I stay on schedule like I planned, then I know the world is mine. Everyone in Vegas will know my name."

The sincerity in her friend's tone sent a chill down Emmie's spine, making the moment even more unbearable.

"I have to go," Nova said softly, taking another step back. "If you're still here when I get back, we'll have a good laugh. When this is all over, everyone will be cheering my name."

Before Emmie could say anything more, Nova hurried away toward the stage, running into Marty near the edge of the curtain. She stood straight as if preparing herself for battle. She seemed to scold the old man, but then, with a bright smile, she stepped forward and disappeared into the glow of the stage lights.

35

Emmie barely had time to react to Nova's exit before two ghostly assistants materialized in front of her. Jessica and Vivian, Max's assistants. Their faces showed something twisted, something dark and raging beneath the glitzy exterior. Their expressions turned to cruel amusement as they approached.

Jason and Sarah stood their ground as Jessica, the taller of the two, eyed them all curiously, before stopping on Jason for a long moment.

"Joker!" she said with a wide grin.

Jason cringed. "Oh great, you again."

"Well, well," she purred, her voice dripping with mockery. "If it isn't our little daredevil. You were so eager to play with us earlier. Did you enjoy the view from the balcony?"

Jason clenched his teeth and glanced at Emmie with a pained expression, as if to apologize for his behavior once again.

Emmie turned her focus back to the assistants. "This isn't going to end the way you want."

"Yes," Jessica said. "Yes, it is. Everything is playing out just as Max said it would."

Vivian inched toward Jason. "Maybe you'd like to have a rematch? Careful this time, you might not be so lucky."

"You caught me off guard," Jason said.

"Oh, sweetheart," Jessica said with a wide grin. "It's adorable that you think it matters. Max has already won, and you're just here to entertain us until the curtain falls."

"Then why are you still here?" Emmie asked in a biting tone. "If Max is such a genius, why are you two still stuck playing backup?"

Jessica's smile faded and her eyes narrowed. "Don't bother standing in our way. Everything is all set, and nobody will dare step foot in this theater ever again after tonight."

"Why?" Sarah asked. "Why is it so important that you kill Nova? And the other magicians?"

"Because we were betrayed," Jessica said sharply, "just like you're about to be."

Emmie took a cautious step forward and spoke carefully, raising her hands slightly while keeping her voice steady. "Betrayed by who? Max?"

Jessica let out a bitter laugh. "Max has never betrayed us. Not Max. *Him.*" She pointed a finger toward the stage where Marty had stood moments earlier, and her gaze darkened. "He abandoned me. He let me die."

Emmie's heart beat faster. Marty's confession came rushing back, and her voice softened. "Jessica, Marty didn't let you die. He's been carrying that guilt with him for decades."

Jessica's form seemed to waver. "Don't lie to me. He didn't really care about me. He didn't even look for me."

"That's not true," Emmie said. "He couldn't bring himself to come back to this place, to the place you died, because of you. He's haunted by your memory, by what happened. He loved you."

Jessica's expression twisted and shifted from deep anger to a softness, then back to anger, and then replaced by something else—grief.

"You're lying," Jessica whispered without conviction.

"I'm not." Emmie stepped closer, ignoring the warning look

Jason was giving her. "He told me himself. He said he never forgave himself for what happened to you. That he could never move on from this place because you couldn't. He never gave up on you."

For a moment, Jessica's form showed a bit of light, her gaze softening as the anger that bound her loosened its grip until Vivian cut in. "Don't listen to her." She reached toward Emmie's throat, and Emmie stumbled back, knowing full well from experience that spirits could get to any of them if they wanted it badly enough.

Jason lunged forward at the same time, stepping between them while facing the spirit head-on. "If you're planning to kill us, you'll never leave this place."

Vivian lashed out, pushing him back, sending him crashing against the wall of props. Sarah cried out and rushed to his side, standing over him with her arm out as if preparing for another attack.

Jessica didn't move. She stood frozen, staring at Emmie, her expression full of pain and heartache.

Emmie jumped at the chance to connect with the woman. "Marty still loves you," she said. "But you have to let go of everything Max told you. Please, let us stop Max before it's too late."

Jessica trembled as she slumped a little.

"You aren't going to listen to them," Vivian growled in frustration. "They all deserve to die like the others."

"Leave me alone," Jessica said, her voice faint but commanding.

"You're pathetic," Vivian snarled as her spirit flared with bursts of dark energy. "Now you've betrayed Max too!" She spat toward Jessica before her physical form faded then disappeared in a burst of cold air.

Jessica turned back to Emmie, her form almost translucent now. "Marty never came back for me. And then this happened." Jessica's spirit wavered between shades of light and dark. "Are you telling me the truth?"

"I promise, and I'll let him tell it to you himself when this is over, but only if we can stop Max."

"I can't." She frowned and looked down. "But maybe you can."

"Thank you," Emmie said.

Jessica faded, leaving behind a lingering sadness that pressed on Emmie's chest and mind. The assistant's spirit still lingered in that place, but at least they had broken through one of the roadblocks on their way to Max. Emmie turned to Jason and Sarah, who were still recovering from the attack. "Are you alright?"

"I'm fine," Jason said hoarsely, his hand pressed on his side where he'd hit the floor. "But we need to keep moving."

The trio hurried down the corridor toward the stage, avoiding eye contact with the stagehands, who looked at them curiously, until they spotted Marty hunched over a series of props, ropes, and pulleys. His face was slick with sweat. The faint hum of the audience filtered through the walls, punctuated by bursts of applause from Nova's performance.

"Marty," Emmie called to him with sharp urgency.

He glanced over, his eyes bloodshot and frantic. "You shouldn't be here." He worked his hands to adjust the tension on a series of ropes that ran along the wall.

"We know about the guillotine," Jason said, stepping forward. "Finn told us what he found. What's going on?"

Marty swore under his breath, yanking on a rope that groaned in protest. "Finn's under the stage," he said. "He's trying to hold the mechanism steady, but it's flawed. The damn thing is rigged to fail. All we can do is…"

"What?" Sarah whispered as her eyes widened.

"I wouldn't have believed it unless Finn showed me Max's notebook," Marty said with a bit of guilt. "I built the damn thing, and I had no idea it was based on Max's design, I swear. It was Nova's trick—she guided me through every step of its design—"

"Max's design," Emmie cut in.

"—but it's a death trap," Marty continued. "If Finn loses his grip on that rope, the blade will drop, and it'll be over."

Marty's words sent a chill up Emmie's spine. She glanced toward the stage where Nova's voice rose over the noise of the audience. "How far is she into the act?"

"Almost at the end. If Finn can't hold on…" His voice trailed off, the unspoken words hanging heavy in the air.

Emmie's chest tightened as she met Jason's gaze. "We need to help Finn."

Marty shook his head. "Nobody can get down there. Not enough room for more than one person at a time. He's got to do it alone. And I'm doing my best to keep things from falling apart up here. If there's anything you can do…"

She knew what he meant. They were out of options, and if there was anything they could do to pull a rabbit out of their hat, then they should do so immediately. Peeking through a crack in the curtain, she spotted Nova on stage but shifted her attention to Max.

36

Thunderous applause filled the theater as Emmie was the first to arrive near the edge of the stage. Her heart pounded as the cheers only reminded her of how close Nova was to disaster.

"We're too late," Jason said with panic in his voice.

"We can't be," Emmie said. Everything they had fought to prevent came down to this moment, and yet they seemed powerless to stop what Nova had already set in motion. They *could* run out onto the stage to disrupt Nova's performance, but Wayne would have security drag them all to jail within minutes. That would only delay the inevitable, anyway. Nova was determined to go through with it. Force wasn't an option. They had to figure out something from behind the scenes.

Peeking around the edge of the curtain while keeping her eye out for stage workers trying to stop them, she spotted Nova near the center of the stage, a vision of confidence and determination illuminated by the glaring lights. The towering guillotine stood behind her, along with Max, unseen by anyone except her and Sarah. The crescent blade glistened ominously overhead.

"Nova," Emmie whispered hopelessly, "don't go through with it."

Her friend's act began with the grace and precision of a professional magician. She had all the talent and skill of a true Las Vegas entertainer. Gesturing to the guillotine, her voice carried over the hushed audience as she seemed to dare the contraption to do its worst. It went on like that for a few minutes as Nova took advantage of every opportunity to stretch out the tension. Stepping up the platform beside the guillotine to reach the wooden arc that formed the base where her neck would rest, Jimmy tied her in with straps on both sides and then secured the top half of the clamp over her neck so she could not escape under any circumstances.

Jimmy stepped back and pulled at the straps holding her in place to prove that Nova was completely powerless and her fate rested solely in her hands. She would live or die as the result of her skills.

The music held an uneasy tone as Jimmy completed the illusion, backing away with grace and a bit of unease.

The lights focused on the crescent blade dangling several feet above Nova's neck.

Moments before the climax of her illusion, the rigging above the stage shuddered with a sickening groan, and the beam of light stuttered like a broken heartbeat. A loud snap echoed through the theater as a piece of scaffolding dropped and crashed to the stage floor, only feet from the guillotine. The audience gasped but stayed in their seats, probably thinking it was part of the illusion.

Up near the light rigging, Emmie spotted Danny Drake. "He hasn't given up trying to stop her."

"It won't be enough," Jason said. "She can't back out now, anyway."

Nova shifted within the confines of the straps, her neck and head stiffening as her beaming face stared confidently toward the audience. The ropes and gears within the equipment stretched tight as the entire guillotine seemed to tremble on its own, its blade teetering at a threatening angle.

"Come on, Nova. Stop," Sarah whispered under her breath.

Max appeared beside Nova, still whispering into her ear, no doubt feeding her a string of lies and false confidence.

"Get out of there," Emmie said.

"She can't see what we see," Sarah's voice broke.

It was all on Nova now, and Finn to hold back whatever Max had planned. They couldn't risk running out on stage or creating a distraction. Nothing would stop her friend. They could only stand and watch and hope that somehow her friend prevailed through the impending disaster.

Something cracked again. Not from above or behind the stage, but within the guillotine itself. It lurched, shuddered suddenly as the blade descended just a fraction, then jolted to a halt. A gasp rippled through the audience as Nova struggled against the constraints. There was panic in her eyes as her confidence seemed to fade.

"She's trapped," Jason said. His body was tense as if he might run out onto the stage at any moment. "The props got her locked in."

One of the ropes in the guillotine snapped, and the blade dropped another few inches. Nova let out a panicked cry and struggled to pull her head away.

"Something's wrong," Nova said within the silence as the music stopped.

"Finn's got it. Finn's holding it," Emmie said. "He's holding the rope. If it wasn't for him…"

"I can't just stand here and watch this." Jason inched forward with his fists clenched at his sides.

Emmie nodded and lurched toward the stage until Max hit her like a wall, stopping her in her tracks. His spectral form stood in the way, while only the shorter assistant flickered beside him this time as they let out a chilling laugh.

"This is it," Max said, raising his hands as if he were putting on the illusion himself. "The grand finale."

The weight of Max's presence prevented her from rushing

out onto the stage to save Nova, who was still struggling within the restraints. She was gasping for breath. Jimmy had run out beside her to help, although he fought to stop the blade from crashing down, desperately searching the guillotine's structure to solve what might have gone wrong while still presenting an air to the audience that everything was alright. A bit of sweat glistened on his forehead. The guillotine shuddered again, the blade rattling in place.

"Finn can't hold that thing forever," Jason said.

The audience gasped and some of them stood while Nova continued to squirm within the device with her head poking out, trying to pull it back through the hole.

"Get me out!" Nova yelled.

The theater's house lights switched on, and from the side of the theater, just below the balcony where Gloria, Wayne, and the nurse had sat watching moments earlier, a single voice cried out, clear and commanding.

"Enough!"

37

Emmie hadn't noticed until that moment that Wayne, Gloria, and her nurse, Camila, were gone from the box seating where they'd sat watching the performance only moments earlier. The chaos seemed to stop for a moment as the old woman's defiant shout echoed off the walls of the theater, silencing even the restless spirits. Everyone turned to stare at the frail figure who had emerged near the side of the stage, walking slowly and unsteadily.

Gloria.

Wayne and the nurse were helping her step forward, holding her arms as she made her way toward Nova. They tugged at Gloria's arms, whispering in her ear, although she scowled and pulled at their efforts to turn her around. The old woman's hair glinted under the lights as she moved forward with shocking determination, her body still trembling from Parkinson's disease. She walked with her chin up, and her presence seemed almost ethereal, as if her renewed life were a part of the illusion on stage—a stark contrast to how Emmie had seen her lying helpless in her penthouse bed only days earlier. Within the glare of the theater lights, the old woman's plastic surgery was clear across her face.

The audience gasped and stared as the old woman headed toward the center of the stage. Her frame wobbled with each step, making frequent stops until she reached the front of the guillotine.

"Grandma, go back," Nova called out as she struggled beneath the faulty guillotine's blade. Locked in place by the restraints, her face was pale but defiant as Jimmy and Marty worked frantically to break her free, disassembling the prop piece by piece with great care while glancing up at the blade every few seconds. The exasperation on their faces was clear as beads of sweat glistened on Marty's forehead.

Gloria stood trembling in front of Nova, eyeing the guillotine's blade. It rattled again as if it might break loose at any moment, just as she spoke again, this time in a raspy voice, "Leave her alone."

"Mom," Wayne said to her, "We'll get Nova out of there. Please get off the stage."

Leaning toward her granddaughter, Gloria pushed aside a clump of hair that had fallen over Nova's face. "My sweet Nova."

"Stay back," Nova pleaded.

"I won't." Gloria straightened and turned her face up into the lights. "Max, stop this madness!"

Marty enlisted Jason's help to dismantle a series of gears and pulleys that fed the guillotine's rigging from the top. Sarah crouched beside the towering device, peering in through an opening in the floor, where Finn's strained cries rose above the chaos.

"I can't hold it much longer," Finn shouted.

Emmie focused on Max and the two assistants. The magician was watching everything with a satisfied grin, relishing the moment while turning his focus to Gloria. The old woman had distracted him for now. Maybe that would buy them enough time to get Nova out of there safely.

Gloria refused to budge as Wayne tugged again on her arm, this time almost pulling her off the stage. She gave a look of disdain and cursed him under her breath before glancing back at the audience with defiance.

"Grandma," Nova paused within her struggle. Her gaze locked onto her grandmother. "We can handle this. You're not safe up here."

Wayne's voice cracked as he wrestled with his mother's resistance. "Mom, what the hell are you doing?"

Gloria raised a trembling hand, silencing him without a word as she stared out across the stage again, stopping on Nova, then at the rattling blade, then back to Emmie, and then stopping at the panicked crowd. Facing them, she spoke with an almost miraculous strength that filled the theater. "Go home." Her voice was firm yet full of exhaustion. "There won't be a show tonight. Go home to your families. And forget what you've seen here."

The crowd broke into soft murmurs, followed by an uneasy silence as the lights flickered and the temperature seemed to drop. Gloria took a step back, her expression sharpening. She wasn't looking at anyone, although her focus was unmistakable.

"I know you're here, Max. You've taken this too far. What do you want from me? You've taken everything away. You can't have my Nova too."

Emmie focused on Max, who stood tall near the guillotine, watching her with an amused grin. She tried to pull him away from the scene, tried to pull him toward her where she might face him alone, but his spirit held so much rage, and his assistants only added to the inferno. They were going to have their way or take everyone down with them.

Emmie gasped as the air pressure seemed to drop, as if the theater itself was holding its breath, and she strained to contain his suffocating force.

Wayne moved in closer to his mother and put his arm around her. "No, Mom, please. We don't have time for this right now."

"Stay back," she snapped, her voice fierce. Staring up again at the lights, she shouted, "You want me to tell them everything? Is that what it takes? Yes, this is my fault... All my fault."

A wave of energy surged around the stage, hitting Emmie and catching her off guard. She stumbled back, sensing an icy presence forming just in front of her. Max was pushing against her face and body, his icy hands clutching at her throat. He wasn't trying to kill her, not yet, but trying to get inside of her, possess her. Emmie pushed him away, forcing his spirit away. The cold force burst across the stage, and Sarah let out a scream that cut short.

Sarah's eyes rolled up in her head, and when her mouth opened, the words that came out were not her own. She spoke in a low, venomous tone, "You finally have the courage to tell the truth. You betrayed me, Gloria, and my lovely assistants."

Gloria's face tightened as she stared at Sarah in horror and disbelief, but took a step toward her. "You threatened me. You were going to take it all away from me. What was I to do?"

"What were you to do?" Max cried out through Sarah. "It was so clear that *I* was the star of the show. All you had to do was stay out of my way."

"You threatened me... and my unborn child."

"*My* child!" Max said. "Did you really believe you could simply make me disappear from your life? So many crimes! None of this belongs to you. The theater, the money... the child. You deserve to lose it all in the worst way. Did you really believe you could hide your lies from the world, from my family forever? I always knew the truth would come out, eventually. So tell them now."

Gloria seemed to wilt under the weight of his words. She spoke slowly at first. "It's true."

Max gestured to the audience. "Tell them your real name. Tell them *everything*."

She nodded. "My name is Darlene Harken. I didn't inherit my fortune. I laundered every penny from a company in California back in the late seventies. I stole millions and then ran away, changing my name, changing my face." Gloria touched her fingers to her face. "I thought I'd finally found my refuge here after buying this theater. Amber House Theater was everything I ever wanted. A stage of my own. A palace where magic and dreams and illusions thrived and, maybe one day, I'd dare to perform in front of an audience myself." She glanced back at Wayne, then at Nova with defeated eyes. "I tried to protect you, tried to warn you to stay away from this place, but these old bones failed me. I couldn't leave the father of my only child whose presence I felt every day. Now it's all gone. My family. My dreams. Max is right. Everything I built in my life, it's all a lie."

Silence filled the theater until Gloria continued a moment later when she turned to face Sarah directly. "Why didn't you just leave me alone?"

"You didn't deserve to be left alone," Max said. "You were as corrupt as any of us and worse. Much, much worse. A heart darker than all of us combined."

"And you were planning to ruin me, expose everything. You blackmailed me, and I couldn't let that happen."

"All you had to do was play along," Max said. "You knew the rules of the game, but then you betrayed us. You murdered us."

Nova's face twisted in confusion and horror. "Grandma, please tell me what's going on?"

"Max is your grandfather," Gloria cried, her voice echoing through the silent theater. "And Wayne..." She turned to him with a warm smile. "You look so much like your father... in the right light."

"Don't toy with their emotions," Max said. "Tell them the truth. Tell them everything."

"Yes." Gloria lost her smile. "I kept this secret far too long. I killed Max, but I didn't mean to kill his assistants. I didn't know Jessica and Vivian were with him when I opened the gas valve into the lounge."

Marty stepped forward. "And you left my wrench at the scene to pin the blame on me."

"I had no choice," Gloria said. "But it worked out okay, didn't it? They didn't suspect you after all. I'm afraid it was necessary, because Max would have destroyed everything I'd built to get his way. That man was charming but ruthless." Her face softened a bit. "I fell in love with him after we met in college, flaws and all. He also recognized my strengths and weaknesses. My ambitions were far bigger than a simple nine-to-five job, so I found other ways to get what I couldn't earn. With my advanced accounting skills, it was easy. At first, we laughed about it as the money started rolling in. I could manipulate the books so perfectly that no one ever caught on—and no one ever did. Early on, Max even helped me hide the money. But when our relationship fell apart, he disappeared, and I didn't see him for years. Then one day, he walked into my casino, applying for a job as a magician. What are the odds? By then, I'd changed everything—my name, my face—but somehow, he still recognized me. I had no choice but to hire him. He made it clear: if I didn't do what he wanted, he'd ruin everything."

"You never had anything," Max said. "No money. No talent. No soul. No better than the rest of us."

"I had love, Max. For you. And your arrival rekindled our romance briefly. Long enough to conceive a child, but it wasn't enough to save me from doing what I knew I had to do."

"Murderer," Max said.

"We're two sides of the same coin, Max. You planned to kill your own granddaughter. An innocent."

"To hurt you." Max's rage filtered through Sarah's expression. "I would have killed her a thousand times to watch your heart shatter."

"And the other magicians?" Emmie asked. "What about them?"

"They stood in my way."

Gloria looked at the floor. "It's over now and Max has won, and now my heart is empty. I should have burned it all down when I had the chance."

Max shouted back, "I would have risen from the ashes."

Gloria nodded slowly. "Yes, and I couldn't let you go. After the others died, I knew you were still here. I could never let you go."

Everyone stared at her for a stunned moment as Emmie's mind reeled from the revelations, taking every piece of the puzzle into account—Gloria's murky past, the mysterious inheritance, the plastic surgery. All of it made sense if Max was blackmailing Gloria to get to the top.

A loud crack filled the air and Marty let out a pained cry. The top latch holding Nova in the guillotine broke open, and she stumbled out the back just as Max turned his attention toward her.

The blade came crashing down, slicing through the opening where Nova had sat helpless only moments earlier. Gloria turned toward the audience and lifted her chin, straightening her wilted frame and trembling as she spoke.

"I'm sorry," Gloria continued. "My lies have destroyed more than my heart can bear. God knows I've paid for those lies since the day I opened this theater." She paused to glance back at Nova. "But my granddaughter deserves better. Neither she nor Wayne know anything of what I did. Nobody does. I hope someday you can forgive me."

Her raspy voice broke into a soft melody, starting a song that was raw and full of emotion. She pulled away from Wayne and Camila, standing on her own for the first time. Her voice wavered as each breath came out as a struggle, but it was a powerful moment. The audience, who had remained in their seats, watched her in shock with wide eyes as the melody echoed through the air.

> I held the stars, but let them fade,
> The lights so bright... now fall to shade.
> Beneath their glow, I lost my way,
> But found my love, where shadows lay.

Gloria's moment in the light seemed to enrage Max after her chilling confession. A freezing wind burst over the stage, and Max's dark spirit flashed through the air like a black cloud of ice toward Gloria. At the same time, the lights flickered then went out. A pained cry filled the air—an old woman's cry—followed by a loud thud. When the lights returned, Gloria lay crumpled on the stage floor, her limp body motionless beneath the dim light.

Max's spirit was gone.

"Grandma!" Nova cried out and jumped forward.

With a stunned expression full of pain and shock, Wayne and the nurse followed, but Nova arrived at Gloria's side first.

Sarah rushed out toward the old woman, broken from her trance, as Emmie and Jason also moved forward to help, but the look on Wayne's face reminded them that he still hadn't yet welcomed their presence.

Dropping beside her grandmother, Nova pulled the lifeless body into her lap as she sat on the stage and cried.

38

Gloria's lifeless body lay in a heap in the center of the stage. Judging from the faces of those around her, they had given up on trying to revive her.

The last of the audience was escorted out the door. Their muffled conversations and shuffling feet echoed through the theater. One of the last to leave, the pregnant mother Emmie had seen near the entrance, gave a nervous glance back on the way out. At least nobody else would die in the Amber House Theater.

Emmie held back the urge to rush over to Nova and say something—anything—to comfort her friend, but what could she do in a moment like that? She could only wait for her to work through the grief. Nova kneeled beside her grandmother and reached out with trembling hands, her fingers hovering just above the old woman. There was so much sadness in Nova's eyes—a stark contrast to the confidence she'd exhibited at the start of the performance.

Jason and Sarah were right beside Emmie, standing near her like two soldiers waiting for instructions. Her friends had watched the spectacle like everyone else, wide-eyed and mouths gaping, and it had taken them all a moment to catch their bearings again. None of them spoke as the scene played out around them until a muffled call came from below the stage again.

Jason jumped forward as though shaken from a trance. "Finn." He exchanged a glance with Emmie, and together they rushed to the opening behind the guillotine. Marty was already kneeling by the trapdoor, working to undo the latch.

"Hold on, Finn!" Marty called out, his voice cracking beneath the weight of everything that had happened.

The trap door groaned open, and Finn's head appeared, his face streaked with grime and exhaustion. His usual smirk was faint, but it was there.

"I'm going to need a... Can someone get me some water?" He winced as they pulled him up. His arms stretched with exaggerated stiffness, and it was clear he was trying to mask the pain in his hands. "I'd really like to never do that again."

Jason patted him gently on the back. "You did good, man."

"Well," he replied, "if there's a reward in this... Maybe the hotel could comp us the deluxe suite next time?"

"Don't get your hopes up." Sarah brushed off his shirt and ran her fingers through his hair. The dust floated to the floor as she stared into his eyes. "I'm proud of you."

He nursed his wounded arms and winced while stretching. "I haven't had an upper body workout like that in years."

As they stepped back to let Marty close the trapdoor, Emmie turned toward the stage. Jimmy had joined the others around Gloria's body. Wayne's face was stoic, although there was a bit of softness in his stare as he glanced over at Emmie. He gave a little smile, buried within a brief nod, while resting his hand on Nova's shoulder. But she didn't seem to notice. Her entire focus was on her grandmother, tears streaking down her face as her lips moved in soundless whispers.

Max's spirit had dissolved into the darkness moments after Gloria's speech, having found his closure after she'd revealed the truth about what had happened. His shorter assistant, Vivian, had also flickered away moments after him. The dark energy that had filled the theater with rage and revenge had dissolved along with them.

But Jessica remained.

Her ghost lingered near Marty. Her expression didn't hold the same malicious intent now. Something softer had come over her. She looked sad, tilting in toward him as if longing for the connection they once shared. Sadness washed over Emmie as the two stood beside each other, Marty completely oblivious to her presence. Although he seemed to almost lean into her in the same way. Maybe on a subconscious level, he could feel her presence.

Nova stood suddenly, stumbling away from Gloria while nearly tripping over the microphone cord. "I need, I need to..." Her voice cracked a little as she turned toward Emmie, her teary eyes wide and filled with confusion and regret. She walked hurriedly toward Emmie, calling out, "I'm sorry, I'm so sorry."

Emmie stepped forward instinctively until the two embraced. "Nova—"

Nova pulled back. "I didn't know any of this about Grandma and Max. I didn't know..." Her friend seemed weak at the moment, and Emmie held her arm while leading her over to the side of the stage where they could talk in private.

"You couldn't have known," Emmie said. "There's always a reason behind spirits when they stay behind. Sometimes it takes more effort to get down to the truth, past all the emotions."

Nova shook her head. "But I should have known. I should have told you about where I was getting all the ideas for my illusions. It makes sense now. Max set up everything for me to find. He betrayed me, too—my own grandfather. He knew Grandma would be in the audience, and he was using me to get to her. It was all there, but I didn't see it. And now she's gone."

Emmie stood beside her friend in silence for a long moment.

"She made her choice. She did what she thought she had to do to protect her family."

Nova met Emmie's gaze. "How am I supposed to move on from this? How do I *fix* this?"

Emmie didn't have an answer, and the silence between them stretched on forever until Nova stepped away, wiping her face with trembling hands. "I need a minute."

"I'll be here," Emmie said.

Nova walked back toward her grandmother, then crouched on her knees before tears started flowing again.

Emmie glanced back at Marty. He was staring at Gloria's body, his face full of disbelief. With so much to deal with, he seemed resigned to leave it all behind. She walked over to him but kept an eye on Jessica, who stayed by his side, her gaze jumping between him and her.

"She did it," Marty said when she approached him, his voice hollow. "She killed my Jessica. All this time I thought it was Max or one of the other magicians, but it was her." His shoulders sagged as he pressed a hand to his forehead. "She built it all and then destroyed everything, didn't she? Max, Jessica, the theater. It's all gone because of her."

"Gloria kept the truth hidden until her last moments," Emmie said, a cold weight settling into her chest. "It took the threat of losing Nova to break it free. She couldn't let it go—the truth or the theater—until now."

Marty didn't look up, his gaze fixed on Gloria. "Jessica was my world, and now I've lost her twice."

Jessica's spirit shimmered faintly, her expression shifting between sorrow and longing as she reached her hand out toward Marty, although she stopped short, her fingers brushing the air just above his shoulder.

Emmie's chest tightened as her gaze jumped from her to him. "Not everything is lost."

Marty looked at her now, his brow furrowing. "What do you mean?"

"There's still time." Emmie stared at Jessica's spirit. All the rage that the assistant held earlier had faded, revealing a face that radiated a warm glow and soft eyes that sparkled. "There's still someone waiting for closure, waiting to say goodbye."

39

Leaving Sarah and Jason behind to take care of an exhausted Finn, Emmie took Marty aside, as Jessica's spirit seemed even more eager to speak to him now. There was so much information they probably had to share between them.

Marty stood frozen near the edge of the stage with his hands stuffed into his overalls, his shoulders hunched as if bracing himself against whatever Emmie was about to do or say. Jessica's ghost lingered right beside him, never leaving his side. She was whispering things to him, and it wasn't until she moved in closer that Emmie could hear what Jessica was saying. But she held back from repeating the words right away, instead taking in a steady breath. She crossed the space between them, and Jessica's spirit inched away, as if sensing what was about to happen.

"Martin," Jessica said softly to the old man, her voice cutting through the silence.

He turned to her slowly. "She's... she's still here, isn't she?"

Emmie nodded, glancing toward Jessica. "She's got a lot to say to you."

Marty swallowed hard and stared past Emmie as if trying to see what Emmie was seeing. "I don't know if I can do this."

"You don't have to," Emmie said gently. "I can help. Just say what's in your heart and I'll make sure she hears it."

Jessica's ghostly figure flickered with a faint light as Emmie tilted her head slightly, focusing on the connection between them, letting Jessica's words flow through her, entering a sort of channel between them, more like an interpreter.

"Martin," Emmie said, her voice shifting subtly with a hint of Jessica's tone. "I forgive you."

Marty flinched at hearing his name and pulled his hands out of his pockets. The years of guilt and regret had all built to this moment. "I should have been there," he said in a trembling voice. "I should have done something to stop it. Maybe if I'd—"

"No," Jessica said through Emmie. "You didn't know. None of us did, and Max used that anger to manipulate us. It wasn't your fault."

Marty shook his head, his eyes glistening. "But I love you, Jess, and I let you down."

Jessica's spirit seemed to change colors as her energy shifted. "You didn't let me down. You gave me everything, especially your love. You supported my struggle through years of alcoholism, and I couldn't ask for anything more."

Marty wiped his hand over his face and let out a choked sound at the same time. His shoulders sagged under the weight of her forgiveness. He nodded slowly.

"Max fueled my anger at this place," she said, "and at Gloria, and even at you for not being there. But it's time to let go. It's time to let me go."

Marty spoke quietly across Emmie again to the space next to her. "I don't want to lose you again."

"You never lost me. I've been with you here all along, but... someone's calling my name now, Martin. I have to go."

"Please don't."

"That's just the way it is." Emmie glanced over toward Jessica as her form started to change. Her spirit grew brighter and streaked toward the ceiling like a shooting star in reverse.

Marty stood motionless, his hands trembling at his sides, and he seemed to sense when she had gone, breaking down and crying only a moment later. "Thank you, Emmie." He put his hand on her shoulder and then walked away.

Turning back toward the others, Emmie noticed Sarah had disappeared. She spotted her friend a moment later at the back of the stage facing a darkened corner with her hands extended toward a shadowy figure. Sarah's hands were radiating a brilliant light into the air between them. The golden glow grew brighter —a psychic energy only she and Sarah could see—until the figure's face became clear.

Trick.

His face showed no signs of trauma now, and even a bit of joy, as Sarah's light flowed into and around the old magician's spirit. With a flash of light, he flared upward and then disappeared.

The sound of footsteps and police radios broke the fragile stillness. Wayne was still at Gloria's side, with the nurse hovering behind him. Nova stood apart from the others, her arms wrapped tightly around herself, with a blank expression. As the medics lifted Gloria's body onto the gurney, Nova took a hesitant step forward.

"Wait," she said, her voice barely audible.

The medics paused, and Nova kneeled beside her grandmother one last time, her fingers brushing over Gloria's hand.

"I forgot to say thank you, and I forgive you," she whispered. "For everything. Even the things I don't understand. Even the things you hid from me."

A tear slipped down her cheek as she stepped back and let the medics continue. Before they wheeled Gloria's body up the main aisle toward the exit, Emmie sensed a great weight had been lifted from the place. But it would take a long time to mend the damage Gloria had left behind.

Finn had managed to sit upright, although his exhaustion was still clear in his slumped posture.

Jason glanced at Emmie with an expectant expression. "Jessica?"

"She's gone," Emmie said. "She and Marty, they found peace together."

"That's something, at least," Finn said.

Sarah came back a moment later and let out a shaky breath. "That's exhausting, but they're at peace."

"I saw you with Trick." Emmie glanced around. "What about Danny and Zack?"

Sarah nodded with a little smile. "I took care of it. They were watching us from over there." Sarah pointed to the other side of the stage. "After Max disappeared, they still refused to approach the stage, but I helped them to move on."

"I couldn't do all of this without you, Sarah," Emmie said. She glanced at Jason and then Finn. "Or you guys. We definitely work best as a team."

Nova approached them slowly, with her head down, as if still contemplating her grandmother's last moments. She stopped a few feet away before she spoke. "Thank you."

Emmie stepped toward her, shaking her head. "Nova, you don't have to—"

"I do," Nova interrupted. "You didn't have to come here. You didn't have to go through all of this just for me, but you did, and if you hadn't..." She stared at the ground while shaking her head. "I don't even want to think about it."

Emmie placed a hand on her shoulder. "You're stronger than you think, Nova. Gloria saw the strength in your character, and that's why she fought so hard to protect you in her last moments. For you."

Nova nodded. "I just hope I can pick up the pieces and move forward."

"I see a bright future for you," Emmie said softly.

Nova smiled and glanced around. "I suppose that's the end of Amber House Theater. Nobody will ever take another step in here, even if the ghosts are gone now."

"I have a feeling none of this will hold you back."

Nova nodded. "We'll keep in touch."

"Absolutely."

They embraced again as the sound of Wayne's voice cut through the air. The warmth between them lasted only a few seconds, but her friend's authentic tone and energy were different now, and hope filled her spirit.

Nova turned back to Wayne, gave a final wave goodbye, and hurried away to his side. Wayne was speaking to the medics and the police, his tone sharp but subdued. His gaze jumped briefly over to the gang. Emmie tensed within his stare, but then Wayne gave a subtle nod—acknowledgment, maybe even gratitude—and then turned back to the medics.

Emmie walked off the stage beside her friends and up the aisle where they had taken Gloria's body only minutes earlier. Glancing back at Nova one last time, her friend was standing alone in the center of the stage, where her grandmother had fallen. She picked up the microphone and began reeling it in.

40

Emmie stared out through the limousine's windows. The crowded Las Vegas streets swept past in a blur. Giant, glittering billboards towered at nearly every corner, each one promising excitement and fortune. The city's endless hum contrasted starkly with the silence that had settled over the group inside.

Wayne had provided the limo this time, even instructing the driver to treat them to free drinks on the way to the airport, although none of them had touched any of the alcohol. What was the point? They were exhausted, and everyone just wanted to move forward. It was difficult enough knowing that Nova's career was in jeopardy, although her friend would somehow persevere over what had happened. If it wasn't Amber House Theater, then probably somewhere else. She guessed within a few years, Nova would headline some other big-name theater or casino. Nothing stops a woman with that much determination.

Finn slouched in one corner and leaned against Sarah. She cradled him against her chest and hovered her palm just above one shoulder. The others couldn't see it, but there was a faint glow coming from her hands.

"You're doing too much," Finn said. "It's not that bad. I'll be just fine. Just some sore muscles."

"It'll help with the pain," Sarah said.

"How can I argue with that?" Finn replied. He looked at Emmie, then at Jason. "Too bad we can't stay and have a little fun."

Jason leaned back and tapped his fingers against his knee. "I would just as soon get out of here... If it's all the same to you."

"We don't have to gamble," Finn said, tilting his head against the window, watching the lights from the strip flash past him. "I mean, there's lots of entertainment and other things to do."

"Jason doesn't have many fond memories about this place," Emmie said.

"I'm aware of that," Finn said. "Maybe just a concert or something?"

"Next time." Sarah put her hand on his arm.

Jason shifted slightly, gazing out one of the windows with an expression of guilt. "It feels different now."

"What do you mean?" Emmie asked.

Jason gestured vaguely out his window. "The city, the lights. It used to be so much fun, you know—electric. Like I couldn't leave without playing one last hand. Now it just feels so empty."

"That's good," Emmie said. "You don't feel the pull anymore? The desire to risk it all?"

"I can't say it's completely gone, but all the pizzazz... it's like it's trying too hard."

Emmie studied him for a moment, opening her mouth a bit to say something, but then she stopped and nodded instead.

She turned her attention back to Finn, who was shifting in his seat to let Sarah reach his shoulder a little better. He let out a little groan. "You know, I'd feel a lot better if you guys stopped looking at me like I'm about to break into pieces."

"You are in pieces," Jason said wryly. "That contraption could have ripped your arms off."

"Yeah, but I'm still here, aren't I?" Finn said. "And I got the best surgeon in the world working on it."

"It's a full-time job," Sarah added.

Finn tilted his head slowly toward Sarah, his voice softening. "Thanks, by the way, for all that alchemy you do."

Sarah didn't look up from her focus on his shoulder, but the corners of her mouth turned upward. "Don't thank me yet. You might need some physical therapy for this. I think you sprained some muscles."

"Great," Finn said, leaning back with an exaggerated ease. "There's another excuse to take a vacation, and another reason why I don't do manual labor."

Jason reached into the small bar at the side of the limo, pulling out a bottle of champagne and several glasses—four glasses. He poured each with precision, handing them out one by one.

"I wasn't going to do this, but... To Em." Jason held his glass up.

"To our team of misfits," Sarah added.

They clinked glasses, and Emmie paused, watching the bubbles rise in her drink. Reflecting on everything she'd been through with her friends over the last several months, she smiled warmly and embraced the energy of their presence.

"I couldn't have done it without all of you," she said. "I couldn't have gotten through that alone. And I think back to that day after I moved back to my childhood home, Hanging House," she looked at Sarah, "when you showed up at my doorstep to apologize for teasing me in school. I'm *so* glad you had the courage to come back into my life."

"And you," she turned to Finn, "if you hadn't been stalking me—"

"I was investigating the house," Finn said defensively.

"Stalking," Emmie repeated with a grin. "I wouldn't have had the same strength to face everything that came afterward."

Then she turned to Jason. "And if this bully hadn't made my life miserable—"

"Sorry," Jason said.

"—I never would have grown into the person I am today. All of you have strengthened me, and it's been such a wild ride so far."

"There's more to come," Sarah said.

"Is there?" Jason asked.

"Someone out there needs us," Finn added.

"I suppose that saying is true," Emmie said. "Whatever doesn't kill us makes us stronger."

They clinked glasses again and drank.

∾

Get a free short story on the next page!

Read more in the Emmie Rose Haunted Mystery series on Amazon.com!

PLUS, get a **FREE** short story at my website!

www.deanrasmussen.com

FREE SHORT STORY!

★★★★★
Please review my book!

If you liked this book and have a moment to spare, I would greatly appreciate a short review on the page where you bought it. Your help in spreading the word is *immensely* appreciated and reviews make a huge difference in helping new readers find my novels.

Shine House: An Emmie Rose Haunted Mystery Book 0
Hanging House: An Emmie Rose Haunted Mystery Book 1
Caine House: An Emmie Rose Haunted Mystery Book 2
Hyde House: An Emmie Rose Haunted Mystery Book 3
Whisper House: An Emmie Rose Haunted Mystery Book 4
Temper House: An Emmie Rose Haunted Mystery Book 5
Raven House: An Emmie Rose Haunted Mystery Book 6
Amber House: An Emmie Rose Haunted Mystery Book 7

Dreadful Dark Tales of Horror Book 1
Dreadful Dark Tales of Horror Book 2
Dreadful Dark Tales of Horror Book 3
Dreadful Dark Tales of Horror Book 4
Dreadful Dark Tales of Horror Book 5
Dreadful Dark Tales of Horror Book 6
Dreadful Dark Tales of Horror Complete Series

Stone Hill: Shadows Rising (Book 1)
Stone Hill: Phantoms Reborn (Book 2)
Stone Hill: Leviathan Wakes (Book 3)

ABOUT THE AUTHOR

Dean Rasmussen grew up in a small Minnesota town and began writing stories at the age of ten, driven by his fascination with the Star Wars hero's journey. He continued writing short stories and attempted a few novels through his early twenties until he stopped to focus on his computer animation ambitions. He studied English at a Minnesota college during that time.

He learned the art of computer animation and went on to work on twenty feature films, a television show, and a AAA video game as a visual effects artist over thirteen years.

Dean currently teaches animation for visual effects in Orlando, Florida. Inspired by his favorite authors, Stephen King, Ray Bradbury, and H. P. Lovecraft, Dean began writing novels and short stories again in 2018 to thrill and delight a new generation of horror fans.

ACKNOWLEDGMENTS

Thank you to my wife and family who supported me, and who continue to do so, through many long hours of writing.

Thank you to my friends and relatives, some of whom have passed away, who inspired me and supported my crazy ideas. Thank you for putting up with me!

Thank you to everyone who worked with me to get this book out on time!

Thank you to all my supporters!

Printed in Great Britain
by Amazon